Windows In The Loft

Windows In The Loft

SALLY GERARD

Dewy Moss, LLP • Indianapolis

Copyright 2013 by Sally Gerard

All rights reserved. No part of this book may be used or reproduced in any manner whatsoever without written permission except in the case of brief quotations embodied in critical articles and reviews.

This book is a work of fiction. References to real people, events, establishments, organizations, or locales are intended only to provide a sense of authenticity, and are used fictitiously. All other characters, and all incidents and dialogue, are drawn from the author's imagination and are not to be construed as real.

About This Book

When Isa's mother dies soon after her father, she is left in the hands of abusive caretaker, Frank. Even more devastating, Frank has his own agenda for the family farm. Isa, feeling alone, turns to her beloved horses for comfort and strength.

When Captain Bane Lucas from the Space Alliance shows up looking for a good horse, he's drawn to Isa's independence and profound equestrian knowledge. He opens her eyes to new possibilities by traveling in space.

The stars offered her hope for a new way of life, a way to escape her oppressor but she loved her horses too much to leave them behind. The farm was all that remained from her family.

Can Isa leave her home planet and beloved horses to explore a completely different world, or will she stay on her family farm where so many of her memories remain? Isa's courage and faith are tested as her decision forces her to discover herself anew.

For Jared and Alex
For Cathy

Acknowledgements

No one writes alone, not really. Every piece of schema comes into play when I sit down and put words together to craft characters and settings, and to tell their story.

To Robert for making the barn loft available to me anytime, for answering all my questions, showing me how an acre counter works, providing just the right word or name when I needed it, for loving me and believing in me, and for so many batches of your famous popcorn. I love you.

To MaryPeg for typing each word from my handwritten manuscript and for the constant conversation in Word to make everything the best it could be, well for that and for being my best friend.

To Karen for countless readings, being my cheer squad, providing me care, friendship and love always.

To Julie because we are sister writers and one day we will write the story of those notorious Prescotts.

To all of my family in every category, words cannot express all of your support and love, oh, and all of those experiences that make my writing so rich!

To Michele for calling me back and not hanging up when I said I had to go up into the barn loft to get a signal, and also Danette and their conception of Dewy Moss Publishers.

There are of course many others I need to thank: Wayne, Julie L, Heather R, Elaine, Jamie, Kali, TJ, countless wranglers, RSITs, campers, and all of my students and the staff at Sunset Middle School. If I've left your name out, please know that I thank you, too.

To Jared and to Alex, not only for their faith and undying encouragement, but for Bounty's design, countless "shots" of whipped cream from a can, and for so many weekends when I was in the loft, writing.

Credits

Photography:

- Dr. Susan Wight (Barn photo)
- Jim Powell Photography (Author photo)
  206 S MAIN ST
  YUMA, CO 80759

Cover art:

- Horse in Barn: By Robyn Porteen, Porteen Photography - www.porteenstudio.com
- Starry Sky: By EpicStockMedia

Cover design:

- Danette Davis

Manuscript Edit & Review:

- Jenn Rosenberger (jrosenbergerbooks@gmail.com)

available from

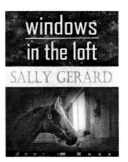

1.

Sentinel over the yard, the barn stood at night with the high yard light illuminating the west side. The cement wall glowed and the light sneaked into the two small high windows flanking the horse door. As the metal roof rose from grey to slate in the late evening, the Eagle's Beak was all but in shadow. On the south-facing front of the red barn, stars shone above, and four black bulls grazed the new spring grass in the field to the east.

Inside, warm in the crisp spring night, the aisle was packed with years of dirt and hay. The hay mangers were empty, waiting. An earthy, musty odor beckoned her to come up the steep stairs to the loft, the rafters rising high above the wood floor worn from so many boots and bales.

A refuge—the warm smell of the work horses, the pleasing sound of their eating—sighing after the day's work. Being shorter than average, she could lie in the largest manger, the muzzles working their way around her to get the last pieces of the sweet grass; soon now she'd have to move, knowing he'd still be looking for her. Chores were finished, she'd left his supper on the stove, but he'd find something she hadn't done right.

Her hands lingered on the soft rumps as she passed between Teyha and Smokey, still searching for any remaining hay. Smokey occupied the stall just as her horse, Hank had before him. As she closed the door behind her, her boots softly scratched along the gravel going toward the house. Letting herself in the back door, she eased it shut, softening the click of the latch as much as she could. Padding down the hall and through the doorway into the kitchen, she began to run the water to wash up the dishes.

He'd left his dishes on the table and she breathed easier when she saw the chair was empty. The house was quiet and, checking for his pickup out the window, she found it gone. Pulling back her brown hair with an elastic band from her pocket, she hummed as she finished cleaning up, enjoying the hot soapy water covering her tired hands. These were her mother's dishes—little blue flowers danced along the edges, partnering with green leaves as they made their way around the rim of the plate. Isa imagined her mother's hands lovingly washing these dishes when she was a young woman. Longing stretched out of her fingers and her grip tightened on the plate.

Her mother, Julie, had died one year after signing papers that gave Frank control of the farm, leaving a grieving Isa in the hands of a guardian who never wanted her. Isa could not, although she tried, remember much of her father. She had the stories her mother had told her and held them fast in her heart, along with the loving warmth she associated with him.

Isa knew her father had graduated from the Alliance Academy, but had come back to his home planet, Mellacross, when his own parents had been tragically killed in an accident. He'd met Julie as he was sorting through his parents' affairs and settling their estate.

They fell in love and James gave up his career with the Space Alliance, deciding that Julie and agriculture would be his life, not traveling to distant planets and more technologically oriented worlds. Isa was glad now that he'd made that choice.

She sometimes wondered when she gazed up at the stars what some of the other settled planets were like. She'd studied them in school books and knew that some were agrarian-based and had been homesteaded like hers, some were technology-based, and some more mixed. All the planets together formed the Alliance. There were some who did not join, but those planets and cultures had not been Earth-settled; they had their own origins.

Putting the dishes away in the cupboard, Isa calculated how much time she had until he came back. He went into town several evenings a week, drinking cheap beer at the local bar; there was a strained peace until he returned in the early morning hours.

Grabbing her jacket, she strode out to the barn, knowing she had ready companionship there. Practicing shadow walking, Isa stayed along the north side of the house, passing by the plum thicket across the short grass to the Quonset. She closed her blue eyes as she paced the distance to the barn's west wall and around to the door on the south side by the corrals where the bulls wintered.

She had oiled the sliding door and it slipped silently open as she squeezed through, closing it behind her. Four ears pricked forward at her entrance, but Teyha and Smokey, accustomed to her gentle presence, made no other movement. Isa climbed into the manger, stood in the grain box, and helped herself on to Smoke's broad back. She liked the way his nickname sounded when she talked to him. Lying there with her arms around his thick neck, Isa whispered her escape plan to him, knowing he would never tell.

The girl often made her plans with this pair, her two best friends. All three knew she had never tried one of her plans, but that they would lay in wait until she was strong enough to try. Making them gave her a sense of power, some control over her life.

Her eyes began to close, muscles relaxing as Isa drifted off into her dreams. Smokey moved slowly over to Teyha in the double stall, providing more warmth to the girl, and stability should she slide. They stood in the warm comfort of the barn that Isa kept well prepared for them, daily mucking and re-bedding them with thick straw. She had always been theirs, and they sensed her need for protection.

Night settled in around the red barn, a cool breeze flowed out of the west as stars beyond counting burst forth in the sky. The air was sweet with the first growth of spring, and newborn calves had bedded down with their mamas in the pasture to the south of the main road into the farm. Spring rains encouraged a thick stand of wheat reaching ankle-high with a promise for a good harvest. A "prairie" owl stood perched and alert on the thick, wooden gatepost near the small east door on the barn, awaiting a feast of any mice that ventured out. She was a very healthy owl.

Too soon the old Chevy could be heard in the near distance careening down the road spewing dust behind it. Teyha's ears perked up hearing the old diesel motor in the distance. She bumped Smokey and he wuffled deep in his throat and shifted his weight to wake the sleeping girl. Isa tightened her arms around him as he stepped closer to the manger. She slid off his wide shoulder and into the grain box. Climbing out of the hay manger, she slipped quietly out of the barn, across the buildings in the yard and into the house, turning her head toward the driveway to check the progress of Frank's pick-up.

Isa scampered up the narrow staircase to her small room on the second floor. Closing the door behind her, she went to the window, seeing that he was pulling up to the house. Getting into bed, pulling the sheet and blankets over her clothes and up to her neck, she lay still, wide blue eyes open to the dark.

The back door opened. Heavy footfalls came across the kitchen floor linoleum, the boards underneath creaking out his progress. He paused at the base of the stairs. Her eyes widened. She whimpered a prayer in her heart. Moments later, Frank's movements filled the hallway downstairs as he clattered his way into his own bedroom. Isa's body unclenched when she heard the bedsprings groan under his weight. She let go of her rigid defense and allowed her mind to wander off into sleep.

2.

Frank was a drunk who thought nothing of pushing the young girl around. He was rough and quick to anger. He was also slick and he easily manipulated Isa's mother into an arrangement in order to possess her farm and money. She was so vulnerable after her husband's death, and desperate for someone to help with the work of the farm as she tried to raise her young daughter. Frank came along with references that appeared to show his hard work and dedication, and his knowledge of running a farm. There were names on his list that Julie recognized, but had she only called she would have heard the truth about him. He did not have experience with horses, but Julie really needed someone to handle the crops and equipment. She thought that with Isa, they would be able to handle the care of the horses. Her heart had gone out of the farm with James' death. She didn't pay attention to what was going on and signed everything Frank put in front of her, never imagining he was taking advantage of her. Julie thought that should anything happen to her, with no other family, Frank would see that Isa was educated and then when she was ready, she could take over the running of the farm herself.

Julie had loved her husband as no other and they were both filled with joy at the loving creation of their daughter. They had worked this farm together just as Julie's parents and grandparents before her. They raised Isa with love and respect for the land and the animals on the farm and those native to the land.

From a young age, Isa had loved the horses and shown a special ability to work with them. The farm had modern machinery, but raised quality workhorses trained to drive with a gentle disposition. With her parents' nurturing, encouraging their daughter's gifts, Isa had her first small horse at a very young age. She spent hours with him each day, riding and simply becoming a herd of two. She could relax her muscles at will, calming herself and thereby calming the horse. The horses were drawn to her and she seemed born to be with them.

Deep love filled this family. They lived with joy a rich, full life. Many people came to their farm. Some to look at and purchase horses, some to consult with Julie and James about wheat, beans and corn crops, and many came at Julie's invitation to share a meal. This was a place where life felt easier, and troubles didn't seem unbearable. Laughter, good food, music and friendship were abundant.

Julie's family had settled in this area a hundred years ago, and this was the family's legacy. Their faith was a source of gladness, their hard work an example and inspiration to those around them. Julie's parents had died when she was in her teens, prompting her grandparents, Ada and John, to continue the work of the farm and finish raising their granddaughter. They sent her off to complete her higher education, and there she met James while he'd been home to take care of his parents' estate. His bright blue eyes sparkled with love and laughter. James became apart of the farm from the first visit, impressing Julie's grandfather with his "jump in and get 'er done" attitude. Grandmother was won over by the obvious love James had for her granddaughter and the gentle respect he showed her.

They married when Julie finished her schooling, in a simple ceremony on the farm with family and close friends. The two couples continued to work the farm together, James and Julie adding their own love of horses and the expertise that experience brought. Ada and John were proud of their granddaughter and her husband, easing themselves out of the business to enjoy their last years together in leisure. When Isa was born, they were overjoyed and loved their great-granddaughter as well. Their passing was grieved by many, but left an awful hole in Julie's life. James and Isa reminded Julie that she would never forget the great love her grandparents had given her and that their spirit lived on here at the farm and in the love James, Julie and Isa shared.

Although Isa had been very young, she had in her heart the knowledge that she was loved and cherished. Her parents continued running the farm and developing Isa's love of horses and her special ability to communicate with them.

James began to tire more easily and to lose his appetite. The family took a trip to a larger medical facility on the advice of their local doctor. Many advances had been made in the discovery and treatment of cancer. His was a rare exception as it had taken over his bones. They travelled home to spend the time they had left together. While he still had strength, James spent as much time as he could with Isa. They cuddled together in the loft, on a blanket nestled in the bales reading her favorite book and talking about horses. He knew that his little daughter would need her horse friends to ease her grief when he was gone. He wanted her to remember how special she was and how much he loved her. Building those memories for her in the barn would help her to find him in her heart each time she came here. James died, held by his wife with his young daughter perched by his side.

Julie's tears had come with her husband's illness, and at his death none were left. She gathered her young daughter close and, putting one foot before the other, they made their way through days that had grown dull for her. The farm became too much for Julie, even with the help of so many caring neighbors. They had their own places to keep up, and soon fell away. Isa turned to her horse and poured out her grief, her young heart knowing that her mother had all she could take.

As Isa started school, her teachers not only noticed her gift in reading, but her empathy for those who had faced suffering in their lives. Isa preferred to talk with the adults at school and had a tendency to see her peers as young puppies that needed her care. They lacked her maturity.

The years passed in a grey blur. Isa began to forget her father's face and touch, but held tight to the stories her mom told her. With each passing day, Isa felt her mom slipping further away from her, and into her memories of her husband, Isa's father. Julie knew she needed help, so she hired a man. Isa felt that this was too sudden. Her mom hired him without taking any time to consider, in a hurry to put the burden of the farm on someone else's shoulders. In the beginning, he worked and completed the jobs Julie put on a list for him each day. He lived in the bedroom downstairs that had been Julie's and James's. Julie had moved upstairs into the small room next to Isa's. Soon enough, he worked off of his own list, telling Julie not to concern herself with anything, that he would take care of it.

Frank did not like horses, and Isa did not like him because of it. Julie and Isa took care of the horses and left the other work to Frank. Isa did not understand why her mother tolerated Frank. Her instincts kept her wary when around him, the soft hair on her neck standing up to warn her when he was near. Her mother had told her about her grandfather's sense for people. How he could meet a person for the first time and just know what they were about. He wouldn't sell a horse to anyone he hadn't met personally and felt a "sense" of first. He'd held Isa at her birth and told Julie that his great-granddaughter had a gift with horses. He had sensed that in her. Isa knew her great-grandfather would never sell a horse to Frank or even let him near the barn. Frank was one of those people who thought force was the way to handle any situation. When he happened to be working out where the horses were, they kept their distance and Isa noted that.

Julie could not see Frank for what he was, so lost in her grief over James. Her blue eyes were flat where there had once been joy and the sparkle of mischief. Her hair, once thick and brown, had thinned and lost its luster. Her slim frame had gone thin, her clothes hanging on her gaunt skin. Her soul longed to be with James, and was slowly taking her body with it. Isa watched as her mother's spirit slowly left. She tried as best as her young self could to bring her mom back.

One night, she repeatedly asked her mom to make popcorn balls. Julie and James had loved to make these sweet, gooey treats and sit out with their sticky mess watching the stars and licking their fingers. Frank had gone to town after dinner, and habit told Isa that he wouldn't be back for a while. Julie just couldn't bring herself to grant her daughter's wish. It was too painful to revisit those memories.

Isa said, "It's okay, Mom, I'll do it myself."

She climbed onto a chair to pull her great-grandmother's recipe box down and filed through it until she found the popcorn ball recipe. Getting out all the ingredients, Isa set to work with her eyes going back and forth between the handwritten card and the pan.

The sweet smell of sugar cooking filled the house. It was a bit tricky to make the hot sugar mixture the right temperature and consistency, but she had confidence in her abilities as she added the popped corn and buttered her fingers so she could form the balls.

"Mom, they're almost ready." No response. Isa placed the balls on a wax paper-lined pan and washed the butter off her hands. Leaving the mess in the kitchen for later, balancing the pan in her arms, she found her mom slumped in James's chair, their wedding photo in her lap. Isa set the pan on the side table. "I did it, Mom. Don't they smell good...Mom?"

Isa dropped to the floor at her mom's feet and laid her head against Julie's knee; the faded blue roses in the carpet giving her a place to focus while tears slid down her cheeks. Each one was locked with their grief: one for her husband and one for her mother.

Outside, a pick-up was weaving down the road to the driveway. It came to a stop outside the two-story farmhouse. Frank stumbled out and up the steps to the small veranda. Coming in the front door, a strange quiet hit him—he didn't like it. He noticed them then; the woman still, the little brat tracing patterns in the rug. He went into the kitchen looking for something to eat and was greeted by a sticky mess. He couldn't believe Julie had left the kitchen in this state.

"Hey, who's gonna clean up the mess in here?"

Hands on hips, he loomed in the doorway, staring at Isa. She glared up at him.

"I'll get it cleaned up later."

"Isa, do it now, please." Isa looked up at her mother and Julie turned away. Keeping her shining eyes downcast, Isa got up and passing through the doorway, was cast across the room. She hit the counter hard and fell. Julie roused herself to address the commotion.

"Isa, what happened? Did you trip? Are you okay?"

"He pushed me."

"Accident. I was trying to get out of her way. It was an accident."

"Well, are you okay?" Julie knelt down by Isa. Her arm was bleeding where it had struck the counter; Isa stared at her mom. No comment. No orders to get out. Something inside her broke in that moment. Isa dared not look at Frank; she didn't want to show weakness.

"I'm fine, Mom." Mother and daughter shared a look in that moment, and as if they had put money in some magic machine, they changed roles. Isa stood, making all her muscles rigid and pushing her pain away. She wrapped her uninjured arm around Julie's waist and walked her back to James's chair.

"I'll make you some tea with honey." Isa went back into the kitchen and put the kettle on. She washed the dishes and wiped down the stove and counters while the water heated. She began to relax as she worked because Frank had disappeared into his room. Isa dropped the tea bag into a deep blue mug and poured the boiling water over it. Adding some of the sweet clover honey, she let the tea steep.

Removing the tea bag to the trash, Isa brought the mug to her mother. Julie wrapped her hands around the mug, drawing the warmth into herself. Isa kissed her cheek and, grabbing a jacket, went out the front door and headed to the barn.

She opened the smaller south door and slipped into the milking aisle, closing the door behind her. Walking the length of the aisle, she opened the door to the separator room, where they kept a first-aid kit. She flipped on the light, set down her jacket and studied her right arm. There was a gash with an ugly purpling bruise. Isa worked to clean off the dried blood. It hurt. But she felt that the bone was okay. She bandaged the cut by criss-crossing adhesive bandages over it and then wrapped it with Vet-Wrap. The support felt good.

After cleaning up, she left the separator room by the west door and let the warm smell of the horses in their stalls surround her. There was a half moon shining tonight and its light sifted through the windows. Isa went to her horse's stall, rubbing muzzles as she went. She pulled the jacket on, going gingerly over her sore arm. Hank's warm breath ruffled her hair and Isa leaned into him. His compact head came around her shoulders, pulling her into his chest. Isa took comfort from her horse, knowing that he would love her even when it seemed that no one else did. She told Hank everything that had happened, from the popcorn balls, to Frank shoving her, and buried her wet cheeks into Hank's warm neck. Hank was getting older now, but had been her friend and confidant, seeing her through good and bad times.

As time went on, her mother retreated further into herself and relegated more authority to Frank. Isa tried to stay out of his way. When he drank, she ended up with bruises. At first, she pleaded with her mom to do something, to protect her, to get rid of Frank. Frank always had a version that made what he'd done an accident. Julie had no energy to dispute him and he began to convince her that he was good for the farm and that it would be a lucrative business for Isa to inherit. Julie loved Isa and all she heard, no matter what Isa said, was that Frank would make sure her daughter had a future.

Isa worked hard to nurture the excellent quality of their horses. Frank never came into the barn, but worked the fields in a haphazard way, producing minimal crops to sell. Business dropped away as the farm fell into rotting boards, weed-choked fields and rust.

While Isa continued to go to school and spend her other time with the horses, her mother signed papers that made Frank Isa's guardian and gave him control of the farm and Isa's future. Julie didn't see any other options with no other family to depend on. She wanted to be sure Isa had a good future, and because she felt the pull of her soul to James so profoundly, it was easy to believe Frank was the solution.

Isa knew that each night brought her closer to being alone and she crawled into bed with her mom, whispering, "I love you and tell my daddy I miss him." Isa felt Julie's last breath just before Christmas and clasped her hand, trying to keep her there, but knowing she had been gone for some time now. She didn't know what to do. She prayed to God to bring her mom back. She got up and sat, staring out the window at the stars and the yard and the barn. She was alone and felt like a big black hole had opened up and swallowed her. Dozing off, she tried to climb up this black hole, clawing her way in the dark, begging for her mom and dad to help her. She woke and wondered if her world would ever be whole again.

In the morning, she called their family doctor and told him that her mother was dead. That set in motion a chaos that Isa could not have anticipated. Frank was furious that she'd called before he even knew, but he played his part well. Julie was buried, in a simple and subdued celebration of her life in the Lee Cemetery northeast of the farm, amid the wild roses and the family that had gone before her –beloved James, parents and grandparents. Isa stood, dry-eyed, thanking God in her heart for the time she'd had with her family, and asking Him to please watch over her mom, dad and great-grandparents, since she no longer could.

What followed should have been Frank leaving, but Isa soon learned of his treachery. Well-meaning folks told her she'd be fine and was lucky this man had agreed to stay with the farm and care for her like a daughter. She just kept telling herself, "I have my horses." She spent the days following the funeral immersed in the horses' care and the barn.

When she returned to school after the Christmas holiday, her teacher, Miss Gates, tried to be a comfort to her young student. Isa had become quiet, more so than usual, and more reliant on herself, physically pulling her small frame up and presenting a straight-spine-chin-up attitude to those around her. It was only with Hank, her special horse, that she shared her tears, sadness and anger.

Frank soon made it clear that she'd do whatever he said or he'd beat her, and many times even if she did do what he said. The first time she didn't clean up to his satisfaction, he slapped her, sending her across the room and into the wall. She cried out, "Please stop! You're hurting me!" He replied by slapping her again.

"Get this sty cleaned up, now! And don't make me tell you again. Don't you tell me to stop; I'll stop when you've learned to do what I say." He shoved her when she passed him to clean the counter that had not met with his approval. He began to keep her home from school when she had too many bruises showing and soon enough it was easier to not let her go at all. He told the school officials he was signing her up for a home-school program, as she didn't wish to leave the farm after her mother's death.

3.

The Space Alliance had a strong presence in this quadrant. Bane Lucas had already been tagged as captain material, with a growing reputation as a leader possessing the ability to bring conflict to middle ground. This planet, Mellacross, with its agrarian economy was a favorite, with lots of open country and quality horses. Nothing brought clarity to Bane's thinking like a long ride.

He made his way onto the dirt road, following directions he'd been given in town. He'd asked around and been told that a young girl, some twenty miles south of town, had the best horses available, but he'd have to drive out and see if she'd lease him a mount for the time he'd be here on the planet. Bane had several days before he needed to report to Alliance officials and he would use this time to think through the recent offer of a Captaincy of his own, which filled him with excitement. Captaining a ship was something he'd looked forward to. Bane was strict but fair with those who reported to him; his reputation for integrity was well known.

Guiding the old pick-up down the dirt road, Bane noticed the crops struggling through thick weeds; odd, most of the surrounding fields were well tended. The drive was marked by the end of the wire fence and a utility pole where he turned north, a quarter mile, went past the white two-story house and pulled up to the barn.

Bane unfolded his long frame from the truck and zipped his insulated flight jacket against the morning chill. His dark hair was combed back, and his deep blue eyes narrowed as he took in the details of the farm surrounding him. The sun was up, but just, as he scanned the yard and back towards the house, he saw no one present. Most country dwellers were early morning folk, not the late-night city crowd still abed halfway into the morning. He'd tried to call ahead, but had no answer. Even with the empty barnyard, he felt an awareness that told him someone was about.

He slid the barn door open, the familiar warmth and scent of horses filling his nose; fresh hay and well-kept stalls stood in stark contrast to the drooping porch on the house, the neglected crops, and the farm implements scattered in the yard.

"Hello?"

The answer whickered back to him, as alert ears pricked in his direction.

"Someone's been out to feed you, eh fella?" He noted the neatly folded blanket in the grain box next to the hay manger.

The stallion had an intelligent face and gentle brown eyes; he was stout-boned and well put-together. By the look of the other horses in the barn, Bane guessed he was the foundation stallion. Someone had put much time and care into these horses. Stepping out of the barn, Bane found a few more horses in the small paddock connected to the east side of the barn, all friendly noses lifting from the morning's hay to greet this new visitor.

Looking farther east and into the pasture, Bane saw a young girl coming toward the barn with four cows. She seemed to be a part of this little herd and a sweet melody reached his ears, the sound of her humming carried on the slight breeze. He watched as she reached the last hundred yards towards him. She was slight, even in the bulky coat, and completely lost in her task, as if nothing else in the world mattered.

Bane noticed when her head turned ever so slightly and she stiffened, stopping in the center of the cows, statue-still. He hadn't meant to alarm her; indeed, he was surprised that she'd moved so quickly from communing with those cows and an obvious joy in the morning to this guarded, almost wary, stance.

"Hello! I'm sorry to disrupt your work; some folks in town directed me here to talk horses. Have I come to the right place?"

The shift she made back to the relaxed young girl came in an instant. "Yep, you've come to the right place. Gimme just a minute to get my girls in to milk."

Her movements were fluid, graceful, reminding Bane of dancers he'd seen at a ballet performance. As the cows followed her into the paddock, her hand gently reached out to touch each horse she passed and receive nuzzles from those close enough in return.

The milk cows filed into the small south door of the barn as Bane let himself back through the main door on the south, under the eagle's beak over the top hay door. The cows had found their place in the milking aisle and the girl was at work filling a bucket under the first one.

"Can I help?"

"Sure. There's another bucket just there at Daisy's head. Watch me for a minute and then you can milk Daisy. I'm Isa."

"Bane. Bane Lucas. It doesn't look too complicated. I'll give it a go."

Bane watched Isa and noted the rhythm and her reassuring murmur to the cows. He took the bucket, patting Daisy as she ate her hay from the trough, kneeled down, positioning the bucket and began to massage her milk down through the teats and into the bucket. Comfortable with animals, he soon fell into his own rhythm and received a nod of approval from Isa. As she moved on to the third cow, Bane helped carry the fresh milk to the separator room, pouring it into the electric machine that would pull the cream from the milk.

As Isa worked, Bane felt a tension in her, as if she was waiting for something and might flee. He knew that at over six feet tall and well muscled, he could be intimidating. He wasn't sure how to put her at ease; he was known to be trustworthy and wished to reassure her.

"This is a beautiful barn. Someone obviously put a lot of thought into its set-up, the aisle for the milk cows and a room for dealing with the milk right here, as well as spacious stalls for your horses with mangers and grain boxes. Do you mind if I look upstairs?"

"My great-grandfather built it to last and nothing much has changed. Sure, go on up. You can open the doors if you like. Great grand-dad built in steps instead of a loft ladder—you won't find another like this in the county." Her freckled face turned toward him with a smile, her curly brown hair falling over her face. She blew it back out the side of her mouth and went back to work.

"Indeed. Or the horses, either."

The loft was filled with hay, baled and stacked. Bane wondered who had helped Isa with this work. Two small windows high on the north wall let in some light, glowing like two bright eyes shining in the dark interior. The roof appeared to have been built in three sections, each one tapering in, finally meeting the other side at the top center. In one corner was a pile of antlers, looked like deer or elk. Bane unhooked the wire and swung the big door out; the horses in the paddock below looked up and nickered at him. Behind them, and in every direction, grasses undulated across the pastures as far as Bane could see, like the unending stars in space.

Closing the door, Bane called down to Isa, "Great view! I don't know how you tear yourself away."

"Well, the critters around here just can't seem to figure out how to feed themselves without me." There was a smile in her voice that carried through the carefully crafted barn and made Bane smile. He stepped down into the aisle between the horses and the milking row. The cows had finished their breakfast, headed back into the pasture and Isa had the place swept clean.

"So, Bane, what is it you need from my horses? Lessons? Are you buying?"

"I'm planetside for several days—Alliance. I'd like to spend a fair amount of that time seeing the country around here with an honest mount. I was hoping you could help me out, with some advice about where to go and one of your fine horses. I'll pay a fair price, and I won't mistreat them or overuse them."

He could see her thoughts playing out on her face, her vivid blue eyes revealing her hesitancy. Bane wondered why this young girl, 12 or 13 years old he guessed, was alone here. He liked her "I'm-in-charge" attitude; it was just what he looked for in his crew.

"My dad was Alliance until he met my mom." She went on to ask him about his horse experience and the details of his childhood, if he was raised with horses, and how that connection followed him into adulthood and through the Academy; to become his priority whenever he found himself on a planet with horses available and time to ride.

Isa observed Bane as he related his life with horses. She liked the way he looked her in the eye, but noticed that as he relived those memories, his eyes shone brighter, became more distant. She felt the heart of him gladden as the experiences came to the front of his mind. Isa gave him points for the straightforward way he spoke to her, as an equal, he didn't simplify like some would because of her age. Bane's eyes had a spark, his quiet passion came through to her in the way he leaned slightly towards her as he spoke. Her throat tightened as she had a glimpse of her dad standing with her in this barn, talking horses. It had been a long while since she'd had a memory so vivid.

"I'm sorry, are you okay?"

"What? Oh, uh, yeah, just thinking about what horse might suit you."

Bane cocked his head slightly, and then looked away, allowing her a moment.

"You seem an honest sort. I think I can help you out. I would request that I ride with you for the morning; I'm fairly selective about who rides my horses. I can show you the countryside, and give you some ideas for places to explore in the time you're here."

"I can live with that, if you can work me into your schedule today. What about price?"

"The deal I make with most folk is a hundred a day, and you pay the feed store in town. There's an account in my name."

"Interesting arrangement, but the price is more than fair."

"Everything I make goes to feed, supplies, shoer, vet and tack anyway, so I'm just eliminating any chance of a middleman. This way, there's no confusion." Bane knew there was more behind that comment, but he let it go as she turned her attention back to the horses. She slipped in with the big black and white stallion.

"Smoke here will be a good match for you. He's smart and honest; he'll go anywhere. He's a bit of a sightseer, but he'll always bring you home. He does have a tendency to be terrified of our large prairie rabbits, don't ya, boy?" She stroked his muzzle, smiling into his cheek.

"Terrified of rabbits, huh? Well, you never can tell when one might jump out and bite you. I imagine we'll get along just fine. Do you mind if I use my own saddle? I'm rather attached to it."

"Long as it fits him, sure. Why don't you go ahead and groom him while I ready my Indian horse. He's young and can use the work."

They worked quietly, currying and brushing the horses; Bane followed Isa's lead as she picked up each hoof and cleaned it out with a pick. She spoke softly to the tall brown and white paint as she worked. Finished, Isa checked over Bane's work on Smokey, and approving, went to retrieve his pad and blanket. Bane went out to the pick-up for his saddle. He'd found it at a sale, tried it out, and it had been with him ever since. The leather was a dark, deep brown, with a rich luster and it fit him like a favorite pair of worn jeans.

Bane carried it into the barn and over to Smokey's stall. Isa was settling the thick wool pad and folded Indian blanket over his withers and across his back. Bane lifted the saddle and gently set it on the pad and blanket. Isa checked the fit, noting how the bars set and how much space there was between the gullet of the saddle and Smokey's withers. "I think you're ready, Smoke; it's a fine fit." She gave him a final pat on his shoulder and went to saddling Indian. Bane fed the long latigo through the cinch ring and tightened the cinch, feeding the end of the length of leather through the latigo keeper. He adjusted the back cinch, checked that it was clipped to the ring on the front cinch and buckled the breast collar.

"You want some help, Isa?" As he turned to move towards her, she had already finished. Very efficient, he thought.

"Thanks. Here's his bridle and he takes it just fine; go slow and be gentle." She watched as Bane held the crown piece in his right hand and put the cheek pieces on the sides of Smokey's face.

His left hand held the bit with his thumb at the corner of Smokey's mouth as his right hand pulled the bridle into position. The bit slid into Smokey's mouth and Bane tucked his ears gently under the crown piece that rested just behind the ears. Isa nodded, turning to open the door so Bane could lead the horse outside.

"Could you hold him a moment while I run to the house to pick up a few things?"

"Sure."

He watched her jog off to the house; her steps on the porch practiced to avoid certain boards. It had appeared rotted to him when he'd driven past. Bane wondered, not for the first time, what Isa's situation was here. He liked the strong conformation of these horses, but found it hard to believe this young girl was solely responsible for the breeding program. Surely, some adult or parent ran the place. She returned, following the same path, but taking care not to let the screen door slam. Her hair was captured in a ponytail and tucked into a cap; a half-eaten cookie hung from her mouth and she was tugging warm gloves onto her hands. This was the young girl he'd glimpsed walking though the pasture with the cows at dawn.

Isa shoved the rest of the cookie in her mouth and reached out for Indian's reins. Bane handed her both sets of reins and hauled his saddlebags out of the pick-up bed. He let Smokey nose them over, and once he had the horse's approval, he tied them on behind the saddle.

Taking the reins back from Isa, Bane slipped them over Smokey's head, turned the left stirrup towards him, put his left boot in and swung up, landing gently. He tucked his right boot into the other stirrup. He knew he'd been approved as Isa turned from him to mount her own horse. Indian pranced around a bit, with Isa speaking to him in a low, firm voice. "Easy, bud. Ooohaay."

She stroked his neck as she spoke and asked him to move forward with her legs.

They set off down the dirt driveway, side-by-side, each taking the measure of their mount. Smokey responded to the slightest pressure from Bane's legs and held the bit lightly in his mouth. Bane felt the contact in his hand through the reins. He relaxed and figured he had a lot to look forward to in the next several days.

At the end of the drive, Isa turned them east. The sun was up now, but the sky still held onto a faint orange glow. A calm breeze from the northwest gave the day a crisp feeling, making Bane glad he had the insulated jacket. Isa was busy with the energy that was Indian and a smile lit up her face.

"Can you imagine anything as amazing as this: a good horse, beautiful country, and nothing but the day in front of you? Of course, a pocket full of peanut butter cookies with chocolate chips is pretty sweet, too!"

"This is definitely on the list of my top five." At her look he added, "Don't get me wrong, I love it. But sailing through the galaxies, surrounded by the light of stars too many to count, can also take your breath away."

"Closest I can come to that is the night sky on the plains, and you're right, it *is* so vast it can fill your soul, it can cause you to dream of rising up and finding one of those twinkling lights. I'd love to sail with them one day."

"Have you thought about Academy training?"

"I don't know how I'd get there. I can't leave here until I know my horses are in the right care. And even then, I haven't yet devised a plan that gets me away safely." Isa glanced away quickly, giving her attention to Indian, as if she'd said too much.

"Who helps you here? I mean, who keeps track of all the breeding, makes decisions?"

"Well, I do, of course. My granddaddy started this place, built the barn. He taught my mom and dad, and after he passed, my daddy took over and he and my mom continued my training. I have all the stud records, notes, and information about every foal that's been born on this place, every broodmare, everything. I've done my best to keep it going and I'm doing my best to find the right person to take it over." Her chin stuck out and her shoulders squared off in defiance.

"Easy. I didn't mean to insult you. It's just hard to imagine a young lady with so much responsibility. Doesn't your mom or dad help?"

As she answered, a deep sigh escaped, "They both died. My dad had bone cancer, no cure, and not too much later, my mom followed him. Before she died, she signed over the running of the farm to Frank. He's my guardian now."

Bane watched emotions play out on her face as she said the name "Frank"; her eyes widened. Fear? "I'm sorry. You must miss them terribly. Where is this Frank?"

"He shows up when he wants, usually late morning, spends most evenings at the bar in town. He's supposed to work the fields, but he's run the place down to the point that I'm sure he's just racking up debt. I do what I can, but I know this place that has been in my family for so many years, will be lost to me."

It came out matter-of-factly. Isa didn't want this man's pity, she'd long passed needing acceptance and had headed sometime ago into planning her escape. She'd tried to run, but couldn't stand the thought of what might happen to her horses, so she came back.

"So, your plan is to find someone to buy out your breeding operation? Any prospects?"

"Some. I'm waiting for what my great-grandfather called his 'sense' of what feels right. He said he had it with my dad the first time they met, and he knew my dad was right for my mom and for this place. My dad was a horse lover; his touch was warm magic on even the most skittish horse, bringing calm. Great-grandfather said he had that same sense when I was born, the first time he held me. So, that's what I'm waiting for. I felt it this morning with you when you helped me milk."

She looked at him frankly, eye-to-eye. Isa had a good feel for people; she was guarded in the beginning, until her heart sent a message to her nerves that she was safe. She knew well how to stay small and deep inside herself until that sense of safety reassured her and she could let down her defenses. Frank had taught her that, and it would be the only thing she'd thank him for. She felt she could trust Bane.

"Thank you. I consider that high praise." Isa could see he meant it. She liked the way he spoke straight out; he was not put off by her age.

"So, you ready for a bit of speed?"

She didn't wait for his answer, squeezing Indian's sides with her strong legs, and a sharp "Ha-tsss" came through her teeth. Bane saw the flash of brown paint pass him and eased Smokey back for a moment, watching Isa lean forward slightly, urging Indian to greater speed. Indian fairly lofted himself down the road, his young, gangly legs shooting out as if enjoying their freedom. Bane could see that Isa was a risk taker—bold, unrestrained in this, her world of horses.

"Okay, boy, let's see what you got." As soon as Smokey felt the okay through the reins, he galloped off after Indian. That's what Bane felt, an ease of gait, incredible balance and powerful hindquarters driving this horse. It felt good; it had been too long and he'd almost forgotten what this was like. He'd found nothing in his life to equal the wild feeling of being alive that was running with a horse. It gave perspective to wants versus needs, an inner confidence from working with a thousand-pound animal, indeed, flying down the road on one. Also providing an empathy and compassion for that which is wild, and yet a wild that will be bridled, but most of all, it gave a respect for life. Bane knew all of this, yet each experience with a horse brought it all back, as well as seeing it played out in the young pair in front of him.

Half a mile later, Isa began to slow Indian's speed as he cantered easily, coming down into a trot and she kept him there for a distance, posting to his rhythm to smooth his giant gait. She spoke to him quietly, reassuring and rewarding him for a job well done. His ears turned back to the sound of her voice and his muscles relaxed beneath her. As he slowed into a walk, Isa dropped the reins around the saddle horn and wrapped both arms around his thick neck. "Good boy. You are such a good boy!"

Bane rode up, laughing, beside her. "That was quite a show, he's all leg." Smokey stretched his head over, receiving the expected pat from Isa.

"You too, Smoke. You know you'll always be my favorite. Time for a Smokey-snack?" As she said this, she guided them both off the road toward the tall, dried seedpods there. Both horses helped themselves. "Yucca seeds, they love them."

"Alright, Bane Lucas, this is where I leave you. Take any road you like, if you go cross-country, close any gate you open. There's a pretty little cemetery, Lee Cemetery, a mile north of here. I like to ride over when the wild roses are blooming and, well, my family is buried there in the southeast corner. I'll hear you when you come back, just come right up to the barn. I like to feed around 4:30, if you could be back by then, I'd appreciate it. You know when I'm up in the morning, so just head on out when you're ready." She said all this in a hurry, with her eye on a distant pick-up headed toward them.

"Okay. Thanks. I'll be sure to have him back before feeding time."

Bane watched as Isa headed Indian back towards the farm. He let Smokey graze as he found a water bottle and took a drink. The pick-up slowed as it approached and Bane could see the driver—and man with a dirty cap pulled low on his forehead and a grizzly beard. Bane waved, but it was not returned. He figured it was Frank, and wondered if he should follow. He decided against it, not wanting to cause Isa more trouble by aggravating the situation.

4.

As Isa headed away with Indian, she tried to calculate how long it would be before Frank caught up with her. She knew she couldn't beat him back; running a horse back to the barn was never a good idea. She went through a mental list: dishes were done, house was clean, she'd taken care of all the chores, but she knew there'd be questions about Bane. She heard him coming up behind her and eased Indian off the road.

He veered as close as he could, Isa taking Indian into the ditch to avoid him. Frank simply stared at her as he passed. Isa continued to look straight ahead as her skin prickled and sent warning signs out to her nerves. She'd be especially careful to keep as much distance as she could from him. He finally tired of his game and drove off, turning up the driveway.

Isa slowed Indian to avoid the worst of the dust settling out behind the pick-up. She relaxed her tensed muscles and cued Indian to side-pass across the road. He was becoming more sensitive to her leg and seat cues and had only slightly forward motion as Isa worked him across the road and back. She wanted him to have a good home, go to someone who would continue his training, ride him well and often, and love and care for him. Isa wanted that for all her horses, but Indian was the youngest and needed the most time and attention.

Knowing there was a possible escape with the Alliance, Isa wanted to think about what Bane had told her, and talk with him about the opportunities she might have on a starship. If she could avoid Frank being present when he brought Smokey back, she'd ask then.

As the horse and girl rode into the yard and over to the barn, Indian began to dance around and rear up. Isa automatically moved her body to stay with him, but she was trying to gauge where Frank was, looking around and finally deciding he was in the house. She forced her muscles to relax, soothing her darting horse, her hand sliding down his thick neck. Indian walked the last few steps to the barn and Isa pulled her right leg over his back, leaned into the saddle, kicking her left foot out of the stirrup and sliding to the ground. She patted his shoulder, murmuring, "Good job, sweet boy. I had you all worked up back there!"

Indian rubbed his head against her shoulder as she led him back into the barn. Isa unsaddled him, turning the blankets upside down to dry over the saddle and hanging the bridle, reins coiled, over the saddle horn. She curried and brushed him as the sweat dried. Isa put away the grooming tools and untied Indian's lead rope. She leaned into his cheek and softly blew her breath into his nostrils. He wrapped his head around her face and they stood in that stillness for just a brief moment. She led him out to the corral and turned him loose where he nickered and trotted off to join the rest of the herd.

Isa watched them readjust to bring Indian back into his position, with a few ears flattened as everyone settled into their new space. She filled her lungs and turned to walk toward the house. Putting one foot in front of the other and then going up the steps, across the porch, she knew where to step to avoid the rotted boards. Opening the screen door, closing it quietly behind her, she came into the house and crossed to the kitchen. As she pulled off her gloves, jacket and cap, turning to hang them on the peg by the window, she stiffened, seeing Frank in her peripheral vision.

"Who was that?"

"He's from the Alliance, here on leave, and wanted a horse to ride."

"Alliance is trouble, all high and mighty. I'm surprised you let him on one of your old nags. How much is he paying?" As Frank asked this, he grabbed Isa's arm and jerked her toward him.

"He's...he's Alliance. I didn't charge him. He's here for several days." She pulled against his grip, unable to stop her reaction, even though it would incite him.

"Stupid girl, get me my lunch." He let go of her arm, and combined with her pull, she fell backwards, hitting her arm on the counter edge.

Isa got up, ignoring the pain; you didn't stay down with Frank, she wanted no part of either his boot or a tussle to get out from under him. This kind of torture had been happening more frequently lately and it kept Isa on edge and her tongue quiet. She could take a beating, but she was terrified of what she saw in his eyes when he'd held her down these last months.

She set the plate down in front of him with the steaming roast, potatoes and carrots that she'd placed in the slow-cooker early that morning. Isa would wait while he ate and then clean up before she went back out to work the horses. She didn't know what Frank did, only that he expected lunch served when he wanted it, and dinner in the evening before he went into town. Isa didn't know a lot about cooking, but her simple meals were good and filling. Having nurtured a sweet tooth her whole life, she was always baking some yummy treat, and she set a plate of the peanut butter chocolate chip cookies on the table, clearing Frank's plate as she did so.

Frank grabbed a handful of cookies and left the kitchen through the door, saying, "I got work to do, you see that this place is cleaned up and then go get those horses ready to sell and the chores done." He said this every day, his way of letting Isa know that he was in control of her actions. Frank knew well that it would be her horses that brought in money, as he'd let the farm go to ruin, preferring to spend his time in the bar. He should have sold the place as soon as her mother died, but he waited, knowing folks around here would be up in arms if he did, for Isa's sake. Well, it'd been long enough, and he wanted the money and to be rid of that brat. Soon, he thought, as he headed over to the shop for a beer and a nap.

Isa cleaned up the kitchen, had a few bites of roast and potatoes and finished off all the carrots, loving the sweet flavor. She shredded what was left of the meat for sandwiches and figured she'd use the potatoes for fried potato pancakes with eggs and sausage for dinner. That decision made, she took a few cookies and an apple and headed to the barn. She'd ask Bane if he wouldn't mind delivering the milk and cream for her and bringing back a few supplies from town. Frank forbade her to go into town, but she still had a few family friends she could trust not to tell him, so she slipped off to town once in a while, trying to tend to her business managing the horses. Adam ran the general store and went out of his way to help others. He wouldn't even question Bane's request on her behalf.

Isa spent a pleasant afternoon working the horses. One at a time, she groomed, saddled and rode each horse. With Smokey out, and Indian already ridden, she had four left: Oreo, Cowboy, Teyha, and Lilly. Isa started each one in the small corral off the barn, reinforcing leg and seat cues and reining. She wanted her horses to be versatile to appeal to the many different ways people liked to use them. She practiced opening and closing gates, dragging light pipes, smooth transitions between walk, trot and canter, all the while singing or humming with plenty of soft pats on their necks and encouragement for the horses.

After the "arena" work was finished, she rode out in the pasture, making sure to cross the small stream or ride or swim through the pond. Having the horses cross the stream was important for their conditioning, but swimming in the pond was her favorite. She would dump the saddle and ride in bareback. As the water deepened, the powerful feel of the horse striking out each leg underwater as Isa held its mane and the horse's neck stretched out was the closest she'd been to defying gravity. Of course, when the horse regained its footing on the other side, she had to relocate her balance quickly or risk sliding off that wet back. On pond days, she'd ride out of the water and let the horse graze as they both dried off. Smokey loved to swim, so on those afternoons, not much else was accomplished.

On this day, she rode all four horses in turn, and was unsaddling Lilly as Bane rode in with Smokey. "Did you have a good ride?"

"Absolutely!" Isa was pleased at the big grin on his face that reached deep into his eyes. She didn't realize the same expression was on her own face and for the very same reason. "You?"

"Well, thanks to you, I was able to work my other four, and that doesn't always happen every day. This mare, Lilly, still has some misgivings about crossing water, so we spent a good deal of time playing in the crick." Bane's eyes noted that her boots were soaked and her jeans up to her knees. They finished unsaddling and grooming and Bane was allowed to help stall the horses and feed them.

With the horses content and eating their grain, Isa turned to Bane. "So, how does this whole Alliance thing work?"

"Well, there's an application process. Once you are accepted, you attend the Academy and they help you focus on a course of study along with your general classes. When you finish there, you are ready for starship assignment or other opportunities in the Alliance."

"How many years does all that take?" she asked with widened eyes, a slightly defeated expression taking her smile away.

"If you take the traditional route, it'll be four to six years, sometimes more. There are other options, not often pursued. Sometimes, and with high recommendations from a respected source, candidates are allowed to do a work-study program. They are stationed on a starship, assigned to a mentor, and they must keep a rigorous study routine and complete the duties of a junior officer." As he spoke, her eyes narrowed and she leaned toward him.

"Okay. How does someone go about getting a recommendation from a respected source in order to get into the work-study?"

"Isa, you have to be sixteen to enter the Academy. I think you have a few years to get to that point." He watched as she looked up, quiet calculation going on in her brain.

Isa's head jerked up at the sound of the shop door opening. "Bane, would you mind dropping off the cream and milk in town for me and bringing back a few things? I made a list." She handed him a small scrap of paper and glanced out the barn door. Bane's eyes were on her as she went from tight, narrowed focus back to her request. She headed to the separator room for the cream and milk.

"Where am I going and what should I say?" He followed her back, taking the cool containers she passed to him, and they both headed out to his pick-up.

"Just past the feed store, there's a small grocery store. Take it in and talk to Adam; he'll still be there when you get to town. Give him my list and he'll put everything together for you." Isa looked at his saddle in the bed of the pick-up. "You can leave your saddle in the tack room tomorrow if you want."

"Thanks. See you bright and early, Isa. Have a good evening and I'll stop at the feed store too and square up."

Bane watched her waiting in the rearview mirror as he pulled out. So, no encounter with Frank, and she continued to monitor him as he turned down the driveway. He hoped she knew that her secrets were safe with him and he figured he better find a way to let her know that even if Frank did make contact with him, he wouldn't let anything slip about the feed store or supplies from Adam. Bane would do what he could to query Adam at the general store and the feed store boss, Mel as to what Isa's situation was and what he might do to help.

5.

"He'll do everything you ask, just give him a chance to understand. He's smart, curious, and very willing." Isa stood with one hand resting on Indian's thick neck, and the other holding his lead rope out to his new owner. She'd been working him steadily over the last two years, and at five, he was ready for anything. Usually, she'd load the horse into the trailer, but today she just couldn't.

Her hand lingered as Indian walked on, sliding her hand over his shoulder, back, and through his long tail. She watched as he was loaded, and when the trailer door shut, she turned and went back into her empty barn. Isa climbed up into the loft, empty of its sweet green bales, and slid down to the floorboards scuffed from years of the boots of her family feeding animals and stacking hay. Isa closed her eyes and sent up a prayer for Indian's new life.

The hardest prayer had been for Smokey. Like her Hank before him, Isa and Smokey shared a bond that still brought memories of both the pain of his leaving and the joy of so many shared moments, on the ground and in the saddle. Isa had hung on as long as she could; now that Indian was gone, she was at a loss for what to do.

She'd received excellent prices for all the horses, and most were going off-world. Isa figured Bane Lucas must have mentioned her horses and if she ever saw him again, she'd thank him. Indian's sale would settle the last of her debt in town and that was important to her. She wondered if Bane had made good on his promise to recommend her for Alliance training and how she could take advantage of it.

Isa stood and walked around the loft, feeling the presence of her parents, grandparents and great-grandparents. "I'm sorry. I tried to keep our farm going. I just wasn't strong enough. I'll always love all of you and I'll carry on with horses wherever I can. Goodbye." She closed the loft doors, went down the stairs and looked around the empty barn. The breath and warmth of horses and cows was the foundation of this barn and Isa hoped someone would continue it.

She slid the big barn door shut and headed to the house. Frank made himself scarce when people came around, but he'd be back and wanting food. It was near dark, unusual for him not to be complaining about a late dinner. After all, he'd be late to the bar and his "girlfriend," for whom Isa felt sorry.

Every muscle went tense when he entered the kitchen. "You get rid of that last animal? Now that you're done with that, I got a new business for you. I got friends who want to meet you." The words made her shiver and Frank was already drunk. She'd have to keep her guard up. She set the hot plate on the table, but he made no move to sit down.

Shooting past him, Isa's only thought was to get out. His foot sent her sailing, hitting her head as she met the floor. She rolled, but he was on her, his large frame pinning her and stealing her breath. The reek of him triggered her gag reflex. She turned her head and focused on the basement door.

6.

Isa shivered and hugged her lanky legs to her chest where she sat in the dark, taking shallow, quiet breaths. She'd gone through the door and had been huddled here for several minutes expecting his footfall on the steps.

Closing her eyes, Isa wished herself in the barn. She could smell the clean hay and feel the warm breath of her old bay childhood gelding, always willing to come put his head on her shoulder for Isa's love and muzzle rub. She had trusted him with the deepest part of her soul. Hank had eased her pain and Smokey after him. She wished them all back in the barn. Her dad's solid image, holding her close, filled her mind.

Isa carefully and quietly brought her hand up to wipe away the warm tears, anger welling in her heart at this show of weakness. Frank had taught her quickly that any tears or pleading would provide a harsher beating. Isa was very strict with herself, developing a steel-hard discipline of her mind and emotions. She'd become adept at hiding bruises, physical pain, and the terrible emotional damage she wasn't even aware of.

This particular night, Isa knew she had to escape. He'd come close to raping her and planned to offer her to other men. Frank's crushing blows were tame compared to the end of the movie playing in her mind that had begun upstairs. He must have been drinking all day, his slower reflexes providing her escape. She prayed he would pass out.

It was still quiet, so quiet that Isa decided Frank must have passed out. She slowly unfolded her legs and crawled out from beneath the old, dusty workbench. There was no way out of the basement, except to go back up the thirteen steps and through the kitchen.

Isa crept up, avoiding the middle of step six and the outside of step nine, making her ascent silent. She stopped on the threshold to the kitchen, listening hard, nostrils wide and testing the air. She tried to see through the dark to detect where he'd fallen. The pungent odor of Frank's rye-whiskey stung the back of her throat. She made her way across the kitchen floor, rough tile scraping her knees.

Forcing herself across the room, she crawled to the small entryway. Outside, the screen door having closed behind her, she found herself out in the yard and headed south. He'd look for her in town, so she'd avoid that. She still had her barn clothes and boots on; maybe she could find work in another stable. For now, she'd make her way to a safe distance before she stopped. She took stock of what she had: pocketknife, six oatmeal cookies she'd taken to the barn after lunch, some gum, and a roll of butterscotch candies. She'd have to ration what she had and move fast. She knew the area in a twenty-mile radius from the barn well. Isa thought she could climb into the nook of one of those cottonwood trees in the grove along the old crick, but wondered if Frank would look there. Jogging across pastures, walking when she tired, she finally stopped in the middle of a pasture. She tucked herself into the tall grass and slept.

7.

Rowan provided a nice mix, a rugged planet topographically with mountain ranges, areas of plains and some well-known fishing lakes. It also had a technological side with an Alliance maintenance base as well as a modern travel complex meeting the needs of many varied travelers and a good number of retired folk who enjoyed the community here. Captain Bane Lucas was looking forward to some time off. He'd been going one hundred percent for the last two years with his crew on the Bounty. She was slightly overdue for some heavy maintenance, which would provide well-deserved leave for his crew, many of whom were heading home to family, having come right out of the Academy to active duty.

"Captain. Incoming message. Marked personal."

"Thank you, Lieutenant, I'll take it in my quarters."

Bane turned back from the path to the bridge and headed to officer's quarters. He flipped on the comm-link. "Captain Lucas here."

"Captain, Mel Placer, the feed store. Isa's friend."

"Yes, Mel. I remember." Bane thought back to that first day he'd ridden at Isa's and his conversation with Mel at the feed store.

He'd asked Mel to contact him if there was anything he could do or when Isa was ready to make a change. Over the week he'd spent riding Smokey, he hadn't been able to learn much from her about Frank, and she had a ready excuse for the bruises he noticed. Mel didn't like Frank, said he was nothing but a free-loading drinker and he did what he could to help Isa, having received her family's business for so many years. Mel had known Isa's mother Julie, and told Bane about how she'd just stopped living, leaving room for Frank to wheedle his way in. He'd gotten the same story from Adam who had offered to help her get out, but she'd gone into her "it's not that bad and someone has to care for the horses" speech and made him promise not to do anything that would jeopardize her life there. Bane knew they both did what they could to look out for her.

"I don't know exactly what's going on, Bane, but Frank claims that Isa went berserk after the folks who bought her last horse left with him and then she ran away. He didn't report it at first, but we figure she's been gone four or five days. I think she's ready for that change, but no one has seen her."

As Mel spoke, Bane's eyes narrowed, his blue veins pulsing at his neck. He knew Frank had done something, forcing Isa to her escape. She had let that slip once, so Bane knew she thought about it. She also knew the area and could hide out for some time if she had to. "I'll check for transports that have left recently, and I assume you'll keep looking. Is she of age yet, or will we need the local judge to release her from Frank when we find her?"

"I don't know. I'll find out and start the process."

"Thanks. I have time coming, but I don't want to head that way until I know she didn't hitch a ride off planet. I'll get back to you, Mel."

Shutting off the comm-link, Bane headed to the bridge. His communications officer was quite good at finding information and she'd be more than willing to help with this query.

"So, anything that has left Melacross in the last five days?"

"Yes, Jamie, and it's very possible that she snuck on, so small spaces need to be checked. My guess is that the girl is terrified and holed up in the smallest space she can find." Bane remembered Isa telling him how she liked to climb into the hay manger and ball up under the feedbox when she was little.

"Right, Cap'n. Those transport crews aren't used to young girl stowaways. So I'll let 'em know to put on the kid gloves. If she's managed to get on, we'll find her."

8.

The noises her stomach had been making would have given her away, but they had stopped, given up. She'd made those cookies last four days as she found her way south to Aborn, and stole on board a cargo transport. Isa had laid low and watched various crews and decided on this one because the crew had seemed to have an easy relationship as they worked, there were several women, and none who looked like Frank. They had all headed off to the local diner, and she had slipped in among the crates, finding her way into a small cubby and closing herself in behind some boxes. It wasn't long before she got tangled up in an uneasy sleep.

"I'll check, Jamie, but I can't imagine that she could've got on—we left planetside late last night."

"Remember, if you find her, she's had a tough go."

"Right. She's got no worries on my ship. My crew's looking now, and we'll let you know."

9.

Bane used his Alliance contacts to find transport to rendezvous with Isa; he used those contacts to insure her safety from Frank as well. This proved to be simple and smooth because Frank wanted to avoid trouble. Isa had the right to press charges, and Bane meant to see that she did.

He'd been right about her state of mind when she'd been found, something about a frightened cat. She'd been very quiet, but had finally come out of the hole they'd found her in. The crew had a calm way about them, talking softly to her and leaving food within reach until she found the courage to trust them. Jamie had Bane talk to her on the comm-link and he had reassured her that she wouldn't be taken back and that he was on his way to meet her and bring her to the Bounty.

"Welcome aboard, Captain, there's a young woman here that is very glad to see you."

"My thanks to you for seeing her safe and cared for. Jamie tells me she couldn't have picked a better ship to sneak aboard."

"Yeah, well, don't let that get around. This one was hard enough—like taming a wild animal, a scared, silent one."

"She had reason to be that wary, self-preservation has been her way of life for a while. Given half a chance, she'll put that behind her."

They went down the hall to the common room. Isa was sitting on a couch, tucked into the corner with her head resting on her knees, wide blue eyes watching. She unfolded as Bane sat next to her. "Hey, stranger." When he spoke, Isa collapsed into his chest.

The crew disappeared, allowing the two some private space. "Bane, I had to let Indian go, say goodbye to the barn, my family, and he was so drunk...tripped me...he was on top of me...he said...I saw the door...had to get down the stairs...hide...I hid...it smelled...he smelled...I'm sorry." Bane felt the warm tears wetting his shirt. Rocking her as the story wrenched out of her in short bursts.

As she spoke, Bane's protective nature rose up.

"I travelled by night. I was afraid he'd be looking for me. Remember that big old tree I showed you, south of that farm by that dry crick bed?" She told Bane her story over the course of the morning.

Over lunch, the crew heard more from Isa than she'd spoken the whole time she'd been with them. She talked about how she'd rationed her cookies and chewed gum when she felt hungry. Isa told them she'd chosen their ship because she'd noticed that they had more women on the crew than the others. That had them all looking at their Captain, laughing.

"I don't know what you're laughing at. We all know women work better than men." He winked at Isa. "I'm glad you chose us, Isa. What you did was very dangerous, so much could have happened. You have great courage and a logical way of solving problems. Those attributes will take you far."

Isa thanked them and she left with Bane for their journey back to the Bounty. On the way, she filled him in on the last two years and where each horse had gone. He'd smiled when she told him that Smokey had sold intact as his new owners hoped to use him for breeding. He'd be working cattle, checking fences, and helping them establish a reputation for quality ranch horses.

Isa spent a lot of time gazing out the view ports, asking question after question, but not waiting for the answer before the next question came. Looking out at all those stars reminded her of the plains and the way they go on forever, both with a beauty to take your breath away. She tucked that thought into her heart to take out when she missed home.

"What do you want to do about Frank?"

"Forget him? Ask him why? Punish him? I don't know."

"The way I look at it, you have the power to stop him from doing this to anyone else. Will it bring your horses back? Your farm? No, but it will guard others who could be trapped."

She stared off into the stars and Bane saw the slightest nod, her chin dipping briefly, head tilted slightly before her shoulders straightened and lifted with the air filling her lungs. "Okay, what do I need to do?"

"When we reach the Bounty, you can give official testimony to Alliance officials. The local law officers are holding him pending your statement. I asked Mel and Adam to give their statements and to scout around town for others who noticed, well, your bruises for one, and your lack of attendance at school and in town. It seems you made more than one deal around town, but nobody talked, so no one knew the whole picture."

"I did what I had to do, Bane."

Over the last few days he'd seen how resourceful she was. She'd even arranged a drop-off point with a trusted teacher, telling her they just couldn't afford the daily trips to town but that she didn't want to fall behind. Isa had spent the last three years schooling herself at the farm. She picked up books and assignments at the mailbox and delivered completed work the same way.

The rural carrier always found a cheerful face when he showed up, and was happy to oblige, having developed a fondness for oatmeal chocolate chip cookies. She had a way of working with people and a simple joy that couldn't help but be passed on. It had paid off with Ms. Gates, who'd smoothed things over with the school's administrator, especially when all the work she turned in was beyond expectations. The school initially had some confusion because Frank had said she was being home-schooled, but Ms. Gates was able to come up with an explanation about Isa needing work beyond what the home-school program could offer.

Bane was relieved that she'd advanced so far in her studies; it would make the next phase of her schooling easier because she had a depth of basic knowledge and excelled at math and science. He was concerned though about her lack of contact with her peers since Frank had stopped allowing her to attend school. She communicated well with adults, but relating to her own age group would be foreign in many ways. He wondered in what direction she would end up going and planned to expose her to many opportunities with various members of his crew. He had formed a tentative plan to present to the Academy president along with the request for work-study.

The Bounty was docked at the workstation on Rowan. This was an Alliance headquarters and Bane knew the protocol well. When they arrived, he thanked the Captain of the transport for making this side trip.

"Oh, no thanks needed, sir. The young girl's awe at my ship and the joy in her eyes when she stood on the bridge gazing at the stars were enough thanks for anyone. My wife will be proud that we took her in."

"Understood."

Listening to Isa give her testimony made Bane's blood boil. Given the chance, he would string Frank up himself. She needed to be as honest as possible and to give as much detail as she could remember in order to lock Frank away. This was important, he'd told her, and he promised he'd stay with her while she talked to the gray-haired, dimpled-faced Alliance child welfare official. She needed the grandmother-like woman, who had an easy relaxed presence.

The session was being recorded for law enforcement officials. Comparing Isa's childhood to his own "normal" upbringing made Bane wonder how courage and fortitude are formed. She spoke of the great love of her family until the death of her father had undone her mother. That love and her strong sense of carrying on the family tradition with horses had filled her life with purpose and joy. No matter what Frank did, he couldn't take that from her.

When Isa finished telling her story, she said, "I know it isn't right for anyone to hurt another. Someone must have hurt Frank to make him so filled with anger and hate. I don't want him to ever hurt anyone again, but who can protect him from himself?" Bane exchanged a glance with the woman.

"Well, Isa, I can't answer that, but knowing you are thinking about what made Frank the way he is tells me that you are going to be okay. I guess it's like that troubled horse you were telling me about and how patient you had to be before he would trust you, you'll have to learn to trust in people again and I think you're in good hands for that journey." She had told Isa that Frank would be put away for a long time.

Their appointment via comm-link with the Academy president was scheduled for the next day. "So, personal tour of the Bounty?"

"Yes!"

Bounty was undergoing routine maintenance and the ship was almost empty as they strolled the corridors. The halls were wide enough for people to walk and talk, with computer terminals at strategic locations to allow for intraship communication. The floors had a carpet with blue and gray squares running a pattern that made the halls look long. As they entered, Isa stopped to breathe it all in. Isa felt the purpose in this ship, to explore, but there was more to it; this was a place where people lived, not just a place to work.

The crew quarters were on the second level of the ship with many places to sit and have a conversation. Comfortable cushy chairs where Isa could picture leaning in close to hear what someone might have to say. She'd enjoy leaning against the wall watching, or looking out the many view ports at the dark prairie full of stars and other things she didn't know how to name yet. This level also housed the medical area.

Bane showed her the different departmental work areas, taking the lift to the first level with geo-research and water reclamation. He told her that it was important for everyone to work as a team, even though each person had his or her own specialty. He wanted his crew to be comfortable in reaching out with information and for it to be easy to do. It wouldn't be difficult to get around, once Isa learned how each area was interconnected.

The fourth and top level held Astro-engineering and the arboretum, with plenty of room for storage. They didn't go into Astro, but Bane had a hard time getting Isa out of the green world held inside the arboretum. She wanted to walk along the wooded paths and study every plant. It held a big garden too and that provided plenty of fresh produce to feed the crew. She could even have her own garden plot if she wanted. The rest of engineering took up the aft of Bounty and covered all four levels with access to the ship's drive and the sensor arrays.

Bane saved the bridge for last. Exiting the lift on level three, he took her past the common room and galley, the recreation rooms, guest quarters and to the fore most part of Bounty, the bridge. He let her go first and watched as she stopped to take it all in. Her eyes moved slowly, narrowing to focus on the details of each station. She stood, inhaling the view of Rowan hanging in the vastness of space.

"It's like looking out the loft door. You are so lucky to see this every day. Your ship has a good presence, Bane. My dad would be glad that I ended up here. He always taught me to do what I'm passionate about. I just need to find something new to care about."

Bane watched as steel formed her spine. She shook her head.

"So, when do I start?"

"Let's go sit down, get something to drink, and talk.

"Can we do that here?"

He cupped her shoulder, smiling. "We can go to the common room. I think I can rustle us up a couple sodas. Do you remember how to get there?"

Isa hesitated at a few turns; once she could remember what was on each level, it wouldn't be a problem. Eventually, she ended up in the common room. It was set up for the crew to relax, talk, and have a bite to eat or a drink. Small tables and chairs, larger tables, comfy chairs and couches arranged in various spaces to accommodate different activities.

A small kitchen was stocked for a self-serve style; some crewmembers were responsible for meals cooked once a day for a community meal, and they used the larger galley. All other meals were left to personal responsibility, with lots of options and several prep stations. Isa liked the informal feel.

She chose an area by the viewing windows and two plush blue chairs with a small table between. Isa enjoyed the viewing windows that were plentiful all over the ship. They were a reminder of everything Bounty stood for and she loved being constantly exposed to the raw beauty of space. Bane set a soda in front of her, sitting down as Isa picked up the glass and studied its contents. She brought it slowly to her mouth, smiling as the little bubbles tickled her nose, pursing her lips as she took a small sip. Swallowing, a little "oh" escaped, "Wow! That's delicious. Orange?"

"You've never had a soda? Yes. Orange. They come in grape, cherry, cola and root beer, too." Isa liked the way his face crinkled up when he laughed.

"Nope. But I have had pink lemonade. It didn't have little bubbles, though."

She had a lot to discover and Bane could tell that much of it would bring out more of this innocent joy. That would be the easy part; harder would be understanding that she would not be in charge or with so much responsibility for a while. Even under Frank's control, she had a lot of time to do what she wanted and took on all the responsibility for the care of her horses and herself. Bane hoped this would help her and not end up a stumbling block. His crewmembers followed orders on his ship, not without input, but once given, they asked no questions.

"So, we have three weeks here on Rowan? May I spend the time learning my way around? I promise not to get in anyone's way."

"I think we can arrange that if you don't mind being on your own. I'll show you your quarters and arrange for you to pick up some clothes and things for your room. My communications officer, Jamie, said she'd be happy to help you. You should also know that Mel is ready to head out to the farm and put together whatever you want, box it up for transport."

"Really? There are a few belongings I'd like to have. I, uh, left in rather a hurry." The smile was strained, but her sense of humor was still intact. They discussed logistics and the fact that Mel would have to send her saddle, and then Bane brought up horses.

"Isa, Rowan has some beautiful mountain ranges and I had planned to see them on horseback while I was here. I've made arrangements for you to come on a pack trip for a few days if you're interested." She pulled her knees to her chest, clasping her arms around them, stared out into space and whispered, "Yes, please." They sat in the silent company of the stars for a while, each lost in thought. Bane hadn't realized the profound effect having horses would have on her and felt some of the depth of her grief at the loss of what she'd worked so hard for, for her family.

Back on Rowan later, they had burgers with Jamie. The two hit it off right away and made arrangements over chocolate malts to make the required purchases. Bane had already asked Jamie to give him a ballpark figure on what it would cost. "You ladies have a good time and Isa, Mel let me know that you came out ahead after Indian's sale, so you should have plenty to cover your needs. Until that's transferred, Jamie knows how to settle accounts using my name."

To Jamie, the imperceptible shake of Captain Lucas' head. "Sure, no problem, and we can have everything delivered to your quarters on Bounty. Does she have quarters yet?"

They agreed to have an early lunch the following day after the meeting with the Academy. Wishing Jamie a good evening, Bane guided Isa to their quarters in the housing provided. Rowan held a housing section for those who worked in the Alliance and he'd asked for adjoining rooms in case she needed anything in the night. "Sleep well; you've come a long way. We'll have an early start tomorrow—knock when you're ready."

"Night. And Bane, thank you."

10.

Ken Wilson had been President at the Academy for years. Bane Lucas was a former student and both men respected each other. Ken had read through Bane's reference, background and study plan, and the testimony Isa Torunn had given to the welfare authority. He was impressed with her story, but also concerned about her emotional stability and her time out on the Bounty. He was a fair judge of character, so was looking forward to the impression she would make, even through a videoconference.

"President Wilson, Isa Torunn."

"Yes, let's dispense with the titles, Bane. Isa, it's a pleasure to meet you."

"And you, sir, I've heard a lot about you and am sorry not to be able to meet you in person."

"All good, I hope! Now, I've read your recommendation, Bane, and your tentative study plan, and of course we can provide the required texts if I approve. Isa, why don't you tell me how you see this course work unfolding and how you plan to adjust to life on a starship?"

A couple hours later, relaxed smiles sat on three faces. "Isa, give me a day or two to mull things over. It's not an easy path through Academy training, but with your discipline and maturity, I think you will succeed. I'll tell you straight out that I think one of the biggest challenges you'll face will be understanding that you aren't a solo act anymore, but rather part of a well-orchestrated team."

She was intent, leaning into the screen as Ken spoke and he knew she was listening seriously. He hadn't found it difficult to read her emotions as they'd spoken and he'd appreciated her honest quality when she'd told him that she really had no idea what this experience was all about or what direction she should go in, but that she was a good student and would do her best. It was a pleasant change from students who thought they needed to impress him to get what they wanted.

"Bane, when you've assigned her a mentor, I'll want to talk with her and I'll get back to you when I've made my decision and decided who on my staff will be her advisor liaison. I'll expect to meet in person as soon as it's convenient for Bounty. We can further discuss those details when I get back to you. Will you be available in the next couple of days?"

"Absolutely, Ken. We appreciate your time and look forward to hearing from you soon." Bane nudged Isa out of her thoughts and she looked up.

"Yes, uh, thank you, sir." The screen went dark and Bane pulled the cover over it. Isa's eyes were on Bane. "He seems nice; I think I'll like meeting him. Do you think he'll approve me?"

"I don't see why not. You were thoughtful and willing to admit when you didn't understand something and you were well spoken. We'll just wait and see. Until then, there's a lot to be done. Let's find Jamie and I'll turn the two of you loose while I do some thinking about a mentor for you and when Bounty might be in the Academy sector."

Jamie was waiting outside the main dining room in the center. "How'd it go? You in?"

"I don't know yet, but I think it went well."

"Well enough, Jamie, she did fine."

Isa picked at the spaghetti, twisting the noodles first one way, then the other around her fork. "Maybe you should do a little less thinking and a little more eating." Bane smiled at her.

"Sorry. I'm just not very hungry."

"Well, I'm ready if you are for this shopping adventure."

Bane watched as they headed out the door, walking side-by-side with their heads together deciding where to go first. Jamie would be good for her. She was one of Bane's youngest officers and she came from a large family. She could be a friend to Isa, someone to relax with and have fun with, as a young woman.

Jamie steered them to choosing clothing first. Isa had been washing out the clothes she had, and as they were borrowed from the crew of her stowaway ship, they didn't fit well. The girls found jeans first, and Jamie advised Isa, putting her at ease with her matter-of-fact handling of the racks and the dressing room. Isa felt like an alien and couldn't get used to seeing herself in jeans and shirts that fit. She'd turn this way and that, wondering who this girl was looking back at her.

Most everything was put aside for transport; some of the clothes were delivered to her quarters here, along with a small satchel to pack them in. She found a beautiful pair of dark brown leather boots with simple tooling that laced up; she'd picked them up and stood for a moment with her eyes closed, breathing in the scent.

Isa and Jamie left, the new boots making a firm thud on the wood floor as the slim young woman in new blue jeans, a pretty blue blouse, and holding a soft blue-green jacket over her arm strode out. In the bedding store, Isa picked out sheets and blankets, pillows and a small reading lamp. She told Jamie she didn't want a spread or coverlet; she wanted the quilt from her bed at home that her grandmother had made and that she'd always slept under. Jamie suggested they take a break, have something to drink and make a list of what she wanted. Settling into a couple of soft brown chairs, they tucked their legs underneath themselves. Jamie wrote while Isa talked.

"It might help to go one room at a time, Isa, that way your memory can guide you through your place."

"Okay, the quilt on my bed, like I said. Actually most everything I want's in my room, Frank sold the rest. There's our family album that my grandmother covered with old scraps of material, kind of like the quilt, and there's a photo of my mom and dad on the dresser. It's my favorite because they look so happy together and it was taken shortly after they married. My journal and a box with pictures of the horses are in the bottom drawer of my dresser. They hold my whole life. Then, down in the kitchen, in the cupboard over the stove, is my great-grandmother's old wooden recipe box, I need to have that."

"All right, I got all that, go on."

"That's all in the house."

"That's it? There's nothing else you want? No jewelry? Stuffed animals? Books? Anything?"

"I told you, anything Frank thought he could sell, he did, so the only books I had were the ones loaned from my teacher, and I returned those."

Isa stared out the window, quiet, her head tilted slightly, chin resting on bent fingers, breathing even and steady. Small white puffy clouds scattered across a blue sky. She was curled up in her dad's lap in the barn loft, all the doors thrown wide to catch the cool breeze. He was reading a favorite book to her about pioneers surviving a snow-laden, cold winter on the plains.

In the heat of her summer day, she could still feel the joy and love shared by that family through the harsh weather and in the simple sharing of warm soup and biscuits, coming to the aid of neighbors in need, and giving thanks for daily blessings. Isa remembered looking out the loft door and seeing what was, to her, the whole world, graceful and beautiful. Through that door, she could see to the edge of her world, grey in the gathering of a summer storm, the bright straw of wheat stubble laid out like a carpet next to the green-brown pasture grasses.

She watched the little yellow-bellied birds flitting past, their "je, je-de deep" arguments moving from fence wire to tree branch. She knew the words her father was reading by heart and loved the way his voice vibrated through her skin while she looked out at the distant farms, each outlined by their trees, towering windmills standing alone in pastures, the play of shadows on the land making her think of pictures she'd seen of the oceans.

Her gaze wandered to the trees she could see in their windbreak. One old stump that she begged not to be taken out; it must have been a fine tree and she liked the smooth feel of leaning against it and its stately weathered look that spoke of time. The horses grazed their way into her view—pale yellow Doc, his white tail flowing out, red-brown Cowboy, bossing the others around, and two paints, one black and white, one brown and white. She saw the hawk soaring low over the ground and the wind rushed out of the southeast; she'd asked her dad where it was going in such a hurry.

Jamie sat, pen resting on the pad of paper in her lap, sipping the soda and waited for Isa to come back. She was happy the captain had asked for her help. Ever since he'd had her contact those transport ships and she'd had a glimpse of what had gone on in Isa's life, she'd been curious and wanting to meet her. At twenty,

Jamie was only four years older, and she liked Isa, thought they could be good friends.

This morning's shopping had given her a chance to do for someone else what her older sisters had done for her; it was fun watching someone else begin to discover herself, with a few nudges in the right direction. Jamie knew if it were her list they were making, there'd be a whole lot more on it; her mother was still complaining about the amount of stuff left in her room at home and asking when they could get rid of it.

Jamie watched as Isa's eyes slowly began to shift from outside the window, back to her. "Last of my things are in the barn. My saddle, it's the only one left in the tack room, along with my mom's Indian blanket, it's woven from thick wool and is light with gold, red, black and sky-blue stripes." She hesitated, looked down, and then grinned at Jamie.

"What? What is it?"

"They'll need a ladder for this."

That book her father had read to her in the barn was part of a set. But it had been her favorite, often requested when they had time together, and always shared in the loft on a soft blanket against the bales by the north door, sometimes with a bowl of popcorn or some sweet grapes. They'd devised a special place together to keep that book in the loft, inside a waterproof oilskin pouch and tucked high above the west window on the north wall behind the heavy wire mesh that protected the glass. Frank had been angry when he had to sell that set incomplete. He was sure she knew where it was. He'd beaten her, but she'd never told him where it was, and hadn't brought it out since her father's death. It was their story, and she'd buried it deep until something chipped its lock loose today.

Jamie smiled back at her, saying, "Well, we'll just have to let them know." She tore off the page and handed it to Isa. "Be right back." While Jamie returned the pad and pen, Isa looked over the list, nodded, folded it, and stuck it in her back pocket. They spent the rest of the afternoon picking up towels, personal bath items, and the study supplies Isa would need for her course work.

"Do you have a workout that you like? The Captain's pretty adamant about the crew staying in good physical condition, so we have a lot of options on board. Depending on your interest, you'll need some gear, running shoes, and shorts at the very least. We'll also stop and get you measured for regs, everyone's in uniform when on duty."

Isa liked the idea of running; it would give her time to think. They picked up shoes, shorts, running pants, a guide to start running, a little device so she could listen to music while she ran, as well as tights and ballet shoes—Isa loved to move and thought ballet would be fun to learn. Last stop was uniforms. An older lady, Jeanne, with graying hair and sparkling eyes, listened as Jamie explained Isa's position on the crew as a student.

Jamie sat down as Isa was ushered into a private area and Jeanne measured her waist, bust, hips, arm length, inseam, height and weight, and shoe size. They came back into the main room and Jeanne asked them to wait while she looked up Isa and entered all her information. "Okay, ladies, you're all set. Everything will ship to the Bounty in short order and I wish you luck, Isa."

"It's getting late, Isa. Captain'll be wondering where we got off to. I'll walk back with you."

"Jamie, thanks for all your help today. I would have been lost. Do you mind if I try to find my own way back? It's time I start learning this new place."

"Sure thing. If you get lost, just ask someone. I'll probably see you tomorrow if you want to spend the day on Bounty. Just give me a call, I'll be around."

Isa took her time getting back, doing her best to reconstruct the path they'd taken. Once she passed the spot where they'd eaten lunch, she became confused. Wandering in circles for a while, she wished she could get up high and find a landmark. Her breathing quickened and she began to chew on her lower lip. With many people around, she spotted an older man and forced herself to approach him. "May I help you?"

"Hi, I'm Isa and I can't remember just how to get back to my quarters. I'm with Captain Lucas." She looked up after spewing these words out, into a welcoming face. He spoke as he reached out his right hand in greeting.

"Well, Isa, it's nice to meet you. I'm Timothy, and I'm retired. Of course my wife hasn't figured that out yet." He chuckled and she felt reassured; her hand clasped his. "I'm sure I can turn you in the right direction. You say you're with Captain Lucas?"

"Yes. Thank you."

11.

Bane set off to look for Isa after he'd spoken to Jamie and she'd told him that Isa had wanted to find her own way back. She must have stopped or taken a wrong turn for her to be gone this long. He stopped when he saw her speaking to an older gentleman who led her to a computer terminal. Bane had been sure she'd be too timid to approach a stranger and was glad she'd found the courage to do so. She would not run into any trouble on Rowan, but he could see she was playing it safe by approaching someone who probably reminded her of a grandfather.

"So, you're on the right track. Just go down this hall and take the first left—"

"Isa." They both turned as Bane spoke. Isa smiled, but her shoulders relaxed some with relief of seeing Bane approach her and Timothy.

"Bane. Captain." Momentarily flustered at mastering this new word associated with her friend, she glanced back and forth at Timothy and Bane, mouth slightly open.

"Hi. Bane Lucas." Bane's right hand shot out.

"Timothy Hamil," he said and returned the firm handshake.

"Sorry, uh, I guess I got a bit lost. When I went past this center for the fourth or fifth time, I decided I better ask for help, so I turned to Timothy."

Timothy beamed down at her. Bane noted a fondness already developing, remembering how quickly he himself had thought Isa's company pleasant. "No worries, Isa. This is a big station and many of the corridors look the same. My wife, Fran, often gets lost. Don't tell her I said that. I'm quite sure you'll find your way around it quickly."

"Thanks, Timothy."

"Yes, thank you," added Bane, "this is a far cry from the rugged plains Isa is used to, and with the people-to-horse ratio so backwards." They all chuckled.

"Where are you from, Isa? I grew up in the farm community on Savarin. My wife and I retired, and we make Rowan our home base now. She would want to hear your story; she loves to be reminded of the life we both knew growing up."

"My family homesteaded on the northern plains of Melacross. Horses were our specialty." Isa's voice drifted off, her eyes cast down at her boots. Bane's hand cupped her shoulder, his and Timothy's eyes meeting over Isa's head.

"She's being modest, Timothy, she raised and trained the finest horses around single-handedly with a horse-sense born from the generations of knowledge in her family. Why don't you join us for dinner and Isa can tell you all about them?" Isa drew in a deep shaky breath and straightened her back and shoulders.

"Yes do, Timothy and bring your wife too. Maybe we can have a soda. Do you enjoy them?"

Laughing, "I'd love to join you, and yes, I do enjoy a soda every now and then. Let me call my wife. Where should we meet you?"

"The café just outside the Alliance accommodations." As Bane said this, he turned to Isa, who nodded approval enthusiastically.

"Fine," a grinning Timothy said, "we'll meet you there in, say, thirty minutes?"

"Perfect. See you there."

Isa smiled as they parted company and strode off with Bane. She had been frightened for a moment by the sheer number of people in the corridors and her inability to see the sun to gauge a direction in order to find her way. She had always relied on her knowledge of the land and a horse that would get you back to the barn no matter how bad the weather.

"Would I have been in much trouble if I had just climbed up on the nearest column to get a bird's eye view of where I was trying to go?" Her words flowed straight out of her thoughts about climbing that solitary cottonwood tree down in the old creek bed gully when she was eight, in order to see the Lee Cemetery archway so she could find her way home.

"I'm sure you would have raised a few eyebrows," chuckling, Bane added, "I think asking Timothy for help was the wiser choice. Rowan is a safe world, Isa, but it's always smart to rely on your own gut feeling when you meet people. Yours is finely tuned; learn to trust it again. I don't think it's failed you yet. So, how was the shopping spree with Jamie? I noticed your new outfit and boots. You look nice."

She studied her reflection in the glass separating the hall from a shop. Making do had been her way of life and she wondered who the girl in the reflection was.

"I had no idea that my feet were a size nine, I just knew that it was hard to cram them into my old boots, which I'd been patching with glue and cardboard. These are amazing and I felt so—decadent, buying all new clothes for me; I've just been wearing my mom's clothes. Oh, and this really sweet lady, Jeanne, got me all set up with uniforms and Jamie helped me make my list for Mel...." Isa dug into her pocket, retrieving the piece of paper and handed it to Bane. "I may have to explain to him how to get the book."

They'd reached the entrance to the café and were greeted by the host, "Two, sir?"

"Actually, four. We're expecting an older couple to join us."

"Very good, sir. Lottie will show you to your table and I'll keep an eye out for your guests and have them join you when they arrive. What is their name?"

Nodding at the host, Bane gave him Timothy's name; ushered Isa ahead and they followed Lottie to a table in a quiet corner by a window. "It's dark," Isa said, surprised. "I hadn't realized it was so late. No wonder you came for me."

Looking over the list she'd handed him, he asked, "Isa, this is all you want?" His hand clasped her shoulder and she turned, meeting his eyes.

"Frank sold everything he could, Bane; that's really all there is. I only just remembered that I still had that book in the secret spot in the barn loft. I haven't touched it since my dad died. It'll be tricky to get to it with no hay up there. It's wedged down between the window and the wire mesh that protects the glass."

The look was honest, but Bane could see the effort she was putting forth to keep a distance, a detachment from the memories. Her eyes had twinkled in a small smile when she explained where the book was, and it was apparent she'd let him in on a secret she'd kept for years.

"I'm sure Mel can figure out a way to get it if you explain it to him. We can contact him in the morning and make all the arrangements."

Isa turned with a glow as the host brought Timothy and his wife to their table. She was slim, graceful, with streaks of grey through her brown hair pulled up in a loose bun.

"Bane, Isa, I'd like you to meet my wife, Fran. Fran, this is Bane Lucas and Isa...I'm sorry, I don't know your last name."

"Torunn. Isa Torunn." She and Bane stood, exchanging handshakes and "It's nice to meet you." Seated again, Isa between Bane and Timothy, Fran across from her, Lottie handed them menus and said she'd give them a few minutes to decide and be back to take their orders. Timothy piped up and asked for two cherry sodas for him and Isa before Lottie left. Fran gave her husband a raised eyebrow.

"Well, I told Isa I liked soda. You wouldn't want her drinking alone, would you?"

Fran took his hand, looked at Bane and Isa, and said, laughing, "No dear, you will just have to suffer so this poor girl doesn't have to enjoy a cherry soda all alone!"

They had a wonderful meal, relaxing in each other's company. Isa thought the bubbly cherry soda just as good as the orange and couldn't wait to try all the other flavors. Bane made a mental note to let his supply officer know to order in an extra stock of soda until the newness wore off.

Sharing her love of horses and the land that was so much a part of who she was enthralled Timothy and Fran. Growing up on rural planets, Isa sent them both back to sweet memories and the simple way they had grown up. Hard work, yes, but rewarding and satisfying in ways different than those more technologically oriented.

Timothy and Fran had met later in life and had no children and thus no grandchildren. They enjoyed visiting a variety of planets, with Rowan being home now. Enjoying Isa's company and conversation gave them joy, not regret over what they didn't have.

Timothy had shared with Fran his encounter with Isa in the busy terminal section. He'd noticed her passing a few times, looking around, apparently lost. Noting the hesitancy in her walk as she approached him, he'd spoken first to ease the wide-eyed look on her face. Fran nodded as he spoke, and "hmm'd," saying "good" when Timothy mentioned Bane's approach, which seemed protective to him. Putting her hand on her husband's forearm, she'd leaned in concerned when he had described the sudden sadness coming over the girl when he'd asked her where she was from and the look Bane Lucas had given him as he tried to give her a moment to recover.

Timothy watched Fran listening and encouraging Isa all through dinner, and knew this would not be the last they saw of Isa Torunn. Fran had a compassionate soul and a heart big enough to ease great hurt. As he sat, knowing this, he had that familiar feeling of warmth and the quickening of his heart that Fran had brought to his life. He wondered how this Captain Bane Lucas, Isa had stumbled over calling him Captain, fit into the picture. It was obvious that he cared for the young girl and in a protective way, and that she felt safe with him.

Bane watched Isa yawning again. "Timothy, Fran, thank you for a wonderful evening. We've had a long day and I think it's time we turn in for the night."

"Oh yes, the poor girl is almost asleep in her chair. We would enjoy having you both over for a home-cooked meal."

"I'm sure Isa would love that, and I'd be happy to tag along. You can leave a message for us in the Alliance wing. Thank you, Fran, and thanks again, Timothy, for helping Isa to find her way."

Isa also thanked them both and the four of them parted at the door.

"They are so kind. I'm glad I asked him for help." She said this, stifling another yawn into her hand.

"I think we'll be seeing them again. In fact, I bet Fran would be willing to help you with anything, Isa." He grinned as he said this, recognizing a mother hen when he met one. Encouraging Isa to contact Fran, Bane thought she could use a person like Fran in her life. Back in their quarters, Bane said goodnight to a worn out Isa and that he'd see her in the morning.

Leaving the door between their rooms slightly ajar, as he'd done the previous night, Bane flipped open his computer to make a few notes. Remembering the soda, he sent a note to Lt. Gary Brown, the ship's supply officer. Bane spent more time thinking about Isa's training and who on his crew might best teach her. Covering his own yawn a while later, he stretched, closed the computer and got himself off to bed.

In her room, Isa opened the parcels from the day's excursion with Jamie, oohing again as she opened each one—it was like Christmas morning when she was very little. She let her hands glide over the various materials, bringing the soft silky pajamas to her cheek. Putting everything neatly away but relishing the feel of her new pajamas, she slid into bed and whispered, "Dear God, thank you for bringing me here. Tell Mom and Dad that I'm okay and safe now. Tell them I'm sorry I lost the farm. Tell them I miss them. Tell them...." She fell asleep with the unfinished sentence in her heart.

12.

Waking up early, even though it had been a late night, was part of who Isa was. Pulling on jeans and the new boots, along with a blue-green blouse, she'd found Bane also up and dressed and asked if he wanted to come outside with her and watch the sunrise. They'd both ordered a hot cup of coffee at a hospitality station and headed out into the morning.

A deck wound alongside the building and above a small stream; chairs every so often invited relaxing conversation in small groups. Rowan was a planet well tuned for the needs of weary travelers and those on Alliance shore leave. Isa was perched on the deck railing, her hands clasping the mug for warmth, sipping coffee and taking in deep breaths of the cool, clean early morning air. Her gaze was fixed on the pink orange horizon and the sun emerging though it. There were still a few bright stars visible in the darkest part of the sky.

"I was hoping to spend most of today on the Bounty. Jamie said she would come, and, well, would it be okay to ask Fran to help me organize my quarters and make them... homey?"

"I think Fran would be thrilled that you asked, and yes, it's fine with me. Jamie can help you find something to eat midday, and we can meet up for a meal this evening, although not as late as last night. I have business to take care of here, including getting supplies for our pack trip. Why don't you have breakfast, contact Mel with your list, and go from there. Did you happen to pick up some warm clothes yesterday?"

"Not really, just the basics. What will I need, and should I help you get ready for this pack trip?"

"No. You spend time getting to know Bounty. If you can squeeze it in today, you'll need to get warm clothes, including thermal socks and full-body underwear, a couple warm flannel shirts, an insulated jacket, raingear, a warm cap of some kind, liners and gloves. If not, we'll work it in tomorrow. Hop down, let's go get some chow." Reaching out for her mug, he held it while she climbed down. She kept her eye on the magnificence of the new day as they disappeared back inside.

Seated in the first eatery they came to, Isa asked question after question while waiting for their meal. "So, Jamie says you like your crew to stay in shape. She helped me choose some running gear and a how-to guide. I know I'll like that, but I also bought gear to try ballet."

"It's important to me that my crew stay physically fit so we're ready for any situation. I also want them mentally fit. When you serve on the Bounty, you need to have something to offer as well as excellence at your job." Isa was beginning to get an inkling of the Captain-side of Bane Lucas. It had come out yesterday when he'd met Timothy—a commanding presence that was in control. "Lieutenant Iridian teaches ballet. She danced professionally while attending the Academy. She was trained classically, and is a very exacting teacher. I'm sure you will enjoy that. She's teaching a master class while we're here on Rowan; we can arrange for you to observe."

"Sweet, I'd love to see what it's all about." Two steaming plates arrived. Isa doused her stack of buckwheat blueberry pancakes with syrup and dug in. Wondering if ordering a soda would be okay, she paused to ask Bane.

The toast stopped halfway to his mouth and he laughed at the totally kid-like look on her face. "Well, most folks generally don't drink soda for breakfast, it isn't like a glass of juice, Isa, it's a sweet treat. There are no rules against it, although most parents would say no. Go ahead, if you like. I'll have another cup of coffee." Thinking this over, staring hard at her pancakes, Bane could see her indecision. He waved the waitress over. "Another coffee, please." The waitress turned to Isa.

"Ma'am?"

"Uh, yeah, I'd love more coffee...and a small glass of grape soda, please." Her eyebrow rose but she said nothing as she went off for the coffee and soda.

"Grape? I guess that goes about as well with blueberries as anything. I do like, though, that you asked for the traditional coffee first, just to throw her off."

"You caught that, huh?"

"Mmhmm." Wondering if he needed to amend his addition for soda supplies to stock even more, Bane appreciated that she'd asked for what she wanted, making her own decision about what was right for her. She'd moderated it by asking for a small glass, and he could see the compromise in that.

When the contraband soda arrived, she enjoyed it, laughing as the bubbles tickled her nose. Deciding that the coffee went better with the pancakes, she waited until those were finished and then drank the rest of her small soda.

Leaving the café, they went back to their rooms, where Bane used the comm-link to contact Mel. He was glad to see Isa was doing so well and told her that the farm had been sold to a family who planned to fix it up and make it productive again. They'd been waiting and hoping for such a place and happened to be in town when the notice was posted a couple days before. With that ever-present hand resting on her shoulder, she was silent for a moment as she took in this news. Then she nodded her head and said, "Good Mel. That's how it should be. You tell them that it's a place that needs a family and that they should love it and love each other the best that they can." She was still nodding.

"I will, Isa. I'll tell them your story—before Frank. And rest assured that I've already let them know there are a few things of yours still there that I'm picking up for you. They won't take possession until I can get out there."

"Okay, my list is pretty short, Mel." She turned to Bane who handed her the piece of paper Jamie had written her items on. Isa read the list as Mel took notes, telling her it would be no problem to retrieve the book from the loft in the barn. "There isn't much left, Mel, don't be upset at the way it all looks. I love you for all that you've done for me over the years, and please tell Ms. Gates and Adam the same for me. I could never have made it without you."

"I wish we had done more, girl. No sense dwelling on that, your things will be on a transport later today. I don't know how soon they will arrive."

Bane's rich, deep voice answered, "She'll have them before we leave, Mel. Thanks again for taking care of this."

"All right, then, keep in touch once in a while, won't you, Isa-girl? Let us know how you're doing."

"I will, Mel. Bye now." Bane ended the transmission and gently taking Isa's arm, brought her to the sofa. Sitting silently, he wrapped his arm around her shaking shoulders, tucked her head into his shoulder and let her cry. He wondered if this was the feeling fathers had for their daughters, and how they managed to get through their daughter's lives without killing anyone who hurt them.

Unclenching her right hand from Bane's shirt minutes later, she wiped the tears away. "Why does it have to be so hard? I should be glad there is a family on the farm and not Frank. And I am—it's just—I miss it so much. I miss my horses so much. I miss, I just want...." She stopped, and a few more tears escaped.

"Isa, of course it's hard. It was your whole life. I know you feel you let your family down." Her look said he was right. "But you didn't. You accomplished so much and with responsibility that should never have been put on your young shoulders. You took what life thrust at you and not only survived, but also produced some of the best horses I've ever ridden. I call that success. Your parents would be proud of what you've done and where you're going."

"I know you are right. I just need to believe it."

"Give yourself time. It will hurt, but slowly and with patience, it will get better." Hugging her reassuringly, he sent her off to wash up.

After they made contact with Jamie and arranged to meet for transport to the Bounty, Bane helped Isa call Fran. Timothy answered with, "Well, hello Isa. How are you this fine morning?"

"Great, Timothy, is Fran busy?"

"She's right here."

"Isa? This is Fran. Is everything all right?"

"Yes, Fran. I was just wondering if you might be available to help me out with something today?"

"Why, I'd love to, shall I bring Timothy too? We aren't doing anything today that can't wait."

"Well," she glanced at Bane, who nodded, "sure."

After Isa explained the situation, Fran insisted on bringing a noon-day meal, picnic style, for all four of them, and promised to fit the shopping for warm clothes in late that afternoon and before the earlier dinner Captain Lucas insisted on. They agreed to meet for transport to Bounty as soon as Fran could put her picnic together.

Bane and Isa made a list of what she'd need to buy for camping and he recommended a place to go where he thought she could find everything. There was plenty of shopping available in the complex, although they could go anywhere on Rowan and find other similar stores. Rowan offered many options for outdoor activities and that made it a popular planet for Alliance ships to stop, so crews on shore leave could take advantage of the recreation available. For those who didn't have the outdoor bug, there was an active nightlife scene too. Isa had slept outside with the horses in the pasture, but she had never done any pack trips and she was excited to learn what this was all about. Bane joked that he'd warn the outfitter to expect both a lot of questions and a shadow. He figured she would come back from this trip ready to lead a group out herself; he'd be surprised if that wasn't the case.

They discussed the plan for the next couple of weeks until the crew returned and Bounty set off once again. They wouldn't leave on the horse trip for several more days, although Isa wanted to meet their guide sooner. She could spend those days wandering the Bounty and purchasing anything she might need that they hadn't thought of—most likely Fran would find some items they hadn't included.

On their way out to the transport site, Bane tried to make it clear to Isa that everything didn't have to happen in one day. She should take her time and find those stopping points, just like when training a young horse, and then find a view port and enjoy the scenery for a while. Perhaps today, with Fran's help, they could simply focus on her quarters and making them a place where Isa could relax and be herself.

Isa agreed to try not to do too much, but her excitement over what awaited shown in the little hop-skip of her step and the arch of the swing in her arms. Talking to Mel had brought her loss to her heart in a way that hadn't been quite so real until that point. She needed time to wrap her head around the idea that a new family would be taking over what she had been born into. That time would come, when she was alone, quiet. Until then, focusing on this next part of her life needed to consume her.

Bane walked quietly beside her and soon they came to the transport site. After introducing Jamie, Timothy and Fran, and admonishments from Bane for them to meet for dinner at 7 pm sharp, they left for Bounty.

13.

"Jamie, let me try to find my way. I've gone over what I can remember from the Captain's tour in my mind, but I'm not sure of the best way to quarters from here."

"Sure thing, Isa. Lead the way." She smiled at Isa and Fran and Timothy fell in step beside her. The halls were laid out in a circular pattern on the four levels of the ship, and corridors bisected the circle for more direct routes back and forth. Isa took a deep breath; the smell was clean but not antiseptic. She wondered how they kept it so fresh. The walls were smooth and the communication terminals recessed to save space. Isa liked the warm light that illuminated the ship as it gave the place a sunny feeling.

All was quiet as Isa talked her way back to her new home. She stopped in front of what she knew was the entrance to her room, quarters, she corrected herself. She had to begin thinking in this new language. Isa pressed the button allowing her entry and stepped in. Looking around, her heart told her this was a fresh beginning, a chance to start again, as she closed her eyes briefly.

"Welcome to my quarters. Sorry for the mess." Isa turned, inviting the others in. They had held back as she entered, but happily joined her now. Everything she and Jamie had purchased was here, on the floor and covering the bed. "So, what's the best way to sort this out?"

"Plunge in," Fran offered, "unpack and unwrap everything and we'll just see how everything will best fit." It was mid-morning by now, and clearing the bed of the earlier purchases, they used it and the other available flat surfaces to place the clothing and gear in like piles. It took some time, even though Isa was sure she didn't need much when she'd done the shopping in the first place. Fran was compiling a list of what she felt Isa would still need for comfort and for practical use.

The room had a built-in set of drawers and bookshelves, a small table with two chairs, the bed, a small desk with a chair, an open area with the personal bathroom behind it. Best of all, to Isa, were three viewing windows with covers that could be moved to any position from wide open to completely closed. There was also a small closet and limited storage in the bathroom.

Jamie hung the new uniforms, pressed and still in plastic covers, in the closet along with the pretty new blouses and the one skirt she managed to talk Isa into. The new shoes found homes on the closet floor. Timothy had set to work with the sheets, pillows and other bedding while Fran helped Isa organize her clothing into the drawers and put the bathroom to rights.

"Well, my girl, it's starting to look like home," Timothy said sometime later, putting his arm around Isa's shoulder, hugging her lightly.

She nodded, grinning up at him, "It will, when I get my things from the farm." They had worked steadily through the late morning and as Isa glanced around, taking it all in, her stomach unleashed a series of growling sounds.

"Fran, love, are you going to let our girls here starve?"

"Goodness, no! Didn't that Captain of yours feed you this morning? Jamie, is there somewhere we can go to sit comfortably and have our lunch?"

Timothy took in the joy evident on Fran's face. She was in her element and loving every minute of mothering Isa. He thought that Isa was glad for the guidance even in the tiniest suggestion that the towels would be easier to reach closer to the shower on the little shelf above the towel rack and that Fran knew just where they could purchase some fragrant soaps Isa was sure to enjoy.

"Sure, we can go to the common room. Isa?"

"You lead, Jamie. My brain is on overload right now."

"Timothy, would you please bring my basket?"

"Got it, love."

Filing out the door, they followed Jamie to the common room. It was on the same level as the quarters. Isa and Fran both oohed at the view and then Fran set about spreading out the lunch she'd made. Timothy opened the sodas for Jamie and Isa, having insisted Fran bring them just for watching the pleasure this treat brought to Isa. He was not disappointed and laughed when she told him the breakfast story.

Chatting, they all made quick work of the fried chicken, a juicy fruit salad, nutty tasting rolls that dissolved on the tongue, and thick slices of chocolate cake with a rich chocolate frosting that had the slightest hint of coffee flavor. Isa ate two pieces. "Wow, Fran, that's the best frosting I've ever had."

"Is that why you left the cake of the second piece?"

"Well, yeah, I mean, the cake was good, but I *loved* the frosting!"

"Had I only known, I'd have made Timothy stop licking the bowl and saved it for you."

"Now, Fran, you know that's my only job in the kitchen, you wouldn't deprive me of that—after all, my dignity would be at stake."

Laughing, they helped Fran pack away the remains of the lunch. With the afternoon getting on, Fran decided they better head back to Rowan in order to pick up the rest of what Isa needed and not be late meeting Bane. Jamie called for transport and showed Timothy and Fran around the Bounty while they waited.

Fran was not overly fond of the small transport ships, but she endured them for Isa's sake. Isa followed behind, trying to figure out where they were going before Jamie told her. She felt she had better spend a good amount of time wandering the ship on her own so she could learn her way around without any help. She didn't want to end up lost or appear ignorant when the crew came back and they were ready to go. Isa put this into her plan for tomorrow.

Soon enough, the little transport ship had them back on Rowan. Fran breathed a sigh of relief. Jamie took off, promising to meet them for dinner. Isa produced her list and told Fran and Timothy where Bane thought they would be able to find her cold-weather gear.

"I know right where that is. Ladies, if you'll follow me?" Timothy led the way with Fran and Isa close behind.

"Isa, I've thought of a few more things you might like to have to make your quarters a little cozier. I think a cover for your bed would be pretty, a few more lotions and luxuries for your bath, more clothes, and some basics for your desk to make your studies easier."

Isa waited politely until Fran finished. "Okay Fran, but I have my grandmother's quilt from the farm; it's on the way so I won't need a bed cover. Do you really think I need more clothes?"

Timothy hummed to himself, knowing that Isa would indeed end up with more clothes. Fran would see to it that the girl would lack for nothing. "Here we are."

14.

Bane figured they would be late, as he waited at the table with Jamie, who knew him well enough to know to be on time. He wasn't angry, but he wanted to be sure there was an understanding on Isa's part that she stick to the plans she agreed on, but also that when she didn't, she could face the consequences without fear. He had been clear that he wanted her to arrive for dinner on time, and wondered how she had handled Fran's excitement at helping her get set up on Bounty. There would come a time when she'd need to learn that orders were carried out with no excuses; however, he understood that today she wasn't completely on her own, and that Fran and Timothy would have an influence on her as well.

He watched as she came in with Fran and Timothy. She was walking slightly behind them, eyes downcast, but casting furtive glances at Bane with no sustained eye contact. Timothy and Fran said hello, apologizing for keeping Isa out shopping so long and for their lateness. Jamie kept quiet, trying to catch Isa's eyes with an encouraging smile.

Bane could see that she was falling back on her survival instincts here, staying small and quiet and hoping she wouldn't be noticed. His style was not to address issues with a crewmember in front of others. He preferred a private conversation to make his point and set things straight, but he could see in the way Isa had her arms wrapped around herself trying to make herself smaller that she expected her punishment right here and now. Jamie was thinking the same thing.

Fran and Timothy were seated and looking expectantly at Isa. Bane held out the chair between himself and Jamie, "Isa."

She slid quickly into the chair, eyes on her napkin in front of her. Was he angry? She waited for him to yell at her or slap her—she'd been late. Frank would have beaten her, calling her stupid and lazy. But with Frank, she would have been alone, no other people to worry about. Maybe Bane would wait until they were alone. She told herself she'd better not do anything wrong during dinner.

Fran retold the story of their day to Bane and he listened, asking questions now and then, noting Isa's quiet one-word comments when Fran asked for her input. "Well, I guess we wore her out. Are you tired, Isa?" She nodded, still studying the napkin now in her lap.

When their dinner came, Isa forced herself to eat some of the vegetable soup she'd ordered, but her stomach was knotted with worry for what she felt was to come. There was always a reckoning. Everyone was surprised when she asked for a glass of water to drink; her lack of appetite and subdued politeness were met by Bane's study of her face.

Fran, Timothy and Jamie said their goodnights and left Bane and Isa, Fran telling Isa to get right to bed and she'd feel good as new come morning. The walk back to their rooms was silent. Bane spoke quietly after they entered. "Isa, would you sit down so we can talk?" She had startled, lifting her hands as if to guard her face when he spoke. She sat on the edge of the sofa, every muscle tense, her eyes moving between Bane and the door, waiting for the first blow.

Slowly, watching her face, Bane knelt in front of her, beginning with, "I would never hurt you, Isa." He said it softly and then reached out to tip her chin up, looking into her eyes, "Never." The air left her lungs in shaky bits when she saw this truth in unwavering blue eyes. The muscles that had been bunched for escape began to quiver and Isa pulled her legs up, wrapping her arms around them to still the shaking, and tried to relax into the soft sofa back. Her head bent forward, resting on her knees. She felt stupid for thinking Bane would beat her, he was not Frank; they were not the same at all.

"We do need to talk." He brought her abruptly out of her tangled-up thoughts. "One, what Frank did to you was wrong, Isa. No one, no matter what, deserves that kind of treatment. It is *not* the norm, and although it will take some time for you to retrain your fallback reactions, that will happen. You'll need to teach yourself, with help, how a healthy person handles conflict. No one should ever hurt you in any way." He let her think that over as he stood, headed to the little sink and made them both a cup of hot tea.

She took the cup, cradling it in her hands. "I hear you, I do. I had you mixed up with Frank when we arrived so late. He would get so angry and I was so afraid. I'm sorry, I know you—well, I—"

"It's okay. It will take time, Isa; it's what you knew. I realize it wasn't personal and I didn't take it that way. I saw you sinking into yourself. I should have asked to speak to you privately before we ordered dinner. Now I know. That part is over, and we'll just move on and keep doing the best we can."

"That part?"

"Yes. There is still the matter of your tardiness at dinner. Was I unclear about my expectation as to the time we were to meet?"

"No, sir." Here was Captain Bane, not the Bane she'd ridden with down the road.

"Look at me, Isa."

Her legs stretched back to the floor while she sat up and turned to face him next to her on the couch.

"There are different ways to handle situations. Some are more effective than others. You'll learn as you go how to deal with whatever comes up, and deal with it in a healthy way. Yes, I run a disciplined crew, a tight ship, but I'm a fair man. When something goes amiss, I'll speak privately with you, and we'll resolve the issue."

She sat, thinking, and she didn't drop her eyes from Bane's intense gaze. There was the strength that had gotten her through the years with Frank.

"Is that how it's supposed to be? Is that what you would have said to me if... So, if I'm late, for example, after agreeing to be somewhere at a specific time, for whatever reason, or if I do something out of line or against orders, then you will take me aside and discuss it privately and just, work it out?"

Isa seemed uncertain in what she expected, not sure how she could count on this. It was opening up her world another sliver.

"Yes. In my world, that is how it is. It won't always be me taking someone aside, as I don't supervise everyone on my crew, so it could be your immediate supervisor who I've trained to handle conflicts in this manner. I believe, given time and experience, you'll find that you can trust this process, Isa, and miss far fewer meals and," he paused, winking at her, "sodas."

Red crept across her cheeks. "I thought if I was really good and kept myself from enjoying anything, oh, it never worked anyway. I really am sorry for being so late." Her harshest punishments would come from herself.

"Thank you, for not making excuses. I appreciate that, especially knowing the excitement for you in all you did today. It was good?" Her smile said it all.

"Yours?"

"Fine. Listen, I know you want to be off and exploring Bounty tomorrow, so how about we leave early, after some coffee on the deck, and hear the news from the Academy on board? I'd like to iron out some details and then you can be off on your own. After lunch, we can head out to meet Jack, who'll be our pack trip guide."

"Okay. What do you think President Wilson will say?"

"Tomorrow will tell. Now, off to bed with you!"

15.

But she couldn't sleep. Pre-dawn was still a couple of hours away. Isa got up, dressed and went silently through the door to Bane's room, prepared to leave the note she'd scribbled and find a spot on the deck to watch the stars. She left the note by the door on the floor and set one of Bane's boots on it, figuring he'd be forced to notice it.

Slipping out the door silently was not a problem for Isa's practiced body. She retraced their path from the previous morning, found one of the soft chairs, and tipping the back down, she settled in with her new jacket for warmth and drank in the heavens, alight with stars beyond counting. Her new home was up there somewhere; she wondered what was in store for her, as nothing so beautiful as that held any fear for her and she was ready to begin. The stars, she knew, would always be a path to take her back to the farm and the many nights she'd filled the emptiness inside just absorbing the twinkling peace of their distant light. Isa would never lose that connection.

Bane stood over her holding two steaming mugs. She had been curled into her jacket, her lips smiling slightly in sleep. Stirring, Isa's eyelashes began to part. "Mornin', sleepyhead." She sat up slowly and he handed her a mug. "Nice trick, leaving the boot where I could trip over it." He lowered himself into the chair next to hers as she brought her legs over the sides.

"I figured you couldn't miss my note that way and I wouldn't get into trouble for sneaking out." Setting the mug down, she adjusted the back of the chair upright. She pulled her jacket on, picked up the mug, took a sip, breathing in the hot smell, and hugged the mug to her chest. "Couldn't sleep, so I decided to come out and stargaze." The stars had faded with the arrival of dawn, leaving only a few still visible. "I think I'm going to like my new home up there, completely surrounded by star upon star."

"Glad to hear it. We can go anytime; I can even make some coffee on Bounty if you're ready now." Isa was on her feet before the sentence was finished. Leaving their half-empty mugs on a counter, they headed to transport.

Arriving in the Bounty's common room, Isa glued herself to the large observation windows while Bane put coffee on to brew. Soon, she held another warm mug, leaning into the window. An easy silence accompanied them and then her soft voice whispered out of the well of the window. "I've always loved the newness of early morning, a chance to start again, leave what didn't work behind to, I don't know, be still in a way that only happens in the quietest part of a day. Alone, but surrounded by so much possibility. There's just something about it I can't explain."

She continued to gaze out as she spoke, and Bane nodded, knowing exactly what she meant. He sat at the computer terminal close to the big window and began to read through the plan he'd begun to devise for Isa's education on board. He had decided to oversee her training himself, with mentors in each department she would rotate through. Although it wasn't ordinary procedure, nothing about Isa's journey had been and Bane already had a connection with and a special interest in her. He was certain that

Ken would not disagree. The study structure from the Academy was cut and dry and would be built into Isa's day. All exams were proctored by whomever Ken Wilson assigned as her Academy liaison.

"So, any chance of breakfast?" Isa had turned from the window and her fascination with the stars, grumbles from her stomach directing her thoughts.

"I imagine we can rustle up something. I happen to know a certain lady who tucked away some food just in case you might be neglected. Fran let me know that she left cinnamon rolls and some sandwiches and other goodies for today." They found plenty of food in the kitchen area. Ordinarily, if the crew were on board this would be fare game unless it was specifically marked.

With the rolls and their coffee warmed up, they sat at the counter enjoying Fran's soft nutty bread with a sweet glaze on top. "Man, she really knows how to bake. These are de-licious! I hope she left some of that chocolate cake."

"I would not doubt she did if she knows you like it. If you're finished, let's go to the conference room and I'll let the Academy know we're ready."

Isa drained the last of her coffee and followed Bane out the door. Exiting the elevator on the upper deck, he led them into a room just off the bridge with a long table surrounded by chairs. On the wall on one end were a series of screens, a large one in the center. Isa recognized this was where briefings were held or meetings with Planetary Officials and other matters she didn't know about yet. She walked around the table as Bane made his contact, letting her hand trail over the smooth surface, trying to get a feel for the room and the conversations this table had hosted.

"He should be in contact shortly. Let's sit close to the screens and, Isa, take a deep breath." The air left her lungs as she sat facing the screen when it came to life.

"Bane, Isa, good to see you again. Isa, I trust you have been spending some time getting to know Bounty." It was not a question as he had seen her determination to be on the Bounty.

"Yes, sir. I don't know all of her yet, but I am finding my way around, and my quarters are arranged with plenty of space to study." Her inference was not lost on him. Bane smiled into his hand as he watched this exchange.

"Is it now? Well, relax, Isa, I've decided that the Bounty and her crew are well suited to foster your education and I think, considering your life experience, you will thrive in the work-study environment."

Sucking air deep into her chest, Isa unclenched her fingers from where they had been gripping the arms of her chair. She looked into Ken's dark eyes, her own slowly widening, answering, "Thank you. I promise I will do my best and work very hard."

"I know you will. We'll meet as soon as it fits into Bounty's schedule, and talk over what my expectations are, as well as introduce you to Professor Kolter, who will be your Academy liaison. He's worked out a course study plan for you, and the materials are on their way to you. You'll have them before you leave Rowan so you can go over them and order any study supplies you might need before you leave. Now, Bane, tell me what your plan is while Isa is with you."

"Thank you, Ken. You've made one young woman very happy, and given Bounty a fine student and crewmember." Ken nodded and Isa beamed at them both. "Ken, I've decided to supervise Isa myself. Of course, my department heads will manage her work in their areas as appropriate, but I will maintain her program and communication with Professor Kolter, as I know him fairly well." Bane paused, watching Ken's right index finger run back and forth across his upper lip, his hand finally coming to rest on the table as he settled back into his chair.

"All right, Bane. If you think that is best, I'll note it in Isa's file as well as inform Alex Kolter. You and he can talk before you leave Rowan, I'll give that responsibility over to you." He bent forward at the table, saying, "Isa, your path lies open before you. Make the most of it."

"I will, sir."

Bane switched the screen off, turned and stretched his hand out to Isa. "Welcome aboard."

16.

She called Jamie, Fran and Timothy to share her news. No one was surprised. Promising to meet Bane at noon in the common room, Isa set off through Bounty. Making her way back to her quarters, she stopped in the doorway, her eyes circling her room, and stretched out her arms to encompass the whole of it.

Easy steps carried her to the desk. Sitting in the chair, she imagined studying here, but she also thought there would be a spot on this ship just for her, a place, some small nook, with a view where she'd feel at home, like in her barn, that would provide a more productive work space. It wasn't that she didn't appreciate or wouldn't use this desk; it would be a place to keep her organized. She just knew how she worked best.

Rising, she glided slowly around her quarters, outstretched fingers moving across each new surface, lingering as she began to learn about this space. Pressing her hands against the smooth view surface, she laid her forehead there, inhaling the view. Smokey, Indian, Teyha, Hank and the others drifted through her mind; closing her eyes, the clear surface transformed into Smokey's warm back. She let herself relax and feel safe.

Then, her head came up, hands leaving the window as she turned and marched back to the door, bidding her room goodbye. Determined to find Astro-engineering, Isa wandered down the hallway and made her way up to the fourth level from her quarters on the second level. Astro was located in the fore of the ship in order to allow for the multiple viewing ports.

Several minutes later, she came through a door and into a world of stars. Uninterrupted views of layers of stars greeted her. She paced the room's perimeter just looking and noting various viewing devices and several workstations—it appeared that several projects were in progress. Whoever was in charge here was lucky, Isa thought, and the team members, too. It was hard to tell that everyone was gone for shore leave; the feeling was more like this group had simply gone out for coffee or a meal and would be right back. Work in progress was everywhere. Isa had a sense that this team hadn't left in a hurry to get away from their jobs, but had simply taken a break and would be happy to return to their projects.

She moved into the arboretum behind Astro. She could imagine the outdoors as she took the path, surrounded by all sorts of growing plants and trees, vegetables, grains and fruits. The rest of the engineering section was astern, covering three of the four levels of Bounty. Isa noticed much of the same—this crew enjoyed their work and that was important to know. Isa wanted to be part of this community.

Checking the time, she decided early was better than any kind of late, so she made her way back to the common room. Chocolate cake and soda would ease the chorus that had taken over her stomach.

Coming through the door, she sought Bane who was still seated at the same table working on the computer. He didn't look up until he had finished. Isa sat in the chair opposite him and waited.

"Guess I don't need to ask if you're hungry. I heard you coming before the door opened."

"Nothing some chocolate cake and soda won't quiet."

His eyebrows rose at that, "So, that's your plan for lunch?"

"Well, yeah. What was yours?"

"I happen to be a fine cook, so I set some steaks out to thaw and thought I'd fry those up for us with potatoes, you can make a little spinach salad and save the cake for dessert."

In the kitchen, Bane beat on the steaks with a knife, rolled them in flour and put them into the sizzling oil, adding cubes of potatoes to one side of the pan. He flipped them once and told Isa it would be ready in about ten minutes. Isa washed the spinach and sliced a tomato and split the pile, putting half on each plate.

"Mmmm. This is delicious."

"You sound surprised."

"No. I just haven't, well, I'm used to my own cooking."

"How was your tour?"

"I want to live in Astro-engineering. Have you looked through some of those viewing devices they have?"

"Matter of fact, I have." She nodded at him, and then kept up a steady stream of observations she'd made in Astro while they finished eating, cleaned up, and savored the chocolate cake.

Back on Rowan, they stopped at their rooms to grab jackets and were off to meet Jack in the pick-up Bane rented from the complex. Bane pulled up to the barn. Isa had stopped talking when they turned into the ranch a couple of miles back, her gaze held outside the window by horses grazing pastures. Bane wondered if this would be too painful a reminder of what she'd lost. "You okay?"

Tears had formed, filling her eyes. "I'm always okay with horses. I miss them." Isa's head came up as she rallied with, "Let's go see if they need help mucking." It wouldn't be the last time Bane saw the strength and resolve of her spirit. He left her with the horses occupying the barn and went off in search of Jack.

"That's Amigo. You wouldn't be interested in him."

Isa turned to the older man, her hands still resting on the thick, grey neck. "Well, that isn't what Amigo told me. He practically stuck his head over that feed trough and lifted me in here to take care of a powerful itch right below his ear." She was scratching that ear as she talked and Amigo was almost in her lap with his head. "He's a love."

The man came around and into the stall and stuck out his hand. "Jack."

"Isa." She took his hand. It was strong, warm and weathered and most importantly to Isa, gentle. Amigo blew warm air at Jack, who smoothed a hand over his muzzle. Jack had short, graying brown hair, dark brown eyes, and stood nearly six feet tall. Isa had instantly recognized him as kind and felt him to be someone who knew horses. That gut feeling garnered a certain kind of trust, while his hand on Amigo's willing muzzle did the rest.

"You think this horse is for you? Most folks don't reckon him of any value; say he's too hard to get along with."

"Hm. I think he and I have an understanding. Maybe most folks don't know how much scratchin' that ear needs."

"Maybe not," Jack nodded. "Bane, I guess this must be that girl you mentioned coming along on the pack trip."

They shook hands as Bane answered, "Sure is. I see you two have met." They both smiled.

"Let's head into my office. See ya later, fella." Isa and Jack both patted Amigo as they left his stall. "She's kind of pushy, Bane, thinks she's gonna ride my horse." Isa didn't comment as they went down the barn aisle, her hand greeting every head that was offered. Bane chuckled, as Isa had passed Jack's test and Jack hers.

They sat at the small table in the office and went over the plan. The first day out would be long, it would take about eight hours to reach the place Jack wanted to camp and it had a lot of gain in elevation. From there, they had plenty of options to explore. "You sure you're up for this?"

"When do we leave? Will you need help getting the horses ready? Do you want me to pony a packhorse? Do you need any other help before we leave?"

Bane said, "You can take that as a yes, I think." All three laughed.

"Isa, you'd be welcome to come out anytime. I won't expect you, though, until dawn the first of next week."

"Thanks, Jack. We'll be here." Bane stood, Jack and Isa following suit.

"It was great to meet you, Jack, and thanks for letting me ride your Amigo."

He grunted at her as they left, watching her stride down the side of the barn, stopping to scratch Amigo's ear. Bane stood patiently, slightly apart, allowing her space. She let her head rest against the horse for a time; Jack could see her breathing deep and even in the movement of her shoulders. Bane hadn't told him much when he'd asked if Isa could come on the trip. He'd assured Jack that she knew horses, and told him briefly that she'd suffered some great loss and horses were just what she needed to give her a lift. Jack had been watching her since she'd climbed out of the vehicle and he'd seen her drawn to the horse no one liked. What most would interpret as an aggressive horse trying to bite, she'd seen as an invitation to scratch an ear. He'd get along with Isa, and it would be worth the look on his wrangler's faces to let her ride Amigo.

As Bane pulled onto the main road from the long dirt driveway of the ranch, he thought about the instant connection Isa and Jack had found. Not sure how Isa would react to males in general after her experience with Frank, he began to realize that although it had gone on for a long time, Frank was an isolated instance in many ways. Isa had spoken lovingly of her own father and Bane knew she'd formed relationships with other men in the small town. Of course, many of them had known her since she was born, so there wouldn't have been any perceived threat from her end. She would have to learn about healthy relationships, but she'd had a good start and in time she would be able to look more objectively at why and how her mother had brought Frank into their lives.

"You must be thinking hard. Your brows are furrowed." Isa smiled at Bane as he looked over at her studying him, smiling back.

"Not too hard."

"I never thought I'd be able to have horses in this life. I don't know why, it just didn't occur to me, and it isn't the same, but it's like a piece of my home, my family reaches out to me, even when turning into Jack's place and seeing horses grazing. I know you told me that you like to ride when you find the time and opportunity, and I'm seeing now that I can do the same."

"Absolutely. In all fairness, you should know that the Academy has a stable. And I think old Jack would hire you in a heartbeat." Isa thought this over, chewing on her bottom lip.

"Well, I can't say that working with Jack wouldn't be tempting and going to a school with a stable sounds good too, but I've looked out at those stars from Bounty. I want to be a part of that."

Bane nodded. She had no idea how many points she'd just scored, saying that to him. Driving on in comfortable silence, it wasn't long before Isa's breathing became slower and deeper. It was early when she'd headed out to the deck this morning, so it wasn't surprising that she slept now. It would take another hour or so to get back to the main complex. That would give her a nice nap.

17.

"Fran and Timothy have dinner waiting if you're up for that, Isa."

"You bet, just let me put my shoes on."

Bane turned back to the comm-link vid-screen, "Timothy, we'll be along shortly."

Bane disconnected the vid-screen as Isa appeared in the connecting doorway. The corridors weren't crowded here, as most people were out eating or taking in some evening entertainment.

Fran had put together a delicious dinner. They feasted on grilled salmon, which Isa had never experienced before; her tentative first bite was followed by "mmmm," and a second, larger, bite. The sweet potatoes had been baked with rosemary and cinnamon and Isa loved sweet potatoes. There was also steamed asparagus. Isa learned to cook at a young age, but mostly very simple meat and potato fare or breakfast foods like eggs and pancakes. She was eagerly sampling all these new tastes and decided she would learn to cook them, too.

Fran was happy to explain the recipes and give Isa copies. She would send new ones, too, while Bounty was out, helping Isa as best she could. Timothy commented that this would keep him from getting into so much trouble and thanked Isa for finding something besides him to keep Fran busy! Fran swatted him good-naturedly and everyone laughed.

Timothy brought out dessert, lemon meringue pie. Isa followed him with a pot of steaming coffee and cups. Fran cut and served pie while Isa filled cups for everyone, except Fran, who preferred tea. No one spoke as they all dug into the pie and sipped their coffee. "Fran, what a treat. Thank you." Bane patted his belly as he spoke. "Let's clear the table and clean up."

"Sorry, friend, that's my job. It's late and I'm sure you have plenty to do tomorrow. We're just glad you were able to join us." Timothy shook Bane's hand as everyone stood. Isa whispered her thanks as she hugged Timothy and turned to Fran.

"Thanks for letting us be a part of your family, Fran, and if you have time, maybe you could teach me how to make that chocolate cake before we leave?" Fran hugged her and assured her they'd find time.

Closing the door behind them, Timothy saw a tear sliding down his wife's cheek. "Oh love, come here." Timothy took her hand and pulled her to him, wrapping her in his arms and tucking his chin on the top of her head. "She crawled right inside your heart, hasn't she? Yes, I know. Mine too. There's no use to it, but I keep finding myself wishing we could have been there when she lost her mother and needed adopting. But we're here now, and we'll do what we can."

"I love you, Timothy. I do."

"And you are the love of my life. Now, I'd better get that mess cleaned up, 'fore the boss fires me." He held her close a moment, gazed into her eyes, found her lips as he had so many times and headed off to clean up from dinner. Fran stood, her fingers brushing where his lips had left their warmth.

18.

"Can we walk for a bit, Bane?"

"Sure. If I sit down with this full stomach, I may never get up again. They're good people, Isa, and they care about you."

"I care about them, too. I'll miss them. Bane, how does communication work on Bounty? I mean, will I be able to talk with people like Fran and Timothy? Or Jack? Or see how the new family is doing or what happens if Frank gets out?" This last thought came out soft and quiet. Bane's hand touched her shoulder, squeezed gently to reassure her.

"In some places communication can be problematic, and you'll have to email. Often, you can communicate directly though, through the comm-link and vid-screen, and that will be required by the Academy. You have a comm-link and vid-screen in your quarters and Bounty has stations in many areas. They won't be lost to you. Now, as for Frank, I will be fully informed if he is ever released and of his whereabouts, and I'll tell you if anything changes. You should know, if he is released, his record will follow him, but if he leaves the planet, it becomes more difficult to track his movements. No need to worry, we'll cross that bridge when we come to it."

They continued down the passage, their pace picking up as the meal continued to digest. The walk brought them to a section in the complex that Isa hadn't seen yet. Bane explained that this was an activities wing where many classes were offered in a variety of recreation forms. Indeed, many people were playing late evening games of basketball and racquetball and Isa liked being able to watch through the clear walls. There was a pool with people swimming laps, weight rooms and all manner of stationary exercise machines. Bane said all of those could be programmed so one could run in the mountains or toward a beautiful sunset or cycle through a forest or any other place imaginable.

He repeated what he and Jamie had told her about providing many opportunities onboard Bounty and how important it was to keep fit physically, mentally and spiritually, and that he didn't know how to stay mentally and spiritually fit without keeping active physically. Bane cocked an eyebrow at Isa when she laughed. She had to explain what Jamie had told her and that she was excited to both start running and take ballet.

Arriving back at their rooms, Bane asked Isa, once again, to sit for a minute so they could discuss plans for the following day. "I think Lieutenant Iridian teaches a ballet class first thing each morning; if you want to try it out, I know she'd welcome you."

"I'd like that!"

"Done. After that, why don't you plan to spend the day on Bounty and meet me back here for dinner?"

Isa had curled her feet underneath her, shedding her shoes, her head cradled on her arm across the back of the couch. Bane said he'd check the class schedule and show her where it was on the grid map. She was nodding, but her eyes were slowly closing and the sounds of agreement were sliding down into her throat. Bane helped her up, handed her the shoes and pointed her toward her room, as a sleepy "night" came over her shoulder.

Checking on her a few minutes later, Bane saw that she'd dropped the shoes and was sound asleep on top of the bed. He covered her with a blanket, switched off the light and eased the door almost shut between their rooms.

In Isa's dreams that night, snippets of her last couple of days melded together into a strange story. She was dancing, floating through turns and airborne in graceful leaps, arms stretched out, rounded at the elbow, fingers extended toward a horse in Jack's barn. Jack told her it was well done as she landed on Smokey's back, her Smokey. Then they galloped through meadows filled with tall grasses, flying over logs, running faster still. Isa could see a cliff in front of them coming closer as they gathered speed. She wasn't afraid, but lifted her arms out along the line of her shoulders as Smokey gathered himself for the mightiest of jumps.

"Hup," she encouraged him as his front legs came off the ground and the heave of his powerful hindquarters launched them both into the heavens. Suddenly, they were surrounded by myriad points of light. Flying past stars radiating bright blues and reds and oranges, Isa gathered Smokey's neck in her arms and whispered, "Thank you for bringing me here and keeping me safe." And she slept there, on his back, as they sailed through space and time.

Isa woke in the wonder of that dream, wrapped in a warm blanket and safe. She remembered the time in her life before Frank when she could sleep safe and dream and she was glad to have it back again. Isa prayed then, quietly in her heart, and she promised that some day she would try to do for others what so many had done for her, to do what she could for those who were hurting or hiding or had no one.

It was still early, but not unreasonably so; Isa rose, washed and changed out of the clothes she'd slept in. She slipped through the door.

"Going somewhere?" Bane's voice startled her. "Don't even *think* about putting my boot in the middle of the room." She could hear the teasing in his voice.

"Well, at least you're out of bed at a reasonable hour today, so no need for the boot. Deck and coffee?"

"Lead on."

Buttoning their coats against the pre-dawn chill, Bane and Isa sat outside, hot mugs in hand and watched the sun bring the day. Isa was full of her dream and the hope that comes with morning.

19.

Lt. Iridian, Mary, told Isa she was welcome to join the class. Later in the morning, she'd teach a master class for advanced students, but this was a class for beginners. Mary explained to Isa that she'd need to dance in the leotard and tights, leaving the warm-up pants and jacket aside, as this allowed the teacher and the dancer to see the line of the body, important in dance. Although she felt self-concious about this, she did understand it. She left the warm-ups by a wall and put the slippers she'd bought with Jamie on. Isa and the other students started at the bar. Mary paired Isa with another girl who had some experience so she could learn the positions. There was a beauty and grace in the discipline of the bar work. Isa was captivated by the line of arm and leg in the first, second, third, fourth and fifth positions. She caught on quickly, especially after the repetition, Mary explaining that they had to create muscle memories. That made sense to her, paralleling her experience as a rider.

When they moved off the bar and began to put arm positions with feet, Isa became fascinated. When Mary was convinced they had the positions committed to memory, she added music and watched her student's joy in the movement. Although this was new to Isa, she had a natural affinity for movement.

The class continued across the floor. Isa felt the floating from her dream when she finally understood the way her arms and legs had to work together. She was sweating, muscles tired as they cooled down with the simple stretching. She pulled the warm-ups on as Mary approached her.

"So, you're hooked, aren't you?"

"This is amazing, Mary. I loved it." The excitement filled her with a joy that had been lacking in her life. Mary asked her about leotards and tights, suggesting a minimum number of each, as well as an extra pair of ballet slippers, jazz shoes and couple of other items that weren't necessities, but would be good to have, like some leg warmers and a simple ballet skirt. Mary left Isa with a warning to stretch later so her muscles wouldn't object to this new use, and an invitation to attend the beginning class as often as she could in the next couple of weeks. Isa would also be welcome to come watch the master class, which would give her a sense of the possibilities of dance.

Isa flew down the hall, humming to herself. When she arrived at her room, she showered, changed, and left a note for Bane, as agreed, that she was off to Bounty and would be back by no later than six for dinner. "P.S. Ballet is just like riding Indian first thing in the morning at a full gallop and in perfect balance. Holy cow!"

20.

Coming together at the end of the day, Isa shared her observations of Bounty with Bane, who found her insight delightful. She had pegged the various personalities of the crewmembers who worked together in each area she had explored. Bane was reminded of the dedication of his crew and the joy they had in their work; when he had an unhappy crewmember, it was usually because they were not working from their strengths and passions, and with some questions, discussion, trial and error, the problem was easily rectified. Bane listened as Isa talked about Astro-engineering, the second time she'd stood and lingered.

"So, you found a bit of Indian in ballet class?"

That set her off telling Bane about the class, what she'd learned, and how she saw it all related to riding. Isa stared at her hands in her lap.

"What is it, Isa? You can tell me, you know. I can help you work it out."

"It's just, well, Mary said I'd need a few more things to be prepared to dance on Bounty, and I don't know if I have enough money, or if I should be buying more or making do with what I have or will I be unprepared if I don't have what she asked me to get?" Bane listened while she struggled, recognizing that all she knew was "making do," and that she'd been overwhelmed by the purchases she'd made with Jamie.

"Isa, you've given this some thought, and I can see you are struggling. Take a breath. If Mary told you she thought you needed these purchases, then heed her advice. I'm certain you won't go overboard because you've lived so long in survival mode. You've no need to worry about money; let me handle that for now." She listened, nodding agreement and the smile was soon back.

The routine established on the night she'd been late for dinner became their norm. After returning to their rooms, they spent a few minutes discussing plans, often with hot tea or chocolate, and then retired for the night.

By the end of the week, Isa had fully explored Bounty, had a few more ballet classes under her belt, baked Fran's chocolate cake and eaten plenty of that sweet frosting, and Mary had gone shopping with her to be sure she was well supplied for dancing class. The dancers in the master class had enchanted Isa. The women were so graceful in their pointe shoes, and the strong, supple men seemed suspended in the air as they moved. She would throw herself into learning ballet with delight.

She wanted to try out the little music player and go for a run. Because she didn't know the country, Bane went with her. He was a runner, doing six miles most days. Isa was in good shape, but she had to learn to breathe and pace herself. Her stride and speed changed with the music she was hearing. Sometimes, she tried to sing along, breathe and run, finding this did not work so well, but she didn't seem to mind. Bane told her if you enjoy running, you could do it anywhere. You don't need special equipment, save for the shoes, he said, good shoes were important. Isa asked him why he liked to run and he said it gave him time and space to think. Isa preferred having the option of music so she didn't have to think if she didn't want to.

On the day before they were to leave on the pack trip, Isa's belongings arrived from Melacross, along with a box from the Academy. She and Bane spent time going through her books and the study plan from Professor Kolter. They were able to contact him so Isa could "meet" him on the comm-link vid-screen. He expected her studies to begin immediately as students at the Academy were already in session. Isa assured him that as soon as they returned from the mountains, she'd get started. Bane shared his plan for Isa to work-study her way through the Bounty's sections; he'd mapped it using the Academy curriculum order and Professor Kolter agreed it made sense.

"Isa, many students arrive with an area of study in mind. Do you have any interests to get you started?" She narrowed her eyes, staring off past the screen, deep in thought.

"Well, sir, I don't know that I do. I want to stay open to possibility and to what I can do best, but I, I don't know where my passion is."

"That's fine, Isa. I'm sure as you rotate jobs and duties, you'll discover what you excel in. You have plenty of time. I think we all have a good understanding of expectations, check-in points, and we'll meet in person soon and check on your progress. I hope your trip is all that you want it to be. Isa, Captain Lucas, I look forward to working with you both."

"Thank you, sir."

"Professor Kolter."

With that, Bane told Isa he had responsibilities to attend to while she went through her possessions from home.

"Come on in when you're ready and we'll have lunch."

She paused in the doorway, looking at the boxes. The large one held her saddle and Jack had already told her she could use it on Amigo. Isa opened the smaller box, kneeling on the floor. When she touched the quilt, she was transported back to her home, her parents tucking in the edges of that quilt around her, enveloping her in love.

Wrapping herself in the warmth of that quilt, she leaned against the bed and closed her eyes. Right now, this was enough—she couldn't touch the other things just yet. Warm tears soaked into the blanket, and she drifted back to the farm.

After an hour had passed, Bane stepped quietly to the door and his heart went out to her. No one should have to face what she had at her age, or any age for that matter. There she sat, wrapped in a blanket, alone, and he couldn't stand to think about the loneliness she must be feeling. He dropped his tall frame onto the floor next to her, taking her in his arms like a father comforting a child.

She rested her head against his chest, asking, "When? When does it stop hurting? I miss them so much. I can't even look at the other things, and I'm not a sissy, Bane. I'm not."

"No, you are not a sissy. Isa, you have to expect to feel sad, and you'll feel joy, too, with your memories. You never had a chance to grieve because you had to carry on. Let yourself be sad, and don't feel like you have to be alone. I'm here and I will continue to be, even when I'm Captain Lucas." A few quiet moments passed, and then Bane had an idea. "Isa, how would you feel about having Fran and Timothy, maybe Jamie too, come over later and we can all look at what you have unpacked and you can tell the stories? It could help you sort out your memories and hang on to the good ones."

Her head nodded against his shoulder, "Okay."

"Do you want me to make the calls?"

"No. I can do it. Thank you for, well, thank you."

"You're very welcome." Isa moved to stand up, Bane gently held her arm, "I mean it, horse lady, you are not alone anymore." She visibly relaxed, laid the quilt on her bed and stepped out to use the comm-link vid-screen.

21.

Jamie's response to the photos of Smokey, Indian and the other horses cemented the friendship of these two young women. They passed around the family album and the photo of Isa's parents with the usual, "Oh, you have your father's nose, mother's eyes, grandfather's hands" comments. Isa told them a few stories and the one her folks had told her about her grandfather holding her the day she was born and telling everyone that she had that special "knowing" about horses.

Bane recalled the test she had given him when he'd showed up to rent a horse and how she had told him that when Smokey approved him. They laughed at that, and then continued to share Isa's stories with her. Her saddle and the Indian blanket hung over the back of a chair, and Timothy admired the dark brown leather and the intricate detail in the flower pattern, with little arrows spiraling around.

When Isa brought out the wooden recipe box, Fran moved everyone else out of the way so she and Isa could study each card. Isa showed her the ones she'd made all the time, food that could be put on in the morning to slow cook all day. These cards were well worn, but many recipes in the box had simply been too complicated for a young girl to manage, and Frank preferred beef and potatoes and would tolerate having pancakes for dinner once in a while.

The popcorn ball card elicited silence. Watching Isa's reaction from where he, Timothy and Jamie were looking at the saddle and blanket, Bane glanced at Timothy and Jamie, and the three of them quietly moved to the sofa to listen. Isa, assured that they would understand, started by sharing her family's popcorn-balls-on-the-porch tradition. When she described that evening's crossroads, with her child-like attempt to cheer her mom, Frank's reaction to the kitchen, and then her mother's inability to defend her daughter, her fingers were twined together and turning white. She focused on Bane while she talked; he held her gaze.

"It wasn't her fault. My mom left when my dad died. She couldn't go on without him; didn't want to. I haven't ever tried to make those popcorn balls since, but I think I will now. We sure had a lot of fun with them." Fran had an arm around her shoulder, teary-eyed for that lost little girl.

"You bet we will. And your mother and father and grandparents will be smiling down at you, happy that you have continued their tradition of fellowship and love."

"Heck, I can't wait to taste them!" Jamie grinned at her.

"I bet they'd go real good with grape or cherry soda." Timothy had everyone laughing.

The only item Isa hadn't shared was the oilskin pouch with the book. It was a special secret and she wanted to open it and savor its meaning before she shared it.

Sitting on the sofa later with Bane, she was quiet. Safety for her had always been in the barn, yet she was also safe here and with these people. She was glad that Bane had come her way that day looking for horses, as it had been a new beginning for her.

"We'll have an early start tomorrow; are you ready to turn in?"

"Sure am." Standing, he walked beside her to the door of her room. "Goodnight, and thanks, for tonight."

"Sleep well." With that, she wrapped up in her quilt, and fell into a sound sleep.

22.

The horses were up and fed when Isa and Bane arrived at the barn at dawn. They groomed and saddled the animals, each caring for their own horse. Jack watched his two wranglers watching Isa with Amigo. The horse was doing everything she asked and seemed happy to be doing it. Every so often, she would reach up and scratch his ear, whispering to him and humming while she worked. "What'd you do with Amigo, Boss? This looks like him for sure, but it sure don't act like him. He must have had a twin out there somewhere."

Once Isa secured the saddlebags on Amigo, she helped Jack with the packhorses. They placed regular saddles on them, although Jack gave her a description of the cross-buck, a special saddle designed for packing, especially with mules. Jack showed her the large panniers that would carry feed, equipment, and supplies, emphasizing the need to have even weight on both sides.

She watched as first one, and then the second horse was packed, the rigging adjusted and the ropes securing the loads tied in special knots. They would be taking one of Jack's wranglers, Josh, with them, and the other, Mark, would stay behind to run the barn. The sun was up as everything was checked one last time.

everyone's horse was watered, they mounted and Mark bid them farewell.

"You're full of yourself this mornin', aren't you, fella?"

Amigo was dancing around, clearly excited to be out of the barn and onto the trail. Isa kept her breathing slow and relaxed, checking to be sure she wasn't tightening her muscles in her own excitement. The four riders were headed across the pasture, with Jack and Josh each leading a packhorse. Once they crossed this, they'd go through the gate and continue on a dirt road for a short time, leading up to the trail taking them into the mountains.

Bane dismounted, opening the gate and closing it again after they had all passed through. Isa moved up next to Jack on the road and mined his brain for his knowledge of packing with horses. They were well up on the trail when Jack called a halt for lunch. They dismounted, tying the horses in the trees and retrieving the lunches they'd packed from their saddlebags. Jack had cautioned them to leave a space on top so lunch would be easily accessible.

Settling down on rocks and against tree trunks, they talked about the morning as they ate. The men had made hefty meat sandwiches, while Isa savored her chunky peanut butter with honey on hearty whole wheat bread. "This is the best sandwich I've ever eaten! It just tastes better after a ride and in the midst of all this beauty."

The men nodded, except Josh, who joked, "Are you nuts? Give me a hot double cheeseburger with onion rings any day."

"Is that what you're making us for dinner then?"

"Who me? Cook? I feed horses, not people."

That brought a snort from Jack. Josh seemed to need someone besides Jack to give him a hard time, and Isa caught on right away.

When Jack had finished eating, he stretched out, telling them to be ready to head out in fifteen minutes, said he needed his FOB time. Josh translated, Flat-On-Back, and each of them lay back where they were for a short rest. Isa looked up through the tangle of branches to the bright blue sky, imagining she could step from branch to branch like a ladder to the sky.

The trail had brought them through groves of deciduous trees with pale green bark and smooth trunks to evergreens with friendly green needles, and past small streams falling over glacier-sanded rocks. As they had ascended in elevation, they found more switchbacks, providing a gradual climb; on one corner, Isa had been delighted by a hollow trunk on the ground, with wildflowers growing in the center.

"Look," she'd pointed it out to Bane, "God's flowerpot." Smiling to herself, she'd reached down to pat Amigo's neck.

Startled suddenly by Bane's hand, her eyes opened wide and her arms came up reflexively over her face.

Bane knelt next to her saying, "It's time to ride."

He waited while she came back, dropped her arms and stood up. Standing, he offered a hand and helped her to her feet.

"Okay?" She nodded, red creeping across her cheeks.

He didn't let her hand go until she looked into his eyes, "Jack, how far to that view Josh was telling me about?"

"Oh, I'd say another hour or so. Isa, you want to pony my critter for a while?"

"Sure I will."

She went over to ready Amigo.

"That girl sure grows on you. She gonna be okay?"

Bane was watching her blow into Amigo's nostrils and then checking her saddle and bridling him.

"I think so, Jack, especially if some care is taken with her now."

Ponying the packhorse, Bud, proved to be easy. Isa had often done this with her own horses in order to work more than one at a time without having to go back to the barn.

When they rode up out of the tress, the high tundra was alive with life in miniature. Tiny flowers blossomed in different hues of purple, yellow, and pink. Isa stared in wonder as they reached the top of the ridge, stopping to let the horses breathe. The mountaintops were so close, Isa felt like she must be in a land where giants live. Looking back the way they'd come, she could see plains spread out until they touched the sky.

"Pretty sight, isn't it?"

Jack held out a bottle of water to her. She tipped it back, swallowing what didn't run down her chin.

"How do you drag yourself away from here?"

Passing the water back to him, she took the other offering he had.

"What's this?"

Unwrapping the small red and white candy from its crinkly wrapper, she popped it in her mouth.

"Mmm, cinnamon, thanks."

It wasn't long before the horses were ready to move on, and each turn of the trail brought more delight to Isa in the marvel of creation. Coming down from the top of the ridge had been tricky, the horses picking their way through loose rock. Amigo would find his way and then slow when Isa asked him to allow Bud to choose his footing.

Soon, they had ridden back down into the trees, massive pines lending a completely different feel to the forest. It seemed more rugged or wild, somehow, and was certainly less traveled. Hearing the water before they got to it made Isa think this forest must be magical, with hidden secrets. She thought of stories about woodland creatures, like elves; surely they lived here if anywhere!

The water flowed down a fairly steep ravine, with room to cross one at a time. It took some time, as each horse lowered his head to drink before moving forward to allow the next horse in.

Jack and Bane had been talking about the Alliance and recent developments in contact with a warring race. Bane was often called on for mediation and Jack asked if this situation had come to that point. There had been many deaths along with gruesome stories from those who had witnessed it and somehow escaped.

Every so often, Jack, riding in front of Isa, would point to a branch where he'd balanced a cinnamon candy for her to pick up when she passed it. She hadn't missed one yet, remarking on how delicious they were and asking where he'd found them.

"Oh, well, that's a secret I can't just share with anyone, girl, otherwise there might not be any left for me."

"Well, they must be very rare. I'm honored that you're sharing them with me." She grinned at him.

"Maybe you could trade him some of your oatmeal chocolate chip cookies for the information," Bane piped in.

"We might just be able to bargain at that!"

They had come to a part of the trail where the growth of the trees was stunted. Twisted and gnarled by wind and time, they grew thick, saddlebags, panniers and knees catching on them. Then a long stretch downhill led them across more rocky terrain and finally onto a wider section with a gentle gradient. This opened up into a meadow with a river flowing close by.

They rode down the bank and into the water, deep enough to cover the horses' knees, and let them drink. Jack asked to have the horses stand in the water, the cold of it easing any stiffness or possible swelling from the strain of the long day. He told Isa if she felt part polar bear, she was welcome to swim.

In the most serious voice she could muster, she said, "Darn, and I left my swimsuit in my quarters!"

Unloading everything onto a big tarp Jack had lashed over Bud's load, they let the horses stand to dry so the sweat of the day could be curried off, making them comfortable. Sorting the gear, they brought out the tents and put them up. Josh and Jack worked together to set up the camp kitchen with Isa and Bane bringing each requested item from the tarp. Sleeping bags went into tents atop sleeping pads, along with personal gear. The saddlebags, after being hung up to dry, could be tucked into the tarp with the saddles for the night.

Each horse was tended to with a feedbag and curried and brushed while they ate. Legs and hooves were checked. As each horse finished their grain, the feedbag was removed so they could graze, three at a time so they didn't go too far. Josh and Isa tended the horses, while Bane helped Jack work on their supper.

"So, I guess you've done a lot of riding. You're not too bad."

"Yeah, I've ridden some. You're not too bad either, Josh."

"You know he never lets anyone ride that horse?"

"Amigo? I heard that no one wants to ride him."

"Yeah, I guess that's so. Let's switch 'em, let the others graze."

They worked together to catch and tie the grazing horses and then turned the other three loose to enjoy the grass. Josh told her he'd been working for Jack for a couple years, that he liked the work and Jack was a good boss. Isa told him a little of her history, impressing him with her story, although he'd never admit that to her. They watered all the horses one last time, and tied them for the night. Gathering saddlebags and feedbags, they organized the saddles and blankets and folded everything inside, placing large rocks on top of the tarp in case of wind or rain.

Arguing the merits of various horse breeds, they headed over to see if supper was ready. Jack had cooked up a batch of beans and coupled that with hard rolls and coffee. He served them up in tin bowls and cups. They ate as the sun set behind the peaks, cleaned up, and settled around the fire Bane had built to enjoy hot coffee. Isa was having trouble keeping her eyes open. Bane took the cup from her hands, suggesting she turn in. She wished everyone goodnight, unzipped the tent door and then zipped it shut behind her. She would share the tent with Bane while Jack and Josh shared the other.

Thankful for the warmth of the sleeping bag in the cool of the mountain night, she snuggled down, closing her eyes and listening to the crackling fire and the low hum of the voices around it. Sleep came fast. Dreams were peaceful. Waking early, she stretched inside the bag.

"Sleep well?" Bane's voice was quiet next to her.

"Very. You weren't kidding about how cold it gets up here. I'm so glad to have this warm bag."

"Morning can be very brisk until the sun's been up for a while. Dress warm. It's early to get out yet, still dark."

"That's fine with me. I'm not ready to give up this warmth yet."

That day they rode west into the mountains, Jack and Isa leading the packhorses, with Josh heading up the line. The river met them several times, becoming smaller as they gained elevation. The horses drank every time they came to the water, working steadily up the grade. Isa grew quiet as they wound in and out of the trees, except for her soft voice singing to Amigo and Bud.

There was a peace in these woods that sunk into your bones, and she felt connected to the land. It gave her pause to consider that she could feel this wholeness anywhere other than her farm. She belonged and the possibilities of all the places she had yet to discover that belonging in brought joy to her spirit. There was healing in land, in creation—for Isa, it was plain that a God who could create such lush and diverse places, each with its own distinct beauty, was also a God who intended it to bring joy to heal the spirit.

Looking up, she could see Josh on a bend in the trail ahead, winding in and out of branches, the needles sparkling with the reflection of the sun. Bane followed, the branches weaving in and around him, then Jack, who turned back to her. His lips turned up and he winked at her, she winked back. Coming out into the sunshine, they found scraggly bushes lined the small stream. Jack called a halt and they got off and stretched a minute, got a drink and listened to instructions.

Jack pointed up to a peak that looked like the tooth of an old saw blade, saying, "We'll be up on that pass next and it's a tough climb on a narrow trail with a long drop-off on one side and rock face on the other. We'll take it slow, but steady, stopping is not a good idea. Once we're at the top, we'll rest the horses. Now, it isn't quite noon yet, but this is as good a place as any to have lunch."

Securing the horses to the short trees, the group sat to eat the lunches they'd made that morning after breakfast. Isa hadn't realized she was hungry until the first bite of rich peanut butter on the roll soaked with sweet honey hit her tongue.

"This is the best sandwich I've ever eaten!"

"You said that yesterday."

"Well, Josh, this is a new day!"

"Hmm, whatever."

"You have any more of those cinnamons?"

"Sure. Just remember that I'm keeping track and expect to get it back in cookies."

Jack gave her a couple, saying they would get her to the top of the pass. He wasn't kidding about this trail. It was narrow and rocky. Isa could touch the cliff on one side and didn't want to look down the other.

She was bent forward from her hips, keeping her weight centered over Amigo's center of balance, helping him, encouraging him with her voice. She was also keenly aware of Bud and his lead rope, so all three of them would stay out of trouble. The few times she did look down, dizziness overcame her as the rocks below moved in and out of focus, making her stomach shift as if it wanted to empty itself; she quickly shifted her eyes forward through Amigo's ears.

Maneuvering between two rocks, they were very suddenly on top, as waves of peaks unrolled to the west and they'd reached a wide space of tundra. It was as if they had crossed over into a brand new world. The steep edge of a rocky world lay behind them, having ushered them into an easier land. Isa wrapped both arms around Amigo's neck, whispering, "Thanks, boy. You too, Bud." She reached over to pat his neck.

Bane handed her a bottle and she swallowed several mouthfuls, wiping her chin across her shirtsleeve.

Handing it back, she said to him, "Thanks. This is amazing."

He nodded.

The trail led them to the next river, the path, wider, more gracious. Thick grass grew beneath trees; trunks were wide with years of living. Perfect tree-house trees, Isa thought. Afternoon was running into evening when they rode into a clearing. Following the routine of the previous evening, everyone knew their jobs and camp was soon set up for the evening.

While Bane and Jack worked on supper, Isa and Josh grazed the horses. Isa had found a big log down in the meadow and was surveying the horses from the top of it. Josh stood in the grass next to the log as they bantered back and forth.

"Where did you learn to ride?"

"My mom and dad have always enjoyed riding, so I rode on and off as a kid. My dad's a pastor and they knew Jack; he's taught me a lot of what I know."

"You're lucky. He's a good horseman. So, what are you gonna do with your life?"

"Don't know yet. I'll continue with this until I figure out my next step. You're goin' Alliance, I guess?"

"Yep."

Dinner that night was pasta with a creamy sauce full of garlic. It had been a long day and the group was silent as they ate. Once they were cleaned up and settled around a warm fire, Jack surprised them by pulling out a bag of marshmallows, sweet crackers and flat bits of chocolate.

They roasted the marshmallows over the fire, Isa making hers golden brown and Josh burning his black. Jack took Isa's and layered it on top of chocolate sandwiched by crackers and handed it to her. The first gooey bit covered her cheeks and lips with strings of marshmallow and smears of chocolate. Her blue eyes were shining in the firelight as the deep "mmm" came through the sweet mouthful.

"I take back everything I said about peanut butter on the trail. This is the best thing I've ever eaten!"

"Have s'more—that's what they're called 'cuz that's what you want after you've had one. It's a camping tradition."

She didn't have to be told twice, but already had two more marshmallows roasting.

"Just to clarify, there will be no campfires aboard Bounty."

They all chuckled at Bane's comment. Isa and Jack took advantage of the treat's name and then Isa helped herself to several more marshmallows, discovering that once the outside was roasted, you could pull it off and then put the white center back over the fire to start all over.

"You sure do know how to make a mess," Josh teased.

There was a slight pause as something flickered across her face, "Yeah, but it will be a delicious clean-up."

Bane smiled at their interchange. Josh was only slightly older than Isa and she could handle her peers; indeed she was simply being herself. She was even now attempting to lick all the marshmallow off her face, sticking her tongue out trying.

"Where's a camera when you need one?" Jack was shaking his head, grinning.

The company was easy, sitting with their warm tin cups enjoying the moment. Isa leaned her head back, gathering in the stars, listening to the settled sound of the horses shifting their weight now and then and the water softly wandering down the meadow. She filled her lungs with it, making it part of her. This time she didn't flinch when Bane touched her shoulder and said maybe she should turn in. She wished everyone a good night, walked over to check the horses and crawled into the tent, letting the sounds of the meadow lull her to sleep.

They rode to a lake the next day, ponying some very happy packhorses. Keeping the camp set up in the meadow for the next couple days meant no load to carry, so the horses would have a break. The riders only carried what they needed for a day ride.

Arriving at the lake, they were greeted with a clear reflection of the surrounding peaks on the water's surface. Isa wondered if they could swim the horses, but Jack told her a hot summer day would be a better time to swim up here. Although the day was warm, the water was icy cold, and he didn't want to chance a rider sick with a chill this far out. Isa saw the wisdom in that but told him if she were alone, she probably would have done it.

"Good thing you aren't here alone, then. Conditions can change fast up here, girl, even on the best of days, you can't go off half-cocked. Ain't no one to call for help."

"I know you're right." Her tone matched the gravity of his, but the inflection implied that if she had the choice, she might not make the smart one.

They turned the horses loose to graze and carried lunches over to sit in the warm sun by the water's edge.

"I know, that's the best peanut butter sandwich you've ever eaten," Josh intoned and rolled his eyes.

"Why, Josh! That's exactly what I was going to say. I'm glad you're finally coming around." She grinned and he groaned.

After lunch, Isa took off her boots, stuck her socks in them and rolled up her jeans. No one scolded her, so she walked gingerly over to the edge of the water and stuck her toes in. It was icy cold. She waded out to just below her knees and stood still. Looking down, she saw tiny minnows darting around her legs, which had caused a sort of small fish frenzy, or at least that's how it seemed to her.

She picked her way over to a rock big enough to sit on and climbed up, stretching her numb legs and feet across the sunny warm surface. Goosebumps shot down her wet skin and she shivered, basking in the early afternoon rays. The mountains here were as beautiful as the plains of her home. Different, rugged, but similar to the changing seasons at home with so many varieties of life, each one adding the spark that brought the whole together. Along the shore of this lake, Isa had noticed delicate pink blooms, low to the ground and plentiful in small patches. They brought her the subtle sweet smell of the wild roses that grew by the Lee Cemetery back home.

"Better wade on over, it's time to head back to camp." Jack's voice carried her back to this place. She waved at him and immersed her now warm limbs back into the wet chill. Scampering back to her boots, she dried her feet with the socks, pulled them on and laced up her boots.

"That was quite invigorating!"

"Those are not the words I would have used," Josh put in, "cold and miserable come to mind."

"Ah, come on. I had no idea you were such a sissy." They continued to banter as everyone prepared to go, watering the horses before they set off down the trail.

23.

Her studies kept her busy when they returned from the packtrip. Isa felt a lift in her spirit and her new friends remarked on how much more at ease she seemed. She had been back out to Jack's a few times to help at the barn or to ride; he'd even made his famous top-secret chili for her, and was teaching her to play poker. Of course she showed up with the promised cookies. She also found time to continue the beginner ballet class and promising to stick to the route Bane had shown her, she'd gone on several early morning runs.

Bounty's crew was making their way back from various places and shore-leave activities. Isa had met many of them as they'd checked in with Captain Lucas, and found they were welcoming, expressing their own excitement about their work on Bounty and assuring her that she would love it, too. This was a first for most of them, having a junior officer working outside the Academy, and they seemed genuine as they set about making this new experience positive. For Isa, this spoke volumes about Bane as a captain.

Bane was proud of his crew, and investing in her as a top-quality future officer. She'd spent a lot of her time since they'd returned from the mountains on Bounty, exploring and studying. Alex Kolter was a hands-on professor, and he and Isa had already had a few sessions together via vid-screen in the conference room on Bounty. Alex preferred to see her there. It was more formal and that was one thing Isa's education had lacked and one in which she would need more practice.

Fran and Timothy had been back on Bounty too. Fran was working on a supply of sweet treats for the crew with Isa alongside to help. The kitchen in the common room was fairly well equipped, and essentials that Fran thought were lacking, she brought up herself, leaving them behind for the crew's use. She met several of the crew, and said she felt much better about letting Isa head off into space. Timothy didn't remind her that it wasn't their decision.

Jack contacted them early one morning saying he was going to be in town and wondering if Isa wanted to tag along with him to the barn. If Bane could join them for supper, he could bring her back. They settled on a time and Jack said he'd pick up Isa before noon. She spent the morning reading, went to ballet, showered and changed into jeans and boots. The day was chilly, so she took her warm jacket when she left to meet Jack, telling Bane she'd see him later.

Climbing into the pickup with Jack, "So, what are you up to?"

"Oh, just pickin' up supplies and my best hand," he answered her.

"I must be the luckiest girl around, then." She looked across at him and waited.

"What?" More silence. "I put it on 'fore I left. It should ought to be ready when your captain gets there."

"Good, otherwise, I might have to get out of this pickup."

"I hope you kept up your end of the bargain."

"Oatmeal chocolate-chip suit you?"

"Hand one over and I'll let you know." Isa opened the container she'd brought and offered it to Jack, who claimed one; she then set it, open, on the seat between them. "I guess you can have some of my chili when we get there, long as you leave some for supper. How 'bout you make some of that honey cornbread to go with it?"

"Sure, after I spend time with Amigo."

She was working with Amigo on jumping, logs, ditches, whatever they could find. At first, Isa had saddled him for these little adventures. Once he figured out that jumping was fun, he'd get so excited that it was difficult for Isa to slow him down after the jump. They had built a great deal of trust with each other; now, much of the time she spent riding him was bareback. Jack had ridden with her the first couple of times she came out to show her the ranch and the way it was run. She'd also ridden with Josh and Mark and they teased each other unmercifully. She'd made a point of bringing Josh a peanut butter and honey sandwich, asking Mark if he knew they were Josh's favorite. Mark said he'd be sure to remember that next time they went to town to eat, earning them both a look from Josh, and for Mark a punch in the arm.

Today, she rode alone after "taste-testing" the chili. She and Amigo rode down to the river at an easy gait, taking pleasure in the warmth from the sun on this brisk day. The sky was filled with the brightest blue, only fading low on the horizon. They breathed in deeply the clean, cold air. Amigo's back was soft and the heat of his working muscles kept the chill at bay. Isa recognized the grace in this moment, and knew that she was loved beyond measure by the God of her faith. She sent out a silent thank you, and prayed she would remember this place in time and the peace of her spirit when she needed it most. She had many moments of her life stored, she just hadn't realized that the love in those memories had given her strength every time she'd been in need.

Back in the barn, she brushed Amigo, gave him some oats, and turned him out in the pasture with her customary hug 'round his neck. She watched him from the top rail of the fence for a while then headed across the yard to Jack's house.

It wasn't dark yet, and Isa cleaned up and found Jack stirring his chili and having another cookie with his coffee.

"Stirring chili is hard work, kiddo, and it must be done with precision, so I've got to keep my strength up!"

"Right. Anymore coffee?" He nodded toward the stove.

She filled a mug and sipping from it, put together the honey cornbread to bake in the oven. It wouldn't go in until Bane arrived, so she set the pan on a shelf in the fridge and sat down across the table from Jack.

"Good ride?"

"Always. I made a memory down by the river."

"You made a memory?"

Her hands wrapped around the mug, soaking in the warmth.

"Yeah. It was just so still and we could see our breath. I...I felt loved, blessed to be right where I was with Amigo. I knew it would be like a photo I could pull out of my heart when—if—I needed it. To help me...." Her voice trailed off.

"I can listen, if you need me to."

He refilled their mugs and sat down, waiting. She talked. Jack hadn't asked her anything about why or how she came to be on Rowan with Bane. He was not like Fran or Timothy, though he had just as much caring and compassion. He was one you knew you could count on and no spoken words could change that.

Bane let himself in, as Jack was not one to stand on ceremony. Jack had, as promised, listened as Isa shared her story with him. When she'd finished, he'd said that no one could know why hard things come into our lives, why we lose those we love most, or why anyone would want to hurt another; they just did and trying to blame yourself or someone else wouldn't bring anything but guilt and misery. You had to find what strength you could, muster up courage and move on with your life. From all he'd seen, Isa had done just that, and if memory-making pulled her through, then by all means, make more.

"This looks pretty serious," Bane observed as he filled a mug and joined them. Isa nodded at Jack, addressed Bane.

"I was just sharing my ride with Jack. We're thinking about writing a book together on the philosophy of life." Jack chuckled at that.

"Sounds intense. You two spend the day getting into trouble?"

"If she hadn't produced those cookies, there would have been trouble!"

"I wondered what happened to those cookies."

Jack slid the container over to him and Bane helped himself. Isa turned the oven on and pulled the pan out of the fridge, setting it on the stove while it preheated. The boys had gone into town for supper, hoping to take some potential girlfriends out. Isa's attention was caught by their conversation, as she had no experience with dating or good relationships except what she remembered about her parents when she was young. She'd decided to ask Bane about it on the way back to town.

When the cornbread was ready, they all filled bowls with Jack's zesty chili and Isa's cornbread. It was a pleasant evening at Jack's table, and Isa simply listened to them talk. She cleared the table, filled coffee mugs and set a plate of her cookies in front of them.

Jack walked them to the door and they both thanked him. Bane's hand moved to her back to usher her out, but she paused, turning back. Her blue eyes caught Jack's and an emotional pact passed between them; she stepped forward into his embrace and he hugged her. She stretched up and kissed his cheek and then turned to leave with Bane.

They drove down the long drive, Bane turning onto the main road from under the archway. "How do you know when you want to date someone?" He seemed to consider her a moment; she was biting her lower lip, but looking at him, not down at her lap.

"Why do you ask?"

"I was listening to Mark and Josh talk about their plans in town tonight. They were hoping to run into some cute girls, take them to dinner and then maybe a movie. I've just been, well, wondering how all that works."

"I see. It's pretty simple in a lot of ways: You find yourself attracted to someone and reach out to get to know them. You spend time together and see what you have in common. It'll just come naturally, no need to hurry."

"So, that's it?"

"To start with, yes. Of course, it doesn't always work, and hearts get hurt and bruised—it can be the best and worst experience, sometimes all at the same time. It takes years to know who you are and what you want. Over time, that can change, too. Just be who you are, Isa, and never let someone push you into something you don't want to do." She turned away, gazing out the window, and he left her with her thoughts.

24.

Goodbyes were hard; those Isa was leaving behind had come into her life when her need was great, giving her more than she could realize. Love and acceptance were rebuilding the demolition Frank had caused. Fran held tears back as she made Isa promise to stay in touch and to be safe. Jack had found her in Amigo's stall, telling him she would never forget him. Jack tucked a photo of them from the pack trip into her pocket, embraced her in a hug and said he'd keep the coffee on so she should stop by whenever she was back on Rowan.

That last night, as they'd sat on the sofa and discussed the next few days, Isa had been quiet.

"You'll miss them; they've all become family for you and that will never leave you. Now, your family expands even more as you work with the crew and find your place here."

"I'm so excited. I feel like I've been waiting a long time for this moment. I'm sad to leave and I can't wait to go. Is that weird?"

"Normal, I think. Just remember to let yourself feel, don't shove it aside—it's easy to do because you'll be so busy. For a while, I want you to come to my quarters at the end of your day. We can check in that way and you can let your guard down safely."

He wasn't sure how she'd react to that, but Bane thought it important for her to be able to share her day when he could take his Captain skin off, or at least set it aside temporarily.

She'd agreed and he made sure she understood the plan for her first week on Bounty. It would consist mostly of studying six or seven hours a day, and then learning the duties of science officers.

Sleep came fast, but didn't last. Everything was packed and moved to Bounty, so she had only one small bag to bring today. Dressing, she'd asked for one last look at the heavens from the deck that had become such a favorite morning spot.

"Give me a minute and I'll come with you," Bane had said.

It was too early for coffee, but they both held steaming mugs, sitting on the deck and studying the stars. Three weeks ago, he'd met her, scared and confused, for transport; she'd come so far in that time and he was glad to see the confidence of that young girl galloping down the road on Indian returning.

The stars filled her vision, a dim moon shaping the fuzzy outline of a large evergreen tree. Thick, scraggly branches nodded up and down, back and forth in the breeze she was protected from on the deck. This place had been good to her; she nodded acknowledgement of that out to the world around her. However, once onboard Bounty, her relationship with Bane would change. He would be Captain Lucas and she hoped she wouldn't disappoint him.

He was looking out over the railing, "Everything will be okay. You'll be fine."

Dawn approached in the slightest softening of the dark on the eastern horizon. They watched until it became orange and pink, Isa walking backwards as they headed in and back to their quarters for the last time. Taking their small bags, they left to join the crew for a last planet-side breakfast. There were many conversations about the work in progress and senior officers directing who would be doing what as they departed Rowan.

Isa was assigned to the common room to assist in inventory and to put away supplies. Lt. Hamilton was in charge and he was delighted to find all the baking Fran had done and that it had all been packaged and labeled for easy use. Most of it was in the deep freeze to be thawed and served as needed. Across the hall from the common room was a well-stocked galley where larger meals would be cooked and easily brought across to serve. This floor also housed the recreation rooms, guest quarters, the conference room and the bridge. Crew quarters were one floor below along with medical.

Those assigned with Isa worked together to sort everything out, organize and put everything away, and to log the numbers in the computer for easy tracking of what was used, as well as double-checking that everything ordered was onboard. This had been confirmed on delivery, but Lt Hamilton liked to double, sometimes triple-check. It made sense to be well prepared out here.

By midday, they had finished and been sent off for new duties after being advised to eat first as nothing would be served in the common room until evening. Isa grabbed a grape soda and a sandwich from a tray Fran had made up and headed off to her quarters for an afternoon of study.

She sat at the table facing her viewing windows, eating and basking in the comfort of her quarters. She liked seeing the quilt on her bed and various photos of her family and the horses up around the room. Pulling her books out, she tucked into the bottom of a window and began to read, making notes in the text. Isa had found that making a book her own by adding comments, and marking what struck her as important or remarkable in some way, helped her to learn and retain the concepts and information.

Finishing the chapter, she moved to the desk to write the required response and solve the problems set apart for her to complete. She brought out the keyboard and turned on the view screen, typing her work as she thought about the questions and referred to her notes. She would submit this directly to the folder Professor Kolter had set up for her, and receive feedback from him shortly.

Isa liked Prof. K., he had a strict style that wasn't bothersome for a student like Isa, and he liked to engage in discussions that got her thinking. Since she'd studied on her own, she'd missed that; oh, her teachers would write comments and questions and she'd write back, but it wasn't the same. Working with Prof. K. was all "yes, sir; no sir," but Isa had picked it up fast and he'd told her that she'd be expected to address everyone on Bounty in this manner while on duty, just as she would if she were at the Academy.

Moving through her work, she saved the literature and writing for last as it was her favorite. The readings assigned were many and varied, but she'd found freedom in how she responded to them, as being able to communicate verbally and in writing were important skills to master. Prof. K. also told her that being able to work effectively on a team depended on the team's ability to communicate, which included listening skills.

Today, she was reading poetry from several sources, and Isa enjoyed vocalizing them out loud as she paced her quarters. She liked the way these authors used images to show what they were writing about and the pictures in her mind went from meadows full of colorful flowers and waving grasses to the emotional suffering of loss and persons reduced to feeling less than whole from their grief. She decided to try her hand at writing poetry and gazed around her room for some ideas.

Her eyes arrived at the pouch with her special book in it. Isa thought about that pouch and how it came to be the special hiding place for the story she loved to hear her father read to her. She wanted to convey the way she felt, wrapped in her dad's arms, safely tucked into those bales in the loft; how she was transported out the loft door and into that other world in the depth of its winter; the way she shared that secret with her dad as they placed the pouch inside the window cage until the next time they could sneak away together; and finally, guarding that small piece of her dad and their love from being severed from her. How, even after the dismantling of her life, that pouch remained whole and untouched to remind her of who she was and what she could become.

So engrossed in this process, she jumped when the comm unit sounded, "Ensign Torunn."

"Torunn here, sir."

She wasn't in trouble, but had been missed at the start of the meal. Indeed, it was getting late, so she left her work on the desk and started off for the common room. Upon her arrival, a lieutenant motioned her over, told her to fill a plate and join them at the table.

This was her assigned science team, those whom she'd begin work with the next day. In charge was Lt. Sanborn, who explained the project they'd been working on before leave and what Isa's responsibility would be as they continued. There were five on this team, and with all the joking and teasing going on while they ate, it promised to be a good team.

Isa would spend the first part of her days with the science team, and then be released to her studies, which would continue into the evenings. She didn't know yet what Prof. K.'s expectations were for face-to-face contact, but she knew she would hear from Captain Lucas when that was set up.

Lt. Hamilton had brought out Fran's chocolate cake and the crew was really digging in. Isa found a piece with lots of frosting and a cup of coffee, and sat down in a viewing seat to savor them. Finishing, she returned the dishes and went back to her quarters to continue her work.

It was fairly late and Bane had been expecting her for some time; he could see the fatigue in her eyes. Telling her to sit, he fixed hot cocoa and, handing it to her, sat beside her. Isa sank back into the cushion, drew her knees up and sipped the warm chocolate, letting it soothe the length of the day away.

Halfway through the mug, "I wrote a poem." She was looking into the swirling chocolate. Bane waited. "Do you remember that oilskin pouch that came with my belongings from the farm?" He nodded as she went on, "My lit. class work today was all around poetry—beautiful words crafted so fine that I found myself in them. Prof. K. said I could respond to the readings in many different ways, so I tried to write a poem and my eyes landed on the pouch. Sometime, would you read it and tell me what you think?"

"Of course...Prof. K.?" His left eyebrow rose slightly as she said it, and now he waited for an explanation.

"It's my nickname for him. And no, I would never call him that to his face." She leveled her gaze at him, then giggled.

"Hmm. How was the rest of your day?"

She recounted it for him and shared her perceptions of her science team and the schedule set forth. Bane had spoken with Alex Kolter and they'd decided that once a week, after the midday meal, Isa could use the conference room as their virtual classroom. In ten days Bounty would bring her to the Academy for face-to-face meetings, but Kolter had said she was doing a fine job so far and he was pleased with her attitude and work ethic.

"So, tomorrow after lunch, come to the bridge and I'll go with you to the conference room and sit in." He took the mug from her and sent her off, admonishing her to get some sleep and let go of the day.

She did fall asleep fast that night, surrounded by stars moving past the opened windows, with dreams filled with horses and rides past rivers rolling over smooth round rocks.

The smell of the quilt was familiar, but as Isa's eyelids began to slide open, she felt disoriented and lay still, keeping her breath slow and even. Looking around without moving her head, it came to her where she was. She slowly relaxed her tensed muscles, stretched and got up. She just stood in the center of her room and took it in. It had been her first night in her new home, her new life, and she wanted to brand it into her memory.

Leaving her room in her running clothes, she hooked up her headphones and started the player. Isa played with the speed on the machine, running four miles at differing intervals. Stretching, she decided to try the free weights, following the charts the ship provided. It felt good to use her muscles and she wondered when ballet classes would begin onboard. Finished, she went off in search of coffee.

No one was about in the common room, so she brewed a pot and, taking a cup, pointed herself back to her quarters to shower and change. She wasn't sure if she'd need anything for her work with the science team, so the empty cup was all she carried.

Making her way back, she saw some of the crew were now joining in the morning's pilgrimage. She filled several eager cups, put another pot on, and rummaged around for a bite to eat. Oatmeal. Isa loved oatmeal in the morning, with brown sugar and blueberries and a little milk. Taking the thick, bubbling oats from the burner and getting bowls out, she dished herself some, added the sugar and milk, and found a table by a window.

Noticing a few longing looks, she said, to no one in particular, "Help yourself, there's plenty."

Joining her at the table, her new companions complimented her cooking and dug in.

"You can do this anytime, and I'll even clean up!" a young lieutenant announced. Isa enjoyed sharing breakfast with this group and decided it would be fun to cook for them once in a while, after all, what was so hard about oatmeal?

After a morning studying soil samples and nutrient value for optimal growing conditions, Isa picked up some fruit, stopped for her books, and sat alone in the conference room to enjoy the crisp, sweet apple and the grapes. She stood, as she'd been taught, when Captain Lucas entered.

"At ease, Ensign." They sat. "Didn't have time to finish lunch?"

"I wanted to be ready, so I just brought fruit with me."

"And are you ready?"

"Yes, sir." He didn't mention that she'd neglected to come to the bridge.

While Bane set up the vid-screen, Isa moved the rest of the fruit away and positioned her books in front of her. She stood, awaiting Professor Kolter's invitation to be seated. Bane spoke directly with him for a few minutes, and then Prof. K. turned his attention to Isa. Going over the work she had sent, he complimented her on the poem she had written; he was a teacher who believed in giving credit for a job well done or calling you out for work not performed to his high standards.

They spent time going over her history lessons. Isa was struggling with so many dates and events. There was so much to learn about various cultures on distant worlds and she would get caught up in the individual stories and lose sight of the bigger picture. At one point, Professor Kolter made her stand at attention and told her not to speak, but just to listen, and then repeat what he said. He had said her name so sharply that she snapped to her feet, head down and tense. Professor Kolter's voice had softened slightly, telling her to face him and listen. Bane stepped back as the exchange took place. She needed this experience and ultimately, it would help her fear reflex.

After she repeated what Professor Kolter was trying to explain, and was once again in her seat, Bane left them to their work, returning to his.

That night, Isa asked Bane about cultures with wars and why they still existed, where most had seen the value in peace. It was hard to understand, he agreed. The Alliance continued to labor at mediating with these worlds, and on Bounty, she would experience this work first hand. It was a tricky business when the atrocities of war were all people knew. Once these situations were ended, warriors often felt cheated; peace had to come with education and training in order to avoid trouble later.

This was part of the conversation Isa had been having with Professor Kolter when she began arguing with him and had stopped listening.

"It's good to be passionate, Isa, but you must be open to what you might not have considered. That was the point Professor Kolter was trying to make. That was why he called you out; you had quit listening."

"You're right. It scared me for a minute, but then his voice changed and when I looked at him, I realized I was being foolish. He assigned more reading to broaden my perspective, and a paper discussing the benefits of war for a given society." She made a face of disgust, pushing out her lips and rolling her eyes.

25.

Anticipation of meeting the Academy President and Professor Kolter provided a very restless night for Isa. Adding two miles to her morning run took her mind off it for a while. Bounty had arrived and established orbit. Captain Lucas and she were to have a breakfast meeting with the President and her professor, and then Isa would spend the next few days attending classes and meeting her fellow classmates. Professor Kolter had decided that, as much as possible, Isa should have a sort of virtual classroom experience, which included her peers, to give her and them the benefit of learning from each other's insight and opinions.

The visit from Bounty would also give the Academy students a chance to explore a starship, and to work with Bounty's crew in their areas of expertise. President Wilson was quite pleased with this arrangement, and wanted to bring as many of his third and fourth year students aboard as possible in the next few days. Bane had been clear that he wanted his junior officer grounded in everything "Academy," as he couldn't be sure when Bounty might next return to this sector. The Alliance was willing to adjust Bounty's schedule due to the strength of both Bane and Ken's request. It paid to have students with an interest in a career on a starship to be able to have a personal glimpse into how one worked. Some might find it wasn't for them and that would give them a chance to focus their goals elsewhere for the Alliance.

Isa slowed the machine's speed as she cooled down, and stopped it as she stepped off. She was startled from the song she'd been singing by the towel that was extended towards her. She pulled the small speaker from her right ear, taking the towel and wiping the sweat from her face.

"Was I singing too loud?"

"Not at all. I noticed you were slowing down when I came in and thought you could use a towel. That must have been some run." Her shirt was dark with perspiration and her face was bright red. "You better do some stretching; how far did you go?"

She pushed against the wall, one leg behind with the front leg bent at the knee, taking turns stretching each calf muscle, then straightening the front leg and lifting her toes to stretch each shin.

"Six miles," she answered, "I'm a little nervous about this breakfast meeting." Bane waited until she continued. "I guess I'm feeling sort of restless about what's going to happen here, what I'll be doing. How I'll fit in. What if everyone thinks I'm—" She sat down, leaning against the wall with her arms around her legs and her head on her knees.

Bane looked down, her eyes going back and forth as she chewed the inside of her lower lip.

"Come on," he said and grabbed her hands, pulling her to her feet, "You'll never know until you get there. So, go clean up, grab whatever you need, and meet me at transport in twenty minutes." He propelled her out the door.

Nineteen minutes later, in a fresh uniform with a satchel of books, she and Bane took the transport to the surface and made their way to the main Academy entrance. They were ushered into the administration conference room, where Ken Wilson and Alex

Kolter waited for them. After formal introductions and assurances that Isa could be at ease and speak freely, they sat to have breakfast and to talk about what would happen over the next few days.

Isa listened, fingers entwined around the coffee cup, sipping the hot, black liquid and wishing it would soothe her nerves. She picked at the food on her plate, managing a couple bites of pancakes and some small sweet strawberries. The men were thoroughly engaged in their discussion of schedule and what would work best, as Isa wandered away into her thoughts, remembering that the Academy had a stable and what the possibilities were to spend time there.

It took a few minutes for the silence to sink in; when she looked up, all three men were regarding her. Bane was hiding a smile, and the other two seemed to be waiting. "Uh, could you repeat that, please?"

"Are we boring you, Ensign?"

"No sir. I...just lost track of the conversation. I'm sorry." No one spoke. Her grip tightened around the cup. She met their gaze. "Actually, I was thinking about your stable, and wondering if I'd have any extra time to spend there." Straightening her spine, she waited for a rebuke. After all, she was not here to play with horses.

"We know you have some great skills and experience in that area, so I'm sure we can work something out, especially if you're willing to include some teaching there."

"I agree, Ken. I have other priorities for her, but we can make those arrangements."

Bane spoke up, concluding, "All right, gentlemen, you seem to have Ensign Torunn's best interests in mind, and I have a ship to ready for students. The only thing we didn't cover is sleeping arrangements. Is she to return to Bounty each evening?"

"No, Captain, I think it would be best for her to stay here, in the girl's dormitory, while she's with us. I'll send her to Bounty later to get what she needs." This was news to Isa, but not surprising after hearing Prof. K. talk about her lack of experience with Alliance protocol and wanting her inundated with this while she was here.

"Very well." Bane walked around the table to where Isa stood, rested a hand on her shoulder and, looking into her eyes, said, "You're in good hands here. Make the most of it." She nodded. "When you come to get your belongings, find me and check in before you leave."

"Yes, sir."

Professor Kolter took her to a large outdoor area, explaining that she'd be starting out her days with the rest of the students in morning drills. Leaving her with an older student, Mika, he said he'd see her in class.

Mika introduced herself and explained the drills to Isa. Although most in the Alliance had not seen war for many years, military precision was still a priority, teaching discipline in the uniformity of movement and the ability to move efficiently as a group and follow orders. There was an appropriate place to move with practiced precision, just as there was to be an individual. Isa likened it to a herd of horses.

In the wild, the only way to survive was to follow the lead mare and stallion, as horses knew instinctively that there was safety in the herd. Isa figured out fairly quickly that the more regulated your movements were, the less you were called out. Morning drills went on for an hour and by the end, Isa felt like she'd done well for a beginner. Professor Kolter had observed the drills from a window over the courtyard. He'd watched her struggle with the movements, listen, and then try again as Mika demonstrated what to do. When the drillmaster singled her out, she tried even harder. She noted his attention, and it seemed he was satisfied with what he saw as he went off to prepare for class.

"You did fine for your first time."

"Thanks for all your help, Mika."

"Not bad at all. Tomorrow will be easier, and I'll be happy to run you through the drills after dinner if you want." She and Mika both turned toward the deep voice. "I'm Cade."

"Hi, Cade, I'm Isa. Sorry if I messed up your drills."

"We don't expect you to be perfect your first time out." Isa relaxed, falling in step with Cade and Mika as they entered the building. Cade's dark brown hair was short and wavy, and he stood a head taller than Isa. His hazel eyes were kind and his smile came easily. They parted ways to go to their scheduled classes, Cade promising to find Isa later and help her with the drills.

"I think he likes you." Mika laughed at the perplexed look on Isa's face. "What? You don't think he's cute?"

Isa's cheeks felt hot and she covered them with her hands. "I...I don't know." They'd reached the classroom door and Isa had no time to respond further, or even think about what Mika had said. She filed it away for later. The day flew by in a flurry of classes, discussions, and the constant meetings and introductions of new faces. By the time everyone had gathered for the evening meal, Isa was tired. She'd been with Mika all day and was glad Prof. K. had assigned them together. She would stay with Mika in the dorm and spend the few days she had here shadowing her.

True to his word, Cade sought her out and sat with them at dinner. The warmth from her words with Mika earlier crept into her cheeks, and she found her words became jumbled up. Mika had a wide grin on her face when she told them to have a good practice and she'd see her later.

In the courtyard, Cade took her through the routines, helping her remember the basic forms from the morning and showing her how to make the movements precise. He demonstrated, she followed, trying to copy the way he moved. His hands left hot spots where they touched her, guiding her steps. "Yes, that's it, you can't try to match my stride, you need to find your own—it'll be somewhat shorter."

"Okay, I get it." She continued to follow him but stopped trying to match his stride. They kept at it until Isa had the same cadence that she'd felt in the group that morning. "Cade, thanks. I have to get back to transport so I can grab what I need from Bounty and get back here to see Professor Kolter."

"No problem. Come on, I'll walk you there, and if you want, we can work more on it tomorrow." Side-by-side, they went off, and not only did Isa find herself in that regulated pace, but the side of her closest to Cade felt tingly. Mika was right; he was cute! When they reached transport, he gave her a lopsided grin and said he'd see her at breakfast.

Isa smiled herself back to Bounty, humming as she made her way to her quarters. Pulling out the overnight bag she'd purchased on Rowan, she packed more uniforms, her jeans and boots for the stable, and a sky-blue blouse that set off her features, but more importantly, made her feel pretty. Satisfied she had everything, she went off to find her captain.

Reaching his quarters, she pushed the entry button and waited. No one answered. She set her bag down by his door and wondered where to look for him. It was past time for the evening meal, and she didn't think he'd be in the common room. She left for the bridge, trying to remember the proper way to enter and ask permission to enter at the same time.

Bane saw her heading toward the bridge, observing a difference in her step, but he wasn't quite sure how to describe it. He could hear the humming, punctuated by the occasional word slipping out. It must have been a good day.

"Hello there, stranger."

"Oh. Sorry, sir. I went to your quarters, but you weren't there, so I was coming to find you and, uh, I did!"

"Come on. I was just on my way."

They walked back the way she'd come. Measured, that's what it was. Of course, she'd gone through drills this morning, and she was practicing. Bane remembered how difficult it was for some to pick up that drill pace, and how the drill master's stern voice calling you out for messing up was a great motivation not to do so a second time.

He picked up her bag and set it down inside his door while she tucked herself into the cushions on his couch.

"So, talk. I can see you have a lot to say. Tea or cocoa?"

"Cocoa, extra chocolate, please."

"Sounds serious."

"You didn't tell me about drills. I got called out, but it turned out okay." He took note of her tone; she was focused on her feet, pointing her toes back and forth with her fingers. "Cade helped me practice after dinner—he's the drill master. He was nice. He sat with us to eat. Mika said he must like me. He, I, it was different. I felt different, sort of warm." She was getting flustered, her face flushed.

Bane sat, handing her the mug, "Extra chocolate." She sipped, then held the mug to her cheek. "Did something happen? Did this Cade...?" He paused. She beamed.

"Nothing happened, unless you count me being ultra-sensitive and completely embarrassed. I just didn't expect to have that reaction to him. I think Mika planted the idea and, he was so helpful. He walked me to transport when we finished going over drills and said he'd help me again tomorrow, did I do something wrong?"

"No, Isa. It's like we talked about that night coming back from Jack's. You like him, he likes you. Just take it slow and remember that you won't be there long. This is how a relationship starts, so enjoy it, but," he waited for her to focus, "don't let this get in the way of your job at the Academy right now. I'm glad you're having this experience; I also know it's new to you. And who is Mika?"

"She's the student Prof. K. hooked me up with. I'm sort of shadowing her and I'm to stay with her in the dorm. She's fun to talk to and she's smart. Her family is very involved in the Alliance and have all gone to the Academy. I think Prof. K. is hoping that will rub off on me."

"Indeed. You should talk to her about this Cade and about dating. She'll be much more helpful than I am. And the rest of your day?"

She filled him in on her classes and where she would be for the next several days. When she asked, he told her the crew had had a day of organized chaos with students coming and going, but that it had been a good experience, he thought, for students and crew. The exchange had value and tomorrow would bring smaller groups with a field focus working in those sections.

"It's getting pretty late, and there's a strict adherence to lights out. Let's head to transport, and I won't plan to see you until Professor Kolter releases you; however, I'm here should any need arise." She downed the last of the warm, rich chocolate.

26.

She and Mika talked and giggled well into the night. Mika teased her about Cade, giving Isa an opening to ask her about boys and how to deal with them. Isa was rather overwhelmed with all the advice and options, and Mika was delighted to share all her experience with such an obvious beginner. Mika didn't ask why because it didn't seem to matter to her. At seventeen, Mika had already had four boyfriends, so had much to tell a wide-eyed Isa. Sleep overtook them both before the conversation was finished.

"You better get up, breakfast's in half an hour."

"Where were you, and I am getting up."

"I went for a run, and I didn't even get lost. Those paths are great!"

"Do you have to be so awake?"

Breakfast was a hearty meal, with sausage, fried eggs and potatoes. Isa did find the coffee and, complimenting the cook on the fine meal, also thanked her for having a pot on early.

She was nervous about drills, mostly due to seeing Cade and trying not to screw up the maneuvers. The practice had helped, and although she couldn't match the precision of the others yet, she did not fall out of step. It felt slightly more natural to her today; like dance, her muscles had to learn the rhythm and cadence.

"You did great today."

"Thanks to your help last night."

"I'm available today again if you like. We can go down by the lake to practice, so you can see more than this courtyard."

"I'd like that."

"Okay, I'll see you at dinner."

As Cade was leaving, Mika's "ooh-la-la" sounded in Isa's ear, and they were off to class arm-in-arm. After lunch, Professor Kolter called Isa over and told her she'd be spending the afternoon at the stable, which would not excuse her from her assigned work. She was to meet the stable manager, and help with the afternoon lessons.

"Yes, sir."

"And wipe that smile off your face, Ensign. We don't allow any fun here." His lips turned up just slightly as Isa put on her most serious face.

Sarah, the stable manager, was thrilled to have Isa's help for the afternoon. She had a large class of new beginner riders coming, all between eight and ten years old, and the farrier was coming to shoe some of the private horses boarded for older students. These were all kids who lived on the planet and took lessons from the Academy stable. They worked together to groom and tack the ten horses Isa would need. Sarah, after learning Isa's background with horses, gave her free reign to run the lesson however she saw fit. She would have three hours with the group, including ground lesson, arena work, and a trail ride.

When the kids arrived, eight girls and two boys, after introductions and admonishments to be on their best behavior for their guest teacher, Isa gathered them around the horse that Sarah had suggested for this lesson, Echo. She was a deep, claret bay and looked every inch the quarter horse that she was, and she was quiet. Isa demonstrated to them how to approach and lead a horse and then had each one try it in turn. She talked to them about where a horse could see and how they should move to let the horse know they were there, and had them practice going from one side of Echo to the other. They liked the way the mare licked her lips and sighed.

Isa moved on to teach them how to groom, giving each of them an area to curry or brush, telling them how important it was to remove dirt and anything else that might rub against the tack and cause a sore. Echo was gleaming when they finished. Hooves were more difficult. Beginning at the top of Echo's shoulder, Isa ran her hand firmly down the leg, lifted Echo's foot and bent it so the bottom of the hoof faced up, showing them how to clean out the foot with a hoof pick. She also pointed out to them that they should be diligent about keeping their feet out from under the horse's because it was easy to get stepped on and the horse would not know they were standing on your foot. She knew this would be scary, especially for the smaller children, but she assisted them as they tried, to give them a feel for it, and then told them they should work in teams for grooming and saddling, as that way it was easier to help each other.

Echo proved to be a model of patience, putting the students at ease as they breezed through saddling, fastening and unfastening the cinch to gain some experience. Isa showed them the process for bridling, but said they'd need instructor help to bridle until they had a few more lessons.

Sarah had gone over each of the various horse personalities with her and Isa had sized up the kids in that first hour, so she told each one which horse to get, reminding the kids how to lead. She went with the smallest girl, Ella, to help her with her horse, Badger. Once everyone was present in the arena, Isa asked them to stand next to their horse and face the center while she showed them how to mount. Then, she walked around boosting each one up after a tack check and gave basic instructions on how to stop, turn and go.

Standing in the middle, she praised each one for whatever she could find him or her doing correctly and called out encouragement to those whose eyes were still big.

"Horses do best in a herd. You and your horse are a herd of two, and you must be the leader, giving your horse confident, calm guidance as well as praise for a job well done, or immediate correction if they do something they shouldn't. A pat on the neck or a 'good-boy' will do, or a sharp 'quit!' Let's practice that circle again. Prepare to circle, and...circle your horses."

They worked on turning and stopping, sitting up straight, keeping their heels down and their hands quiet. Isa took more time in the arena, building their confidence, and then taught them some trail basics. "Sit up straight going downhill, lean slightly forward from your hips going uphill, stay in the middle of the trail, and don't let your horse eat—this is not a snack ride! Stay in order and keep the same distance from the horse in front of you like you did in here. Okay?"

She swung up on Echo, opened the gate, and led them out. It was a sunny day, providing plenty of warmth, and the kids were afraid and excited at the same time. Ella and Badger followed behind Echo and Isa could hear her talking softly to the horse, it sounded like a description of her lunch. That made Isa smile; she'd told the kids that if they were nervous, they should talk or sing to their horse and it didn't matter what they said, it could even be what they had for breakfast, but it would make them feel better and keep the animal calm.

It didn't take long for everyone to relax with the sun shining through the trees and a brilliant blue sky. The trail was perfect for a first ride; gentle slopes allowed them to sharpen up their leaning forward and sitting up straight skills. Going in a large circle, they were back in the arena forty-five minutes later.

"Stay on your horse until I come around to help you dismount, then return your horse to the tie rack and wait in the center of the arena." She was late, but Sarah would have the parents wait until the kids came back down to the barn. Gathering them all around her in a large circle, she asked them to share just one thing they had learned about their horse today.

"After all, this will be your horse to take care of and learn from, so you need to get to know them. I'll start. My horse is Echo and she is very patient with lots of noise and movement."

Ella was last, "My horse is Badger and he's the biggest horse because he likes to take care of the smallest riders."

"You guys were great today, and whether or not I work with you again, I hope you'll always have a horse in your life." Isa herded them back to the barn, while the older students began bringing horses down, untacking and preparing to feed and perform the evening chores. Kids were sent off with parents, but Ella waited.

"Your mom's not here yet?"

"I don't have a mom." Isa crouched down next to her.

"Neither do I, little one, but I have so many horse friends who are always there when I need to talk or I just need a hug. And the best part is, they never tell me to be quiet, or that I'm stupid, or a cry-baby; they just listen and take all the love I have to give." Ella threw her arms around Isa's neck and they held each other. "Now, who's picking you up?"

"I live in the group home, and I'm not sure."

"Then let's find Sarah. She'll figure this out, and in the meantime, you can help feed the horses and get the barn ready for the night." Sarah had seen the exchange, and much of Isa's lesson, too. She assured Ella that she would find out how she was to get home.

"Not to worry. You go on with Isa until I get this sorted out."

They measured oats and put out hay, and found the manure rakes to clean the stalls. Isa knew she was very late for her meeting with Prof. K. already, but she would not leave Ella alone.   There had been some glitch at the home, so Isa volunteered to see Ella there herself, it wasn't far. Dropping her off with a hug and a promise to see her again, Isa resigned herself to what she was sure would be her doom with Prof. K. She fell into the regimented stride from drills and forced herself to rehearse an apology with no excuses. She would make an effort not to cringe, knowing there would be no physical punishment.

Reaching administration, she went straight to his office and knocked.

"Enter." She stood before him at attention and waited. He was typing on the computer, and did not seem inclined to stop. She waited.

"Three hours, Ensign Torunn. Speak."

"I'm sorry, sir."

"That's it?"

"Yes, sir." Alex respected that answer. He'd gone from annoyed to angry to concerned to waiting. This was a turning point, and she'd done well.

"Very well. You are confined to quarters until morning when you will meet me back here. Dismissed." She turned and left his office, and went directly to Mika's room.

Mika came in after dinner and found Isa reading her history lessons. After some questioning and assurances that Isa was okay, the story came out. "Well, why didn't you tell him what happened?"

"Because it would have sounded like an excuse, and Captain Bane doesn't like excuses, so I figured Prof. K. wouldn't either. I was late and that was all that mattered."

"I still think he would have listened to you. Cade was looking for you at dinner. I told him you had a meeting with Prof. K. and it must have run late. Do you want me to find him and tell him what happened?"

"Would you? I feel terrible about not meeting him at dinner, and for practice," she explained. "We were going to work on drills again tonight."

"Sure. I'll be back, and I'll see if I can bring you some food."

"I am hungry. Thank you."

Males and females weren't allowed in each other's rooms, so Cade sent a message back with Mika that he was sorry to have missed her and he'd find her tomorrow. Mika managed to bring Isa an apple, some cheese, and half a bar of chocolate with almonds, which Isa ate, savoring the creamy bites of chocolate and crunchy nuts. Not long after that she was asleep.

27.

As Isa left his office, Alex sat back in his chair, thinking. He knew there was a story and he was curious to learn what it was. When Ken had suggested they let her spend time at the stable to allow her to build confidence using some of her strongest skills, he'd agreed. He'd also had reservations, thinking it would be good for Isa to find her way around here, depending on herself and her peers and not the comfort of a horse. The compromise had been having her teach, so she would have to come out of herself and interact. If she had gone off on her own with a horse and lost track of time, he'd be very harsh with her. His gut told him that was not the case—only one way to find out.

"Sarah, Alex Kolter. How are you tonight?"

He listened as Sarah recounted the story of Isa's afternoon at the barn. Alex listened, asking a question now and then to clarify or draw out Sarah's impressions. Sarah concluded the story with the phone call she'd had from the group home, and the little girl, Ella, asking to say goodnight to Isa. How, upon finding out that she wasn't there, she'd told Sarah that it was all right because Isa had promised she'd see her soon. Alex thanked Sarah and said he'd send Isa back the next afternoon to work again.

Hanging up, he made some notes in Isa's file and tried to decide how to approach this with her.

28.

Confined to her quarters until morning, Prof. K. had said. Isa figured that meant she did not have permission to go for a run. She spent that early morning time reading and doing bookwork.

She and Mika left together, parting ways as Mika headed to breakfast and Isa to administration. Professor Kolter was outside his office with President Wilson as Isa came up. "Good morning, Ensign."

"Good morning, sir."

"All right, Alex, you can fill me in later."

"Ensign, come in and sit." She did as she was told. "Now, before we start, I want you to speak freely and honestly. Understood?"

"Yes, sir."

"First, I respect the way you took responsibility for your tardiness yesterday and the apology. I expected you to try to give an excuse, or to claim unfairness when I confined you to quarters. You are ahead of many of your peers in that respect."

"Thank you, sir."

"Now, I want you to tell me what happened out at the stable. What was more important than being on time for a meeting with your Academy-appointed liaison? I am supervising you and ultimately deciding your future on Bounty and with the Alliancee. Forthrightness is key here." He'd put an extra measure of pressure on her to see how she would handle a possible threat to her status on Bounty.

"It was my decision. Sarah didn't know I was supposed to meet you. I want you to know that first. After I finished teaching the lesson..." she recounted the story, emphasizing the plight of the little girl and giving an honest look into her own thoughts about not being late and asking someone else to stay with the little girl, and then deciding that Ella needed her more in that moment. She told him she knew she would have to suffer the consequences, but put that out of her mind until Ella was safely home.

It was still. She sat across the desk from Prof. K. who sat back in his chair, one leg crossed over the opposite knee. "Well, Ensign, it sounds like young Ella needed a friend and you were well suited for the task. Sarah spoke highly of your work at the stable. She also told me that little Ella called last night, to say goodnight to you."

"She did? Oh- I hope Sarah reassured her. She will continue her lessons, won't she?"

"To be sure. As for you, Ensign, I'm assigning you to the stable after your classes this afternoon. You made a promise to a little girl, and that cannot be taken lightly. Now, I expect that if anything should come up to delay your return by dinner, you will communicate that to this office in a timely manner. Get off to breakfast now."

"Sir?" Brows together, she was baffled.

"Is there something you didn't understand?"

"No, I, uh," a pause, "if you are confined to quarters, are you still allowed to go for a run in the morning?"

"No, I shouldn't think so."

"That's what I thought." She left with the impression that he was somehow pleased with her. Isa couldn't believe she was being ordered back to the stable, but she was relieved to be able to make good on her promise to Ella. Entering the dining room, she found breakfast was just about over. She grabbed two pancakes, tucked a sausage patty between them and ate on the way outside for drills.

29.

"When will you be coming back?" Sitting on the edge of the lake, hand-in-hand, Isa smiled at Cade.

"I don't know." She squeezed his hand and they locked eyes. They'd walked down to the lake each evening after dinner, sharing bits of their lives with each other and simply enjoying the quiet company. His finding her hand, and she returning the light touch, had just felt right. It was a sweet feeling and gave Isa the sense that the world was good, safe.

This was their last evening, and they were both lingering, not wanting to let go of their crush, or the moment.

"I want to kiss you. May I?" She didn't know what to do; she had never been kissed.

"I'd like that, yes." His arm came around her shoulder as they turned to face each other. Cade's lips were warm, covering hers gently. He pulled back, smiling at her upturned face—her eyes fluttered open and she smiled back at him as a wave of pink ebbed through her cheeks. She closed her eyes, leaned in and whispered, "Again, please."

It was so simple, and yet the warmth of that connection of lips moved her beyond words, and as she and Cade strolled back, she couldn't stop touching her fingers to her lips, feeling his still there, and smiling.

"What? Did I slobber?"

"You might have," pause, "I just didn't know how precious a kiss could be, so captivating, delightful, uh...."

"That was your first kiss, er, kisses? I hope it was, well, everything you wanted it to be. I wish you weren't leaving, I think we fit well together. I'd love more time with you." She squeezed his hand, at a loss for what to say. He stopped before they reached the doors and they kissed again.

She whispered, "Thank you," into his shoulder and hugged him goodbye. Mika was just inside the door waiting.

"I saw you, girl. Tell me!" Blushing as she told her story to Mika, Isa still couldn't stop touching her lips and that made them both giggle.

"Mika, I'm so glad I was assigned to you. Thanks for everything. I'll miss you and I already can't wait to talk. You will visit Ella for me?"

"I promised, didn't I? I'll see you soon enough, since Prof. K. wants us to keep working together; I'm sure we can sneak in some girl talk. You'd better go so you aren't late."

She slung her bag over her head and shoulder and walked briskly to admin. Captain Lucas was in the office with Alex Kolter. "I trust you've said your goodbyes, Ensign?"

"Yes, sir."

"Good. I was filling in your captain on the fine job you've done the past several days, and the outline of your studies for the next few months."

"Thank you, sir. I've enjoyed my time here and learned a lot. Mika was a great partner, helping me more than you could know."

"Noted, Ensign." She wasn't sure if there was some protocol for leaving your professor, so she stuck out her right hand.

"Goodbye, sir." Both men stood and Professor Kolter took Isa's hand, beaming at her.

"Goodbye, Ensign. Captain, I return your junior officer to your command."

"Thanks, Alex, and I know you'll keep me posted on her academics as I will you on her training."

Isa and Bane left for Bounty, the transport ride quiet. He watched her lost in her thoughts, remembering what Alex had told him about her experiences over the last few days, and wondering how she would frame those and what she would share with him. He was just glad that an evening pick-up had been arranged, so they'd have a chance to catch up before the start of a busy day.

Back on Bounty, she fell into step beside him, saying nothing even as they came into Bane's quarters. She dropped her bag on the floor, sat down and tucked her legs underneath herself. Bane took the chair opposite her.

"I don't know where to start. There's so much to tell."

"Why don't you start with that fixation you seem to be having with your fingers and your mouth?" Crimson crept over her cheeks and a shy smile had her hesitant to reply as she looked at him and yet past him.

"How do I explain? How my world was so completely altered, how one person could be so knit with another—it was about joy, belonging, warmth, impression. It was stirring, remarkable pleasure. He kissed me, my first." As she spoke, she was transported back to that moment, her eyes wide and alight. She had spoken slowly, softly, pausing between each word.

Bane was smiling and nodding. "Believe it or not, I do remember what kissing is like, although I'm not so sure I would describe it quite that way. I will assume, Isa Torunn, that kissing is *all* you did and that this boy was a gentleman."

She saw the grin forming on his face, knew that he was teasing and yet she felt he was serious as well. It was probably good that Cade was not onboard; he would be sure to get the third degree from Captain Lucas. She felt protected, somehow, by both the tone of his voice and the expectant gaze he was directing at her. "Oh no, we did so much more." Captain Lucas started to come out of his seat. "We held hands and walked by the lake, and talked. Cade was very nice, told me if I were at the Academy, he'd love to spend more time with me. I can see how having a best friend who likes to kiss you would be wonderful, kind of like Smokey."

"I'm not sure Cade would appreciate the comparison. Isa, I'm happy that it was special for you, and that it didn't go further than what you were ready for, I hope you discussed it with your friend, Mika, was it? Because that is important, friends you can talk to about, well, about girl things. You haven't had that. Although I am here, and willing to listen, I realize it isn't the same."

"We did talk, and it was good to have a friend to be silly with and to show me how to be—I can't explain it."

"No need. I understand. So, not surprisingly, it was noted that you've an aptitude for teaching and working well with others, especially children. I hear that you had a small taste of what happens when your superior officer is displeased with you." She straightened up; both feet hit the floor.

"I didn't make excuses and I didn't cringe."

"Little by little. You also did well in marksmanship."

"That was fun. I've never really shot a gun, but I got better. I hope I can practice more."

"Mmm. I'm sure you can. All right, it was a good opportunity for you and worked out well for a number of reasons, and now everyone is comfortable with this situation. Tomorrow, you're back to the routine you started with, so sleep well." He walked her to the door and handed her bag to her.

"Good night, sir."

Both Alex and President Wilson had been impressed with Isa. Alex had been concerned once he'd heard the barn manager's story on why Isa had been late and that she hadn't said anything. Bane related to him the story from Rowan and the discussion he'd had with her. They both felt that with time and experience, she'd learn the right time to speak up for herself, or that there were more options when handling difficult situations. Her maturity came through loud and clear in many areas, and her record already contained notes of her strengths and skills for future Alliance work. She was on par, academically, with the third and fourth-year students. If she continued to work hard, she'd be ready for commission as an officer within sixteen months to two years.

30.

Astro-physics. It felt more like home to her than any other department. The team had a real awe of stars, not just how they worked or were put together, but of their beauty. These were kindred souls who also spent their childhoods gazing up, astounded and captured by the brilliant, glistening heavens, no amount of science took that from the stars.

This was her last rotation, and she was happy to end it here. She was certain, now, that this would be her place. She'd done so much over the last eighteen months, finishing her required academic courses just under a year after her first visit to the Academy. Bounty had returned there twice, the last time leaving her for three weeks while they were on a mission and she had testing to complete. Mika had become as close a friend as Isa would ever had, though they were bound in different directions with Mika preferring planetside duties to being aboard a starship full time.

During those last three weeks, Isa and Cade decided they would always be friends; he would be that special someone in Isa's heart who had shown her young love, their kisses still brought a smile to her. She also spent several afternoons helping at the barn. Little Ella had found a home and a mother with Sarah. Sarah joked that after that first time with Isa, she couldn't keep Ella away from the barn and Badger, so they'd decided they might as well adopt each other. Ella had blossomed with Sarah's love and Sarah couldn't imagine her life without this incredible little girl. Isa decided that Badger was pleased with the situation as he had so much attention showered on him daily.

She'd also honed her skill with a rifle over the last year. Every Academy student had to pass a marksmanship skills test. Professor Kolter took her out himself one sunny afternoon, as her visits did not coincide with Academy's schedule; many of her final requirements were completed with Professor Kolter as he fit them into his schedule. They did not go to the firing range, and he did not offer any explanation. Isa carried the rifle he'd handed to her in his office. The smooth walnut stock felt right in her hands. Its style was familiar, similar to some of the other rifles she'd fired.

They approached a fenced pasture and Professor Kolter pulled a half-liter bottle of water from his pack and placed it on a post. There was a slight breeze out of the southwest and it felt good out in the sunny warmth of the day. He signaled her to follow. A hundred fifty yards away stood an old building with a small deck on the second story; a piece of the railing had been removed. They climbed the steps and Professor Kolter handed her two bullets. "I don't expect you'll need more than one: one bullet, one kill. Sometimes, you won't get the chance to reload." She didn't care to consider those implications, preferring instead to concentrate on the task he'd given her. That was a small target and, clearly, passing this test meant hitting it the first time. He put his ear plugs in, pulled out a pair of binoculars and said, "Whenever you're ready, Ensign."

She loaded the bullet, the bolt-action smooth as it guided the cartridge, sliding it into the barrel, locking the bolt into place as she clicked the safety on. Isa lay down on the platform, set the butt of the rifle into her right shoulder and, closing her right eye, looked through the scope with her left. At first, it had been a bit awkward shooting right-handed but left-eyed, now it was second nature. Some of the best advice she'd taken in learning to shoot was to throw the rifle up to her shoulder and look through the scope—it was a way to practice the rhythm and teach her eye to utilize the scope. Through the scope, she found the plastic bottle. Ignoring Professor Kolter's presence behind her, she set the crosshairs centered side-to-side, but slightly lower than center top to bottom on her target.

Her thumb moved up and flicked the safety off, her index finger still resting on the trigger guard. A lot was at stake here, and she took several collected breaths to contain the excitement she felt when she shot. *Keep it smooth*, she told herself, *don't hurry, take your time.* Pulling in one more breath, she held it as her finger left the guard and slowly squeezed the trigger.

Isa's aim had been true; she didn't know it for a split second because she had closed her eyes—a habit she was fiercely trying to break. Sitting up, she ejected the empty brass, took out her earplugs, stood up and turned to face Professor Kolter. He was grinning from ear to ear.

"I love the way they shoot up like rockets with water spewing everywhere! Well done, Ensign. You pass. Now, let's go take a look at how you hit it."

Back in his office, he had asked her again if she had any idea where she wanted to focus. At that point, Isa still had a few more rotations to complete. She told him she couldn't really say yet. He'd responded by telling her that she would know when it was the right fit, and she could simply arrange to contact him at that time.

She had known since that day she had spent exploring Bounty back at Rowan. She remembered the impression she had had when she entered the Astro-physics lab, surrounded by a space that was full of the light of stars and the perception that this was a group of people who loved their work. She had never admitted to herself that she knew where she would fit, but it became clear when she passed through the lab doors for a second time.

It was exciting; they were mapping the lives of stars and charting complex systems that Isa had never heard of. She would be helping in the process of investigating various moons for possible habitation. Sending off and retrieving probes provided an incredible amount of data to sort through and analyze. Dissecting and separating the bulk of information received had Isa fired up to get started.

31.

Bane was looking forward to seeing Isa tonight. They had kept up the tradition of meeting in the late evenings, but it had become less regular as time had passed. He was pleased and proud of all she'd accomplished both as a student and personally. She was a confident young woman, much more than she had been that morning they'd first met when he'd seen her bringing in the cows. She was far less apt to go into her protective mode, becoming more open with everyone and less on her guard with older males. He could still recognize the signs that she was wary, but that was because he knew her so well. She'd at least become better at disguising those reactions, even if still wearing many of her emotions so openly. She had not yet mastered that poker face that Jack had tried to teach her.

Today had been her first day with the Astro-physics team, and she'd asked him at dinner if he had time to talk later. It had been obvious to him that she was excited beyond what he'd seen thus far in her assignment to this department.

"Enter."

"Hey Captain."

"Hey Captain?" The other change he'd noticed lately was her bending, so to speak, certain protocols.

"I meant, good evening, sir."

"I'm sure you did. At ease, Ensign, and as we're both off duty, I can excuse the irreverence, this time."

"I brought you some chocolate chip cookies, made 'em myself. They'd go great with some hot cocoa." A pleading, wide-eyed look accompanied that statement.

"Well, I wouldn't want to ruin such a great combination." He set out two mugs and put water on to heat, measuring the cocoa powder into each mug, adding the steaming water and stirring the rich mixture. She set the plate of cookies out, still warm, as after she'd cleaned up what was left of dinner, she'd felt the urge to bake cookies. The sweet smell had drawn a crowd and she'd been lucky to get out the door with a plateful.

"I took my life in my hands trying to smuggle these out of the common room, you know."

"Quite a sacrifice, I'm sure." He handed her a mug, as she sat tucked into her usual spot on the sofa. Taking the seat opposite, he pulled the plate of cookies closer.

"Don't worry; I ate enough dough to make myself sick."

"So, what's the occasion?"

"I know where I want to focus." No lead in, no working up to the pressing topic on her mind, it just came out. That's who she was. Bane was sure she assumed everyone just followed right along with her thoughts leading the conversation, so it wasn't abrupt to her ears at all. "Astro-physics." It was a statement. He'd known what this was about as soon as she'd asked to talk to him tonight. "The stars. When I walked through those doors today, I remembered that feeling I'd had the day I was exploring Bounty on Rowan and I wandered in. Bane, why didn't I recognize it sooner? I've known that's what I wanted ever since I was a little girl watching the stars with my dad, and then the horses."

"Everything was so new and you wanted to be open to all the possibilities. You said that, you know."

"Yeah. I did, didn't I?"

"So, Professor Kolter's been waiting for a decision. When do you want to tell him?"

"Is now too late?" Her sheepish grin appeared.

"I don't think so. Let me put the request through; he can always not answer." Cookie in hand, he went over to his vid-screen, Isa on his heels.

"Bane! To what do I owe this pleasure?"

"Alex, sorry for the hour, I've a very excited Ensign here with a most important message that just couldn't wait. You can listen to what she has to say while I enjoy another warm cookie."

"Now, that hardly seems fair. And I thought life on a starship was for those who could sacrifice some of life's little pleasures."

"Not on this ship! But don't tell anyone."

Isa was rocking back and forth from foot to foot while this conversation went on. "Well, Ensign Torunn? What's so important it couldn't wait until tomorrow?"

Isa told him of her discovery in the Astro-physics lab, and her excitement about her decision to focus there. She poured out her soul to him as far as what she remembered from her path through the lab when she first explored Bounty on her own and the insights she had shared with Captain Lucas that day, as well as the connection she'd always felt with the stars, their beauty and what that meant to her life, and her excitement over being able to study the journey of a star, moon, planet, or other similar bodies travelling through space.

She kept up a steady stream until she felt Bane's hand on her shoulder and a lukewarm cup of cocoa placed in her hands.

"I'm sure Professor Kolter shares your excitement, but your hot chocolate is getting cold. Why don't you finish it and let him think about what you've said."

She seemed stunned, slowly making her way back from her story, red creeping across her cheeks and then a chagrined smile appeared.

"Sorry, guess I'll stop talking now." All three chuckled.

"Quite all right Ensign, I'm glad to see you so excited about an important decision. I can tell that you've put in some serious time considering what Astro-physics means to you. I knew you would recognize when it felt right, and I'm honored that you had to tell me now. It makes my job much easier in a lot of ways to have a student find her passion after having worked in so many areas. I'm sure you will be good at whatever you chose or are assigned to do, but you will excel when it comes to your passion, some would say calling, and that can only be good for the Alliance."

"Thanks, Alex. We'll let you get back to your evening and, I'm sure, hear from you in a few days regarding a plan for Ensign Torunn's study from here."

"Indeed. Goodnight then, and enjoy those cookies."

"I did."

32.

Mapping the stars in this system was going to aid future exploration and possible settlement. The Alliance wanted to find more options for resettling refugees and for colonization. Isa was glad that Professor Kolter had been so hard on her and stressed the importance of her understanding history. She now wished to anticipate some of the needs of the various cultures who could be depending on her research for new life. None of these decisions were ultimately hers to make, but that did not stop her consideration and empathy.

Bounty stood ready to host Isa's commissioning; Professor Kolter was due to rendezvous shortly, and Isa was still in the lab. "Captain Lucas to Ensign Torunn."

"Torunn here, sir."

"Where are you?"

"In the lab, sir."

"Ensign, be present in the common room and ready in 30 minutes." There was an edge in his voice that Isa recognized, and she went.

"Yes, sir."

She was excited to be an officer, but she hadn't wanted a lot of time to think so she wouldn't be nervous. This was a first for Bounty and she didn't want to mess it up. She'd studied the ceremony protocols with Captain Lucas and thus was clear on what her role would be. Most of the crew would be attending, just as family and friends would at the Academy. She had worked alongside just about everyone and they had become family to her, so she was glad they would all be at the ceremony.

Once in her quarters, she picked up the congratulations card from Fran and Timothy and read it again. She wished they could have come, they meant so much to her. Jack had also sent her good wishes, a picture of Amigo, and a note that said he sure hoped she'd made a bunch of new memories and that the old ones were still doin' their job. He'd whip up some chili for her next time she was out. Jack had a way of making Isa feel like they were just a pick-up ride away and she could see him whenever she liked. It had been a comfort to her many times and when she had been able to speak to him, it was like they were side-by-side, horseback and riding on the ranch. It made her features soften and brought a smile, even now.

Aware of the time, and Captain Lucas, she hopped in the shower, having gone straight to the lab when she'd finished her run. She had laid her dress uniform out when she'd awakened and polished her dress boots the night before. She'd not had many occasions to wear them. But in them, she looked quite smart and that unconscious awareness made her military stride crisper, more exact. As she was a strong presence already, the dress uniform added to her height somehow; heads turned as she came down the passage to the common room. She entered with five minutes to spare of the thirty Bane had given her.

The room had been transformed and the seating oriented toward the large view ports. Captain Lucas looked amazing, every bit the commander of a starship. "Ensign, there's an hour until we start. I'd like you to accompany me as I meet our visitors. I'm sure Professor Kolter will want to speak with you."

Isa didn't know who "our visitors" were, but the thought of more of the Academy or Alliance personnel made her nervous. If she hadn't been so preoccupied, she'd have noticed the twinkle in her captain's eye when he mentioned them. The doors to the conference room opened, and Isa found herself face-to-face with Fran and Timothy. Time stilled, then stopped. Isa's mouth had come open; she stood unable to move. Shaking her head, she did not believe what was before her. Something, Bane's hand, impelled her forward and into open arms. She was shaking. Her emotion was raw, unchecked. She was enveloped in their hug.

Bane was wondering how smart it had been to keep this a surprise. He hadn't considered how deeply it would affect her or how much she must have missed them. He had stopped reminding himself that she'd raised herself, she'd done so well that he didn't think about the lack of a parental support and how that would be missed. He'd done what he could, but as she had exceeded expectations, gaining confidence, he had left it up to her to seek him out in the evenings. He was kicking himself now and making mental notes to fix that gap.

"You look beautiful, love. Doesn't she, Fran?"

"You're all grown-up. She's all grown up, Timothy. And just look at her, all official in her dress uniform. I can't believe it." As they gushed over her, giving her time to gather herself, reign in what had overwhelmed her, she smiled.

"I'm so happy to have you here today. I was just re-reading the card you sent this morning and wishing you could be here. I love you both so much." Straightening up, "Of course, someone is in big trouble for not telling me," she looked pointedly at Bane. Back in control now, she hugged Fran and then Timothy. When she saw Professor Kolter, she came to attention. Fran and Timothy stepped back.

"At ease, Ensign, I've seen family reunions before and I assure you, I understand. Now, why don't we sit and go over the ceremony. I'll assume, now that you know who's here, that you'd like these fine folks to stand for you."

She'd never even considered the possibility that there would be anyone to stand for her. She'd told herself that her parents would be with her in spirit. She knew they'd be proud and that was good enough. God had sent a special gift—she was not alone, which she knew, but here was a physical reminder.

"Would you?"

"You know we will, love. We'd be proud to."

They worked out the details; Fran went off to make sure her directions for the reception were followed. She had been involved even before they knew they'd be coming. She wanted this to be special for Isa.

Isa was nervous, but the ceremony was precise and went exactly as planned. She stood straight and received her commission with Timothy and Fran standing behind to her left and Captain Lucas to her right. The crew clapped and cheered for her at the conclusion and congratulations and well wishers surrounded her.

33.

Sitting around the table in Bane's quarters, Isa, Fran, Timothy, and Alex Kolter were enjoying dinner together after a busy day. Isa was quiet, letting the conversation wash over her as she focused on being Lieutenant Torunn now and how she got here. Fran put another piece of her now famous chocolate cake in front of her and refilled coffee cups. Isa grinned her thanks, sliding her fork through the thick frosting and once it was in her mouth, sighing over the rich taste.

Alex would be heading back to the Academy as soon as they finished the evening; Fran and Timothy were hitching a ride on Bounty to a vacation on Planet Kline. They would arrive in two days. Bounty was taking on supplies there, but not staying long. They'd have two days shore leave before heading off again. Isa had already made plans to ride with a local stable.

"We know you want to ride and we would never want to get in the way of that, so can we take you to dinner when you return?"

"I'd love that. And Fran, there are some things I need, would you be willing to go with me?" Timothy winked at her, she had made Fran's day.

"Well, of course I would, anytime you say."

"Will you be joining Lieutenant Torunn to ride, Bane?" Alex chimed in.

"Actually, yes. One day—that's all we have time for—then I have other matters to tend to, and so does she." Bane turned to Isa, who shrugged in recognition of previous discussion on the topic. "Fran, can I count on you to make sure Lieutenant Torunn has the proper uniform suited to her new station? The matter seems to have slipped her mind, and I'd hate to have to throw her in the brig for misconduct." Again the look, but this time Isa was concentrating on scraping up the last few crumbs of cake.

Timothy laughed, "You know she will, Bane, especially with the threat of the brig hanging over Isa's head."

"Oh you men! I'm sure she's simply had other concerns, working and getting ready for today. We'll manage it."

"All right, now that you have that all figured out, I'd best be off. Fran, Timothy, it's been a pleasure to meet you. Captain, thank you for hosting. Lieutenant Torunn, I'd like you to walk with me back to transport."

"Yes, sir." She stood and hugged Timothy and Fran goodnight, thanking them again and promising to see them at breakfast. Bane said he would show them to their quarters.

Going with Prof. K. to transport, Isa was curious about what he wanted.

"Lieutenant, I wanted a moment to speak to you alone, and I invite you to be completely at ease."

"Yes, sir."

"First, you should be proud of what you've accomplished. I am. You are a strong young woman, smart, and you have a good sense for people. The Alliance stands to benefit greatly from your effort, energy, and enthusiasm. I want you to be open to possibilities that will arise but that you have not yet anticipated, and may be outside the realm of your work as an astro-engineer. Even outside work on Bounty."

She listened and her eyebrows rose on that last statement; she could tell that was the crux of the message, and she wasn't sure what it meant.

"I hear what you're saying, and I will try to be open. Right now, leaving Bounty is not on the list of what I want to do for any real length of time, but neither was leaving my horses and the farm. That was one of the hardest choices I've ever had, and yet, it brought me here. And here is home now." She studied him. "So, I guess what I'm saying is yes, I'll do my best to be open to chance, and if chance ever arises with you in charge, remind me that we had this conversation."

"That's all I ask, Lieutenant It's been a great pleasure to supervise you in this unique situation—please feel free to contact me anytime, and I hope you'll continue to send your poetry to me as well. While we may differ in our tastes for form, I do love words that have been crafted with care."

"Thank you, sir, for everything."

Bane was waiting for her outside transport. Falling into step beside him, she soon arrived back at his quarters.

"Assume the position, Lieutenant." She folded herself into the sofa. "Can I get you anything? Tea? Cocoa?"

She shook her head. He took the seat next to her.

"You're nineteen now, Isa, an officer in the Alliance and on my ship. You've accomplished this through the use of your own grit and determination. I wanted to be of more support to you, but I thought you were doing very well on your own, and our nightly talks tapered off as you grew past what happened with Frank. I didn't realize until you saw Fran and Timothy this morning just how much support you'd missed out on. I'm sorry I kept their arrival a surprise. I know it was overwhelming and that wasn't fair. You handled it well, but it opened my eyes to the fact that you always appear to have everything together, in fact you go full bore at anything assigned, but that you could certainly use more down time to process or just have a hot cup of cocoa with a parent-like friend."

Bane gathered her under his arm, her head on his chest as her tears fell.

"I couldn't believe it was really them. I wanted so much for them to be here. I told myself it was okay, that I would never really be alone, and I knew you would be standing for me, both as my captain, and my friend. Bane, I was surprised that I would react as I did. It was one of those moments, like when you're little and scared, and you never want to leave the arms of your dad or mom. You've taught me that I can come find you any time. But I get so easily sucked into doing everything myself, being independent, that I don't admit, even to myself, I need someone else—some, as you say, parent-like friend to tell me face-to-face that I'm doing okay."

"Timothy, Fran and I were happy to stand where your parents would have been today. Now, we can both use some relaxation, time on a horse, and that will be a good way for you and me to reinstate our evening tradition, say, once a week."

"Okay. That's a deal!"

They talked about plans to ride and the schedule for the next couple of days. Isa would be on duty with her usual schedule until they arrived at Kline and her supervisor in Astro had given Timothy permission to observe. Fran would no doubt find plenty to occupy her in the common room. She had mentioned wanting to revisit Isa's quarters to add a few small touches she'd brought along.

"Well, cowgirl, I think you'd better be off and to bed." They stood as Bane patted her shoulder, and she reached up and kissed his cheek.

"G'night then."

"Goodnight, Lieutenant Isa Torunn."

Lt. Isa Torunn slept very well that night, wrapped in the love of family, both traditional and adopted. Her last thought was a thank you to her God for so many blessings.

34.

Timothy was suitably impressed with the Astro lab and Fran ended up teaching a few young crewmembers to cook; the samples were highly coveted. They arrived at Kline without incident and the crew disembarked in waves. Being an Alliance planet, although smaller than Rowan, Kline offered many forms of relaxation and recreation.

Arriving in the early morning hours, Bane and Isa headed to the stable, having made plans to meet Timothy and Fran that evening for dinner. Two horses were saddled for them, as they'd left their own saddles onboard this time. Isa would ride a sleek thoroughbred mare called Snippet and Bane, a large-boned, rangy gelding called Trooper.

The area was woodlands, with a range of trails they could take any way they liked. Having questioned them both on their skill and experience, the stable owner, Seth, handed them a map and said he'd be around whenever they wanted to return. Packing their lunches in the saddlebags, they mounted up and ambled from the main stable area to the trail. Seth stood watching, satisfied that neither was over their head with the mount he'd chosen for them. Snippet was prancing, tail high and ears erect, but the young woman had a nice seat, relaxed into the saddle. The Captain was having no trouble handling Trooper, who was always excited to go. They had decided to make a rough circle in order to see more of the country, and expected to be out six to eight hours. While most folks wanted to ride "all day," in Seth's experience that usually turned out to be two or three hours at best. However, he was sure he wouldn't see these two back until late in the afternoon. It was pretty country.

They rode side-by-side through the trees, each lost in their own thoughts. Bane was going through his list of what needed to be done the next day, including an Alliance vid-conference for the upcoming mediation Bane was working on and where Bounty was bound next. Isa was busy talking to Snippet and breathing in the freshness of these woods. The trees were massive with wide white trunks. Branches struck out at various levels, climbing trees, Isa decided, and what great trees for tree houses, too.

"So, how's the mare?"

"She's sweet, wants to please. And doesn't seem to mind me talkin' her ear off. How's Trooper?"

"He's honest, full of energy. How about we stop for lunch when we reach the river?"

"Okay, I could eat. I can't wait to tell Jack about this—can you imagine building a tree house in one of these trees? You could have a roof that opened to the stars and your horse could graze down below you. You know, those kids who ride at the Academy would have a great time doing a little pack trip here. We could make s'mores every night and sing around the campfire. Can you imagine it?"

"Well, I see that you can. You know, you do have a special skill you could offer to the crew when we end up in a place like this. You'd have to work at making arrangements with local stables, and it'd mean giving up some of your time, but there are those on Bounty who would leap at the opportunity to learn to ride."

She considered that as they approached the river. They let the horses drink and then tied them long to graze while Isa retrieved the lunches, joining Bane by a tree.

"It would be fun, to teach some of the crew. I always liked people to come out to the farm for lessons, and I had a great time teaching the kids at the Academy. So, how could I go about it?"

"Eat." She'd been waving the peanut butter sandwich around, and seemed surprised to see it there. "No need to worry about it right now, we can work on it, although it wouldn't hurt to talk to Seth when we get back to see what he would need for you to do."

"Good idea. It sure is peaceful here."

They finished eating, readied the horses, mounted and began a moderate climb to the top of the valley. Looking out over hills covered with trees and stopping to welcome the view, they let the horses breathe. Bane held a water bottle out to Isa, who took a grateful drink, mumbling her "thanks." Handing it back, she said, "Prof. K. made a point of asking me to be open to special assignments away from Bounty."

Now he knew what had kept her so quiet coming up the hill.

"Did he have something in mind?"

Bane knew full well that Alex would speak to him first if an assignment came up that he wanted for Lt. Torunn, but he wasn't sure that she did.

"I don't think so, but what do you think he was getting at?"

"I'd say he was planting a seed." She cocked her head, eyebrows coming together as the right side of her lips tilted up.

"He wanted you to consider your possibilities, and it was a good strategy. If something comes up, just this thinking you've done based on his comments in parting will provide for a more open conversation." She nodded slowly, processing the professor's approach.

"Of course, anything that might come up would go through me first, and I have loaned members of my crew on occasion for short term assignments if it didn't interfere with Bounty's work."

She absorbed his comments and, as they began their descent, answered with, "Hm, okay, I trust your judgment, so I'm glad that any prospects would come to you first."

She paused, looking over at him, "But what if I came upon something myself? I mean, a project or activity I thought was important in meeting our goals or that would enhance the Alliance or maybe even have meaning to me personally. What then?"

His smile gentled his direct Captain's eyes.

"What you would not do is to go off and make a decision without gaining approval from a superior officer. Communication would be key, and following proper chain-of-command and protocols. You must always be aware that you represent Bounty, her crew, your Captain, and the Alliance in everything you do—and while that is a good thing, it can also burn you if you don't stop and take a deep breath first. I don't ever want you to stop thinking and being creative and taking action to make things happen and get the job done in ways no one else would have. I do want you, though, to make sure you put thought into possible outcomes and your own safety."

Isa nodded as she was scratching Snippet's back, and they fell into an easy silence. She hadn't really considered that she was a representative now of something more than herself, a serious realization. She knew what it meant to have an excellent reputation, and how one bad move might cause a backlash difficult to repair.

In the river once again, Isa gave Snippet her head to drink, Trooper was soon beside her thrusting his head into the water up to his eyeballs. When he brought his big nose up, he showered Isa with water.

"I smell that bad, huh, boy?" She reached out and patted his neck, laughing at his antics.

"He is a boy, Snipper-girl, he just can't help it." The mare looked even more affronted as Trooper lapped up the water like a dog.

"Not very regal, is he?"

"But personality plus! He reminds me of Indian." She grinned, recalling some of his stunts. "You know, he used to untie himself from a post, and then, just because he could, he'd go around and untie all the other horses. I had to remember to lock his quick-release or come back and have to catch all the horses a second time."

"Hear that, Trooper, you'd better straighten up so you don't get into more trouble." Snippet snorted. "See that, the mare agrees with me."

They rode on and came out of the trees suddenly, and into a small meadow bursting with wildflowers. It seemed to be the season for purple and red as they were greeted with many shades and hues of both, lining fallen logs, woven into the grasses, and climbing over rounded rocks.

"It's magical—like finding a treasure, a richness, a sumptuous feast for a starving soul."

Isa's eyes were wide with wonder, her mouth forming a small "oh," then she closed them and breathed deep, bending forward and wrapping her arms around the mare's neck. After a moment, she came up straight, placed her right hand over her heart.

"Thank you," she whispered up into the blue sky.

Bane was a man of faith, but his beliefs were closely held. He rarely thought consciously about God, yet knew the truth of God in his heart. He'd had moments in his life that reminded him, brought him face-to-face with God, and he recognized them as such. Bowing his head, he gave it his attention.

"Do you think God appreciates it when we enjoy creation and are thankful?"

"I surely do."

"Me, too."

35.

Eight hours later, they rode into the stable where Seth awaited them.

"Good ride?"

"Amazing. This mare is a dream, and your planet is magnificent."

Bane could hear the points being tallied as she went on about the horses and the smallest details of what they'd seen that day, including many he hadn't noticed. They unsaddled and groomed, putting the horses in their stalls for feed, leaning on the fence posts as Snippet and Trooper ate their grain. Isa would not receive her first pay for a while, and Bane had made the payment to Seth, telling her it was his gift to her for her graduation from the Academy.

"Seth, I'm wondering how to request the use of your horses and facility to run a riding clinic for beginner to intermediate riders from the ground up, including some trail time and possibly even with packing and camping?"

"Who would be running it and who'd be taking part?"

"I would organize it and run it, and it would be for other crewmembers, maybe their families, who are interested. I'd like to offer an opportunity like we had today to those who need support to see the country the best way there is—on a horse." That did it, she'd made a friend and ally with her statement.

Seth offered good advice, telling her to write up a contract with the selling points as she'd stated them to him, and to include reassurance to a stable owner that all participants would be fully aware of the risks before agreeing to sign up. She would need to provide verification of her own equine skills and background, too. Once she had a working draft of a contract, Seth said he'd be glad to look it over for her and offer suggestions for revision. She knew how to reach him and, if Bounty happened by Kline again, he'd be happy to host her.

Bane stood back watching the exchange and thought his crew was in for a great new adventure. It was important to him that those who served Bounty continued to seek out novel experiences; it kept them alert and flexible. When encountering the unknown, they were apt to be less anxious or stressed, and more creative in adapting and problem solving. This was why Captain Lucas insisted on a physical workout as well as various teaching skills or seminars in areas where they had expertise and passion. He took advantage of any opportunity for himself and his crew, such as Fran's cooking lessons, even for the short time she'd been onboard. Those who learned from her and were interested would go on to further their skills and eventually offer those skills to others. Of course, he also knew that was the way Isa's mind worked; it wouldn't be long before she'd come up with a way to have horses onboard Bounty.

Smiling at that, he stood up from the post he'd been leaning on, "Seth, thank you for a wonderful day, and for indulging my lieutenant in her new plan to make the whole crew horse-savvy. It's time we head back, even though I know she'd love to stay."

The two men shook hands while Isa stroked Snippet's, then Trooper's muzzle and whispered goodbye to them. She thanked Seth, and climbed into the vehicle to head back.

***

Arriving back at Kline's central station, Bane told her to be quick cleaning up and he'd come to get her in thirty minutes to meet Timothy and Fran for dinner. She found her way to the quarters she was sharing with Jamie, who'd become a good friend over the months, and her source for socializing with her peers on Bounty. She was feeling less and less awkward in that department and more able to be herself and hold her own. Jamie was out for the evening, but they would exchange stories of their days later that night.

Isa showered and changed into a pair of silky blue pants and the new white blouse Fran and Timothy had given her. Fran told her that every woman needed a classic white shirt to make dressing up simple. She added a pretty blue scarf, let her curly hair down, but kept it out of her face with barrettes, and was ready when Bane buzzed for entrance. Opening the door, she smiled at him.

"You look very pretty, Isa, ready?"

The smile grew. "Yes, thank you." He offered his arm and she tucked her hand into the crook of his elbow. Entering the restaurant, they spotted Fran and Timothy and as they found their way to the table, Isa softly said, "You look handsome, too." Bane winked at her as Timothy rose to hold her chair. Bane took Fran's hand offered in greeting and kissed her cheek.

"Fran, Timothy. I trust you haven't been waiting too long?"

They shared the details of the day with each other over a very pleasant dinner. Fran and Isa talked about what they needed to get done the next day. Fran was delighted that Isa wore her new shirt, and remarked, "Doesn't she look beautiful, Timothy?"

"She always does, dear, but especially so tonight." Isa blushed. "My wife has an impeccable sense of clothing style, and spent hours finding just the right one for our girl, here."

"Stop, Timothy. You're embarrassing her." By now, Isa's face was bright red and she was trying hard to focus on the last of her coffee as they finished dessert.

"So, you have a plan for tomorrow, and it is getting late. Are you finished, Isa?"

"Yes. See you in the morning." She hugged Fran and Timothy goodnight and they parted company at the door.

Once again, it was difficult to say goodbye when Bounty had to move on, but everyone promised to keep in touch, and the little poem book Isa had made for Jack would be delivered in person by Fran and Timothy.

36.

Bounty was on her way to help negotiate a treaty with the Savarin race. Its people had known war as a way of life for several generations, but had begun to recognize that they must change or they would face heavy consequences due to the strengthening of the Alliance in their system, as well as certain ages of the population, weary of this unpredictable and violent way of life. Many neighboring planets had amassed a number of young with no surviving parents due to this warrior race, and plans were being formulated to bring them together and under care through an Alliance program where they would board together in an outdoor-based education program.

Bane would be leading negotiations and working with the Alliance's Ambassador Lee Kine to set up the base for the school. This would also be an opportunity for Astro-engineering to study this area of space and begin to map it.

Lee came onboard to accompany Captain Lucas in a meeting with the five planets overwhelmed with trying to raise so many orphans, who also suffered emotionally from the traumatic events they'd witnessed. They gathered in the conference room to form a plan.

Bane respected the way Ambassador Kine moderated this emotionally charged meeting. Each planet representative was given a chance to speak and share ideas, which were all recorded and organized on the view screens to showcase how many ideas they had in common. Each wanted to be sure their culture was preserved and taught, that the children were well educated to become positive, productive adults, that they were cared for and loved in order to overcome what they had experienced, and that they were protected from any further violence.

They took a short break in the afternoon, providing time for everyone to informally discuss the presentation around the table in small groups in Bounty's common room. Bane took the opportunity to show Lee around the ship. Lee was young to have come so far in his career, but Bane could see why as they talked. Lee was twenty-nine and very focused and committed to this work. He felt compassion for these lost children, yet there was an equal measure of determination that they reach their potential, becoming positive influences in their respective societies and not live their lives blaming others for the bad hand they were dealt, or sinking into the depths of self-pity. He thought the planet they chose to host this project ideal. It was an Alliance planet, but not one the other five could lay claim to, and it did not house an Alliance outpost, but an agrarian-based culture, rich in folk arts and a simple lifestyle. The people were open to this project and would be supportive.

As they entered the Astro department, Bane noticed Isa glued to a section of viewport with her hands spread across the clear surface as if she were trying to touch what her eyes were taking in, wide in wonder. Officer Wight nodded toward her Captain, finished her directive, and approached.

"Officer Wight, this is Ambassador Kine."

"Lee, please."

"Lee, it's nice to meet you. Let me know if I can show you anything." She turned in the direction Captain Lucas was staring. "She's always like this when we orbit a new planet; especially so with this one. I'd say she's been plastered to that viewport the better part of an hour. Says the scopes don't give her a sense of the planet the way two eyes looking out the viewport can. I can't argue the logic because her preliminary observations are always spot on."

Bane walked up behind her, Ambassador Kine on his heels. "It's a quiet planet, Captain, with mountains that will captivate you, gentle rolling hills—green in summer, but with punishing winter winds and snow; a peaceful place with a caring people. They live well off the land because they take the time to care for it, and judging by the space we're in, they must never get tired of gazing up at their night skies." She'd said all of that still with her face pressed against the port.

"Ambassador, meet my newest lieutenant, Isa Torunn." She had sensed the captain's presence, but not that of his guest. Her quick retreat from the viewport, although one hand lingered until she stood straight, confirmed Bane's suspicions. Lee smiled warmly at her.

"Lieutenant Torunn, you are right on the mark with those observations, and I am in your debt for pointing that out to Captain Lucas, saving me the trouble of trying to explain why this is the perfect choice for our new project. You've captured it in a nutshell. A pleasure to meet you." He offered his hand and she shook it, her mouth slightly open. Not a sound came out.

"There aren't many who can render her speechless, Lee." Bane was grinning at her.

"I'm Lee Kine."

"Uh, sorry. Good to meet you, sir." She was glancing from Bane to the Ambassador, unsure if she might have breached protocol.

"At ease, Lieutenant. I was just showing Ambassador Kine around Bounty. The planet you've been glued to the window watching is the site for an Alliance project to help orphans from five different cultures, even as a treaty is negotiated with those who caused the deaths of so many citizens."

Something flickered across her face; Lee watched it play out in her eyes, a sadness that reached deep inside. She gazed up at Captain Lucas, steadying herself. "So, you're bringing these children who've lost their families here?" There was a bit of a wobble in her tone, and Lee wondered at it. Something emotional was playing out here, and personal to this young woman; he wanted to assure her that these children would be in his care.

"Yes, and we'll provide for their needs and their safety as well as their education. More importantly, we'll nurture them and help them work through the trauma so they can become who they were meant to be."

That set her back. "Well, I think you have the right spot for just such a project, this planet has healing at its core, and enough beauty on the surface to inspire even those young lives hit hardest. Will you have horses for them?"

"Horses? Should I?"

Before Isa could launch into the power present in partnering up kids and horses, Bane stepped in saying they needed to return to the conference and that he would explain this to the Ambassador. Should he be interested in more information, he could locate her when he was finished. That satisfied Isa, and they left her to her work.

"Quite a Lieutenant you have there, Captain. How did she know about the children? She seemed quite taken with their plight."

"Actually, she didn't know anything until we walked into her world. She lost her own parents at a young age and had a very rough existence. She'd do anything to help kids who've been dealt a bad hand. Horses were a saving grace for her, so she knows firsthand the benefits of a horse in the life of a kid. It would be a great addition to what you want to do here, especially if you have the right person to run it."

"All right, I'll take it to the table and see what happens."

Bane left Lee and the conference room and went to his quarters to prepare for his own negotiation. Representatives would arrive that afternoon to begin talks for permanent peace and for restructuring a society that had thrived on war for generations. He chuckled as he remembered Isa's passion, and he decided that Lee Kine had taken her seriously, impressed by her perceptions of the planet he thought perfect for this project himself.

He focused completely on his task as mediator while he took transport to the planet's surface. An administrative center held rooms available with meeting space and Bane had taken care to be sure that the area would be private and not attract any undue attention or cause fear to the local populace. It was difficult, at best, to reconsider the structure and focus of an entire culture, and then to decide what the next step would be. Many men, especially those who had acquired a taste for war, would be angry and at a loss to understand why they had to change. He must give careful consideration to how to address this and redirect this energy through new channels.

37.

Lee presented the idea of horses to the assembled representatives and said that if they were so inclined, he had a knowledgeable source for more information. He also mentioned the Academy's stable program that Bane had told him about. There was interest, mostly born from curiosity for the new and different. The dormitories were being built for the number of children estimated to need help at this point. There was an old stable in the area, and fencing or whatever else was needed for this program, Lee assured them could be done. When they finished, he went in search of Lt. Torunn, hoping she'd discuss it with him over dinner.

Not sure where to find her, he made his way back to Astro and found someone to help him. Once he had the directions, he went to her quarters and signaled for entry. She opened the door and smiled at him; when he told her what he wanted, the smile rose into her eyes, and the vibrant blue sparkled at him. As they went to the common room and found a table by a viewport, Isa plied him with questions about the orphans, their age range, and his plans for this center.

She listened as Lee described what had taken place, her reactions evident in the way her eyes widened, or her brow furrowed, or her hand came up to cover her mouth; she nodded vigorously as he described the hopes and dreams each culture held for these lost children and the shared vision they had for this project. He would administer, as well as provide ongoing mediation to the various factions involved and act as liaison to the locals for them. If they couldn't make a difference in these young lives, there would be hell to pay in their futures. That was why, he told her, he'd been open to any idea that would bring about the healing these kids needed, and hers was one they were all curious about.

It was fairly late when Bane arrived in the common room searching for Lee. His discussions had gone well and the Savarin were off to a good start with a plan to educate their people and begin a new phase in their history. They wanted to contribute to the orphan project and he wanted to discuss the possibilities with Lee and to learn how he might introduce the idea to the planetary leaders involved. Bane realized this would be tricky, but if they came up with a solid plan, it could go a long way towards forging a peace resolution.

He stopped a moment as he spotted Isa with Lee; she was bent across the table determinedly talking fast as Lee sat forward in his chair listening and nodding. He approached and heard her saying, "So, trust is built mutually by horse and human, and the kids find that they can share anything with their horse and not only will the secret be safe, but there won't be any judgment. When they ride, they gain confidence as they control this thousand-pound animal and recognize that kindness and patience go so much further than anger and frustration."

A familiar hand touched her shoulder, "Mind if I join you?"

"Captain, of course, sir." She started to rise.

"At ease, Lieutenant, I'll pull up a chair." She was still flustered when it came to proper protocol and what was required.

"Isa was just educating me about the benefits of providing a horse program, and I her about why it can only be a seasonal program with the winters on Yenna."

"I take it the leaders liked the idea? I'm glad she could help; she is an expert in this field. I see who has been doing most of the talking. Isa, eat, if it isn't too cold. If it is, warm it up while I chat with Lee." She excused herself to re-warm the soup and the grilled cheese sandwich.

"Bane, she really is on to something, I'm just not sure where to start. I need someone like her to get this moving. How'd it go?"

"Very well." He explained the situation to Lee and when Isa returned with her warmed dinner, they talked strategy while she ate. Isa began yawning halfway through her soup and sandwich; both men stood when she thanked Lee for considering the use of horses and left them to their plans while she headed off to bed.

38.

In three days' time, Lee and Bane had finished conferencing and had solid, workable plans. Lee had come right out and asked Bane if it would be possible to have Isa assigned to run a riding program here when the warm season returned in nine months. Bane had similar thoughts, but said he'd need to think about it and the logistics of making it happen. Lee responded that he'd do whatever it took, provide whatever was needed.

In the end, Bane had agreed that Isa was the ideal person to start this program and train those who could take it over in time. He talked it over with both Alex Kolter and Ken Wilson. Although Isa had graduated, the Academy liked to know about and have some input with their students for the first couple of years. It was the nine-month wait all three men thought would make this doable. Isa needed time on Bounty to grow into being a full member of the crew to establish new norms before becoming as disconnected as she would be on Yenna.

He told Lee this, who was thrilled to have this opportunity for his program. Bane asked him not to say anything to Isa until he'd had a chance to speak to her. He'd make sure they came down so she could help Lee decide what supplies to purchase, as he had so many questions. Bane also wanted to ensure Isa would have what she'd need, and the capability to maintain close contact with Bounty while she was off-ship. They agreed to meet later that day in Lee's office on planet and he could show them the facilities available. Children would not begin arriving for another three months, when their dormitory construction was completed.

Bane found Isa's supervisor and explained the situation to her, adding that he wanted her to be strict with Isa over the next nine months so she'd leave with her Alliance training feeling like second nature. Lt. Becca Wight assured him that wouldn't be a problem as she'd never seen anyone work so hard at adopting a completely new way of living, probably precisely because she'd had no exposure to anything Alliance, so she didn't know, like some of the young Alliance-born crew members, what could be fudged.

"Good. Have her report to my quarters at lunch."

Isa wasn't sure what this was about, but she couldn't think of anything she'd done wrong—it was not usual for the Captain to request her presence at his quarter's midday and she was curious. "Captain, sir?"

"At ease, Lieutenant. Come in. I hope you're hungry, I made some burgers." He gestured for her to sit at the table where two places were set and turned to his small kitchen to retrieve the lunch he'd prepared. She sat, looking at him quizzically. "What would you like to drink? Grape or cherry?"

"Grape. Captain?"

"Relax. I need to talk with you, so I thought I'd make you lunch."

"Did I do something?"

"You're not in trouble, if that's what you mean, but you did start something and now I need you to help get it up and running." Her look turned distant as she tried to figure out what he was referencing. "Horses and kids." Now she was completely focused on him. He took a bite of his burger.

"I don't understand. Or, do you mean here? They're going to take my suggestion? Have horses for this program? The Ambassador? Tell me!" Bane laughed at her excited impatience.

"All right. Yes, Lee wants to have horses as a part of the program, but he needs just the right person to get this going, someone who knows horses, can manage and teach, and who also has empathy for these kids and will relate with them." She was nodding in agreement at each point. "Isa, that someone is you." Her brow furrowed, her head tilting to the side.

"Me? But what about Bounty? Are you leaving me here?" Her voice went up an octave and she rose up out of her chair, her eyes wide, panic in them.

"Hey, whoa, take it easy! No one's getting left, Isa." His tone commanded her to look at him while his hand stopped her impulsion. "I'm not leaving you. Let me explain." He was kicking himself for the way he'd handled this, he hadn't considered the frightened little girl inside her and her tendency to take over when afraid. "The warm season doesn't begin for another nine months. For those nine months, you'll go about your normal duties on Bounty. During those months, you'll also be helping Ambassador Kine and his staff to put everything in place to run a horse program. I will figure out how to get Bounty back here to deliver you in time to direct the program for the three months of the season, and to train other staff to run it in the future. Are you willing to leave Bounty for three months to show these folks the benefits of putting kids and horses together, and to build these children up, Isa, give them hope? Bounty won't be far during the season."

She sat silent, and Bane waited, finishing his lunch while she thought. "So, I'd be assigned by you, to be in charge of a riding program for all the war orphans, and Bounty will bring me, work in this sector close by, and then pick me up?" Again, he nodded. She seemed pensive, her left thumb and first finger pressing her bottom lip. A deep breath released in a sigh. "How will he know what I need? Where will he find horses? What facilities do they have? Is there a barn?" She focused on Bane and said, "I think I can do this. I'd like to try."

"Good, then eat your lunch and we'll go down together and check it out. That should answer some of your questions, and you can tell Lee exactly what needs to be done, what he needs to get, and figure out how to bring in the horses."

She ate the burger with her fingers, leaving the bun, and gulped the soda. Taking an apple, she stood up, "Ready?" He laughed as they headed to transport.

Lee met them at the front door of the administration building that housed his office with, "Hello again, Lieutenant Torunn." He addressed Bane, who inclined his head, "and, I'm so glad that you'll be here to get this horse deal up and running. I thought we'd start by going over to the stable so you can see what we have and gauge what we'll need. I'll have you speak to our construction foreman. It's a beautiful day, today. Are you up for a walk?"

By the time they returned to Lee's office, all seemed satisfied that they would have a barn, a corral, an arena and the necessary pasture ready to go. Lee had showed them the small cabin he thought would be suitable for Isa. It was up the hill from the barn, close enough for her to manage any emergencies, but would still allow her privacy. She loved it, it was cozy and peaceful. Lee assured Captain Lucas that he'd have a com-unit installed for easy communication.

They sat and talked logistics. Isa wanted enough horses to be sure the kids would have plenty of horse time; Lee agreed but also insisted that their other studies continue as he wanted this to be manageable for the first year. They settled on 14 to 18 horses, which would all have to be cared for during the cold season, too. Not knowing much about horses, he agreed to let Isa's be the final word on any horse chosen for the program. The construction boss was "horsey," as Isa put it, and had horse connections on the planet. He'd agreed to keep his eye out for the horses Isa had described. She thought they could purchase tack as they did horses, but gave Lee a list of tack and supplies they'd require. He'd also have to find a farrier, veterinarian for large animals, and a feed supplier.

"Is there something else?" She'd gone quiet and was obviously concentrating.

"Isa." Bane prompted her.

"Sorry. I was just thinking about how I want to handle this. I'll need a graduated program, so the little ones still get horse time and the older kids are challenged. I'll do some thinking and planning, and give you a rough idea of what to expect, schedules, how many kids, and time they'll need to be available. I'm going to want some wrangler help, too. Can you find two or three locals that can be part of your staff, but also know horses and want to help with this? That would work in the off-season, too, as they can assume care of the horses and the kids can still have barn time?"

"I'll work on that, and this massive list you've made me." His smile was indulgent, kind. Bane had noticed his gentle attention to Isa, even if she hadn't.

"You have a start, Lee. We'll work out the rest as we go. Bounty's waiting on us, so we'd better get back. Thanks again for all you're trying to do here." They shook hands. Isa, still distracted by plans she was making in her head, took Lee's hand, promising to get her program design to him as soon as she had it herself.

"I'm hungry." Back on Bounty, Isa blurted this out.

"Really? I wonder why. Off to the common room, then, but I want to see you tonight before you turn in." Bane went to the bridge, not waiting for her.

Isa loaded a plate with roast, potatoes, carrots and a spinach salad with fresh snap peas, tomatoes, slices of ripe avocado and her current favorite – balsamic vinaigrette dressing. A glass of water accompanied all this to a table where Jamie was sitting. She'd eaten half the plate without even saying hello; "You'll never guess what happened to me today."

"I was wondering if you'd ever come up for air. Um, you never had lunch? Or breakfast?"

"No, silly." She told Jamie her story between the remaining bites.

"Wow, that sounds right up your alley, girl!"

"I know, right? I'm gonna go to Astro and think."

"See yah."

Isa stopped at her quarters to pick up paper and a pen, and changed into a pair of soft nylon-fleece running pants with a matching long-sleeve hooded jacket and her supple light walking shoes. She had discovered when she'd started her Astro rotation that the place was empty after dinner most of the time. It was an ideal hideaway for her, surrounded by stars through the oversized viewports, but without the quiet hubbub of the common room.

She sat, leaning against the support, staring out at Yenna. They'd be leaving orbit soon and she wanted to have one last impression, picturing the kids filling that dormitory, going over to the barn early before breakfast to feed horses and then spending much of their day around the corral: grooming, saddling, learning to ride, enjoying the trails, and caring for their horses. Time, that's what she wanted them to have. They needed to tell their stories, and no one was safer than a horse for that. Horses had an uncanny ability to understand pain and to protect, and she wanted these kids to have that experience.

Making a list of skills to teach and appropriate levels for beginner, intermediate, and more advanced riders seemed like the place to start; she also included "ground" skills like feeding, mucking, general maintenance and first aid for horses. She'd ask the Captain if she could contact Sarah at the Academy's stable and run this by her for suggestions. As they left orbit, she bid Yenna goodbye and sank a little further into the viewport well. Letting the stars rush over her, she imagined what it'd be like to live in the little cabin for a season, looking out the window by her bed at night to see the moon rise over the tall pine trees or sitting out on the porch in the early morning with her coffee before walking down to the barn for the day.

39.

"Yes, Captain, we ate dinner together. Well, she inhaled hers. She said she was going to Astro to think. You want me to find her?"

"Thanks, Jamie, no, I'll go. Sorry to disturb you."

"No problem, Cap'n." He winced at that, but let it go with a smile.

Thinking, was she? Well, she'd better think about keeping appointments with her Captain. He had no doubt that she'd become lost in making her plans for those kids and he could forgive her for that. It was very late, though, and she probably hadn't noticed the passing of time. Now he knew where she went to find time and space apart.

Coming through the door, he didn't notice her at first. He stopped himself from calling her name in his stern Captain's voice when he realized she was sound asleep on the floor of the well of the largest viewport. Lying on top of several sheets of paper, Isa was curled up in a ball with her back to the room and her face towards the stars. From the sound of the slow, deep breathing, she must have been asleep for quite a while.

Bane knew better than to startle her, so he sank to the floor beside her. Saying her name quietly, he put a hand on her shoulder and waited for her to wake up and figure out where she was. She moved and her breathing became shallower as one eye, then the other, stretched open and she turned, casting Bane a sleepy, confused look. He grinned at her as she sat up, the imprint of the jacket zipper down the side of her face where she lay on it. Bane moved into the viewport and they sat, side-by-side, with their backs against the stars.

"How long was I asleep?"

"No idea. It's very late; you missed our appointment, so I came looking for you. Good thing, too, or you'd be very stiff in the morning."

"I come here when I need to be alone. I watched us leave orbit, and then I was working on some plans." She indicated the papers strewn around, crumpled from her nap. "Then, I was looking out and trying to imagine living in that cabin—I was drinking early morning coffee on the porch and I guess I fell asleep."

"Maybe the coffee wasn't strong enough," Bane teased. "So, what have you decided after all that?" He wanted her to be sure about this, and he was glad that they had nine months to affix Astro-lab routines into her system.

"I think it will be good for me. Of course, I'll love the horses and the kids, but it also gives me a chance to step out of my safety net here and test my new self. I'm nervous about being on my own, is that...odd?"

"No, perfectly normal." Bane wondered what she thought about all her time on the farm, if that wasn't being alone, he didn't know what was.

"Bane, uh, Captain, can I contact Sarah at the Academy stable to run some of my ideas by her? She's been doing a lot of what I want to do and will be able to point out holes to me. I also want to talk to Jack and maybe Seth on Kline, too."

"I'd recommend waiting for a day, but yes, that sounds smart. Enough thinking and planning for one night, Lieutenant. I'll take you to your quarters." Bane stood as Isa gathered up the papers, gave her a hand up, and they walked through the quiet halls to her room. "Let it rest, now, until morning."

40.

Two weeks prior to the program starting was all he would agree to. Isa wanted a month to spend working the sixteen horses they'd found for the program. Captain wouldn't budge, she'd have to manage with what he gave her and that was final. He never raised his voice, but she figured she'd better stop pushing the issue. That she trusted him enough to continue pleading her case directly and with no apology seemed to please him, showing her confidence in her own resources had grown.

Isa had never shirked any of her duties and had learned so much about the stars and mapping, planets and moons, while also spending countless hours putting together this horse program. Everything was ready, and she'd have to rely on the two wranglers Ambassador Kine had hired to prepare the horses until she could get there. The children were adjusting well to this new life and all reports indicated their excitement about working with the horses.

She knew she'd been driving the Captain crazy with requests and wanted to find time to apologize. She was in the common room making oatmeal chocolate chip cookies to take as a peace offering. Bounty would be delivering her in two days. She was ready, but still reluctant to leave for so long what had become her home. Jamie had promised to fill her in on everything while she was gone, as they could talk anytime on the com-link, and that made her feel better. Bounty would stay for several days to provide shore leave and time for Bane and Lee to check in on her progress. Bane also wanted her expectations to be clear and he planned to be able to help with the horses occasionally.

Isa pulled the last batch from the oven; the sweet smell of warm gooey cookies had crew members in the common room drooling and making promises in exchange for the fresh baked treats. She fixed a large plateful for Bane, and decided whoever volunteered to clean-up her mess could have the first cookie. There were plenty to go around, as she'd made a double batch. She left the common kitchen in good hands, and went in search of Captain Lucas.

Setting the warm cookies in front of his door, she signaled and stepped to the side. His nose led through the opening, "If this is a bribe, I accept." Picking up the plate, he waited for Isa to enter and followed her to the sofa, placing the cookies on the table. One cookie disappeared in his mouth and a second waited its turn. "Mmm. You do make the best cookies and warm from the oven is an added bonus. Would you like something to drink?" He was licking his fingers and she giggled.

"Hot cocoa would be great."

"Coming right up." Placing the steaming chocolate in her hands, Bane sat down next to her and took another cookie. "Before you get started on whatever it is you came here to say, take a couple of minutes to enjoy your cocoa and one of these delicious cookies." He did just that, himself. Isa liked to see him like this; it reminded her of the evenings they'd spent at Jack's. She sipped the sweet chocolate and let the warmth in her hands bring quiet to her soul.

"I don't know what I'll do for three months without being able to come here." Bane just listened. "I know I've been a pain at times with all my requests and plans, and I'm sorry. I want this to offer so much for these kids, to give them a reason to hope and to love again. I can't wait to start and I don't want to leave. I'm ready, but wonder what I'll do if something happens to us that I can't handle. I know horses, but am afraid of what I don't know. What if I forget how to operate as Alliance, how to work with my Astro team, or what it feels like to have a home that moves through space? What if I'm overwhelmed with my memories and ghosts, who will help me find my way back?" With a long sigh and a sip from the mug, her head fell back into the cushion and she stared up, past the ceiling. The quiet filled the room and Isa was still.

Bane put his arm around her shoulders and sheltering her, tucked her into his side. "I don't have the answers. I think you are clear about what you want this to be for these kids, and as long as that is your focus, you'll find the answers to your questions as they come up. The passion you have for what you do will help you power through the hard parts, just as your passion for Bounty and what you do here will bring you back. It will be like you never left. I don't need to remind you that I'm your Captain, but sometimes you forget that I am also your friend. I can't make you hot cocoa, or sit with you like this; I can talk, though, anytime you need—in fact, I expect regular communication through the com-link."

"Thank you, sir." Isa tried to set his words into her mind along with her faith in knowing she was absolutely safe here with him, in every way. She made another memory, folding it into the cache with other special moments that gave her strength and courage.

41.

"Captain, Lieutenant, welcome back."

"Ambassador, it's good to see you again." They sat at the table in Lee's office, Isa helping herself to the fresh blueberries and strawberries. She listened while they discussed logistics.

"Lieutenant, if you're going to keep that tapping up, I'm going to ask you to leave."

"Sorry, sir."

"Why don't you go unpack and we'll come find you later." She was up and out the door thanking them with a handful of the sweet blueberries. She popped them in her mouth one by one as she retraced her steps from nine months ago to the little cabin.

It was much as she remembered, but fit with several innovations to make it comfortable, she owed someone gratitude for that. Her trunk had been placed up on the bed, which was covered with a thick quilt all in blues, and plump pillows lay at the head. Isa unpacked and stowed the trunk under the bed. She changed her uniform to jeans and boots with a long-sleeved flannel for warmth against the chill of the day.

There was a comfy-looking rocking chair by a front window. She sat to take all of this in for a minute. Talking out her doubts and fears the other night with Bane had helped to clear her mind for this new undertaking. She couldn't wait, so she left a note and went off to the barn.

A roan, beautiful with his face and thick neck stretched out over his stall door, greeted her.

"Hello, beautiful," she addressed the horse.

"Why, thank you! Most folks just call me Frankie, 'cept my mom, she calls me Elaine, and a few other names I'd rather not discuss." Isa took the hand offered from the smiling face with the long brown hair and deep brown eyes as she stood in the aisle.

"Nice to finally meet you, Frankie. I'm Isa, and this fine fellow must be Roan, huh, boy?" Isa blew in his nose and scratched his ears. "Is Skeeter around, too?"

"Yeah, he's here somewhere. And if you're ready, we've got several saddled out in the corral. They're all working very well and although we've noticed some quirks, there's nothing that isn't workable. We've been making notes that we can look at later."

"Great. Let's ride."

The three of them got along well; Isa liked Frankie's sense of humor and Skeeter's easy attitude. They picked three horses that hadn't been ridden yet that day and left the corral for a short trail ride. Frankie said it was a good first trail for kids because she felt it had several little challenges, but was still a fairly easy, flat trail. Isa joked with Skeeter about his name, but decided it fit him, as he was all gangly legs and arms with a wild shock of red hair. He and Frankie had grown up on this planet and had known each other for years, as their parents had ranched next to each other. They were both serious about helping these kids and completely agreed with Isa that horses would make a big difference in the children's lives. Although they had two weeks before the riding season officially began, they thought the horses were ready and they just needed to schedule and organize.

When they returned to the barn, Captain Lucas and Ambassador Kine were present. Isa had forgotten to leave a note about going on the trail and hoped they hadn't been waiting long. She told them as much and introduced Skeeter and Frankie to Captain Lucas.

"It's no problem, Lieutenant, Lee and I were looking over the stock. You all have assembled a fine group. I particularly like the tall black and white paint."

"Oh, he's a character, that one is. Steal anything that might be hanging out of your pocket, and so smooth you might not notice."

Bane laughed. "Thanks for the warning, Frankie."

"Say, we'd better get to unsaddling and feeding or we'll be late for supper. And I am *never* late for supper, especially when the dessert is brownies with ice cream!"

"I'm with you, Skeeter." Isa had Skeeter show them the tack room setup, and they all helped put away tack. Isa worked with Ambassador Kine to show him what to do and complimented him for taking to it so quickly. With all the horses fed and turned out for the night, Frankie led the way to the dining hall with meals for staff, guests, and the children, a way to build community, Lee said. Isa liked that. The instant they stepped in the door, they were mobbed by kids who already knew they were "the horse people." That was a title bestowed by the children and carried a great deal of respect. Frankie did her best to introduce Isa to them, and they each sat at a different table to give all the children a chance to "sit with the horse people."

Ignored, Bane and Lee took a seat with other staff and some of the Bounty crew, those who had not already found spots with kids. Bane had cause to be proud of his crew, taking some of their own shore leave to be with these kids. It was a time for suffering to be put aside and filled in with the care and love that goes into a good meal and pleasant company. Lee had broken many barriers with this program and even in the short time it'd been running, it had made a difference.

Alliance officials were watching closely, hoping for a model to follow; Ambassador Kine already had quite a reputation, highly respected and so obviously full of integrity. Bane could see why, having the utmost respect for him personally, he couldn't think of many others that he'd trust to care for Isa. He again wondered if that's how fathers felt about their daughters, figuring this would be the closest he'd come to that relationship. He wasn't sure if this surprised him or not, having fallen into Isa's life without meaning to. He'd always feel protective of her, he knew that the moment he saw her curled up on that couch in the ship she'd stowed away on to escape Frank.

"There's a fold-up cot in her cabin." Lee spoke as Bane watched Isa. Bane nodded his acknowledgement.

Chaos had taken over Isa's table when the makings for brownie sundaes arrived. She'd missed out on so much as a young girl, and her joy was evident in partaking of them now. The kids at her table were teaching her how to build the treat. She was not as adept as they were, so she was licking hot fudge off her hands and sticking her tongue way out trying to get the spots left behind on her cheeks that the children pointed out. The kids giggled at each new attempt.

Once the hot fudge had settled into the ice cream atop the fudgy brownie, it was time to add the whipped topping. It reminded Isa of her first soda. Following the kids' directions, she shook the can and sprayed into her bowl, a bit too zealously and close to the contents in the bowl. Whipped cream spurted out, splattering the faces gathered to supervise. One particular little girl, obviously a rapscallion disguised as a cute little blonde, leapt back laughing, and then proceeded to show Isa how to spray the cream right into her mouth. This produced even more excitement as Isa began the "a spray for you, mmm, a spray for me" game. They were breaking all of the dining room rules, but no one had the heart to stop such pure, unleashed joy. Everyone was smiling.

With the little ones begging her to stay after dinner, she looked beseechingly over at Bane, who shook his head once while holding her gaze. "Kids, I've had so much fun eating dinner with you, especially spraying the whip cream, TJ," this to the blonde, "But, I can't stay tonight, we have so much to do and we want all of you in the barn as soon as possible. I promise I will stay another time and I never break a promise," She took in each face and repeated, "Never."

That seemed to satisfy the children and they went off to evening activities. She arranged to meet Frankie and Skeeter at the barn before breakfast to catch and feed, then headed back to the cabin with the Captain and the Ambassador. They sat at the table in what Lee called the "kitchenette." It had the basics in case Isa wanted to eat here. "Thank you so much for making this place so cozy and snug. I really appreciate the thoughtfulness in all of these additions: the quilt, towels, kitchen things—the coffee pot." She added dramatic emphasis to the last, causing Bane to chuckle.

"It was Frankie's mom, so I can't take credit. She insisted that she be in charge of shaping this up for you. You can tell her when she comes to take Frankie home on her time off. She'll be so happy to hear you like it. I'm under orders to tell her if there's anything else you need, so please don't hesitate to ask."

"I can't imagine what it would be, but if I think of anything...."

Captain Lucas thanked him as well and Lee left them, saying he'd see them at breakfast.

"That was quite something watching you with those children at dinner. I believe you single-handedly broke every rule of etiquette they'd taught those kids."

"You're right, I kind of feel bad about that, but did you know that whipped cream came in a spray can? Whoever thought of that had to realize how it was going to turn out."

"I'll be sure not to mention that to Lieutenant Hamilton. We certainly don't need any of that on Bounty." Isa took his mock stern face for what it was and smiled.

"Will you run with me early? I'm not quite sure where to go."

"Sure. We can work out a route. Lee says there's a fold up cot in the closet, so I think I'll sleep here, if you don't mind." She let out the breath she'd been holding, her shoulders and back relaxing.

"It's not that I'm scared, it's just—"

"Okay. It's okay."

They found the cot, set it up, and Isa got ready for bed. It was still early, but she was tired. She climbed into bed to look out the window and was fast asleep.

42.

The cot had been reasonably comfortable, yet it had taken half the night for him to find sleep. He'd thought through several things he wanted to do, and tried to imagine as many scenarios as he could for situations Isa might find herself in and managing those. In the end, he decided she'd have to think on her feet, she was quite adept at that.

Bane heard Isa stirring and the footfall she tried to quiet, saying, "I'm awake. It's a bit dark yet to run."

"Yeah. Thought I'd get some coffee going so I can have a cup before we go."

"You always do that?"

"Sometimes two, and a banana." Her tone suggested that the banana more than justified the coffee.

"Right, because bananas are so...."

"Potassium."

They stayed on the road to be safe, and turned back after about 20 minutes, and Isa figured they'd done a little over four miles. Cleaned up and ready for the barn and the day, they sat on the porch sipping hot coffee. Isa went to feed the horses, leaving Bane who said he'd see her at breakfast.

With two weeks practice, the horses had the morning routine down. Skeeter opened the gate and they came into the corral, making their way to their stalls in the barn. Most went to the right stall; a few had to be moved, causing some confusion to the horses trying to enter occupied stalls. Once the animals were haltered and tied, the sound of contented horses grinding grain filled the barn.

Isa stood by the roan's stall, closed her eyes and, smiling, breathed deep. Home. She was constantly re-framing what that word meant. Bounty was home. She recognized and appreciated that barns would also always be home for her. There was Jack's, the Academy's, Seth's barn on Kline, and now this barn would be hers. It brought an abiding peace to her soul, as her heart gave thanks to God.

Breakfast that morning was more dignified, how much trouble could you get into with eggs, toast and sausage? Bane was going to help them at the barn today, so rather than spend the morning at a table working out schedules, they went to grooming and saddling right away. Wanting to see more of the trails, the four of them packed water and snacks and spent the morning exploring the hilly country at the base of the mountain range. The horses were willing and in good spirits and dealt well with the more rocky sections of trail.

The riders came to the top of a ridge, stopping to rest the horses, get a drink, and enjoy the view. Frankie pulled out their bag of nuts with little pieces of chocolate, each of them munching a few handfuls. Isa was busy talking to the roan. He loved to go, but needed to learn to slow down, as every time someone else gave a vocal cue to his or her horse, the roan responded with a trot or canter. This would be a wrangler horse, and a good one, he wasn't afraid of anything and did all Isa asked him to, except maybe slow down. She felt the pull of this horse, liking the challenge.

"We better head back if we don't want to be late for lunch." Skeeter was all about regular meals.

"You like him." It wasn't a question. Bane saw Isa working with this horse the same way she had with Indian. But it was different somehow. She loved to ride any horse, yet that bond she'd had with Indian, and then Jack's Amigo, was what she had here.

"Yes, very much." This insight made her glad, and she could see he was pleased as well. It would make Bounty's departure that much easier for both of them. At this point, she was much more comfortable in the safety this kind of relationship provided her.

The roan was just as much horse on the way back; the hills they'd ridden didn't seem to affect his energy and impulsion. The other three were quiet. Back at the barn, they loosened cinches, watered, and put up their mounts. Once cleaned up in the barn sink, all four commented on how hungry they were. Skeeter was hoping for roast, Frankie for grilled cheese with tomato soup and Isa said, "Something chocolate would definitely hit the spot." They agreed to go over schedules after lunch, but Bane would not join them for that.

With an hour to work horses before evening chores had to be done, Isa rode three different horses, putting them through their paces in the arena. She wanted to have ridden each horse a few times so she'd have a feel for what they were like and what sort of rider would work for them. After she, Frankie and Skeeter had taken a ride on each of the three, they stopped, shared impressions and made notes.

In the process of finding the right horses for the program, she particularly sought out horses who could help beginner riders gain confidence and a soft hand, but who could also be responsible for more advanced riders. Horses are very good at sensing their rider's abilities; the trick was finding those who wouldn't take advantage of a green rider.

As they unsaddled and fed, they discussed how they would work as a team, all three saying they were pleased by how well they had already come together. Each would have a day off during every week, but once the kids started helping, there would be plenty of hands to get the work done. "By the way, Frankie, I need to thank your mom for making my cabin feel like home. She must be the nicest lady. The two of you are welcome anytime."

"Thanks. Same to you, and I'll tell her you like it. Believe me, she loves a project and had fun decorating that cabin for you."

"What do you guys think about telling the kids at dinner that we'll start 'horsing around' first of next week?"

"A week early? They'll love it! I think we can start barn chore rotation in a couple days, once we have it down."

"I like that idea, Frankie. Skeeter, can you put that schedule together and post it in the barn and dorm?"

"You bet."

They turned the horses out and went off to dinner and Isa was filled with satisfaction for the good work they'd done that day, as she sat down and smiled over at Bane before the kids commanded her attention.

"They really like her, Captain, and from the looks of it, I'd say she's pretty happy to be with them, too."

Bane turned his look to Lee, hearing something different in his tone and again noted fondness for Isa. He thought about sharing some of her story with Lee, but decided it was really up to Isa whom she chose to know her that well. He'd considered whether it might help for someone here to know, in case anything came up, but since he'd never discussed it with Isa, he remained quiet. She had been the one to let Fran and Timothy, and later Jack, into that part of her life, but she was very selective about sharing her most private self. Her judgment had been sound in those choices, and Bane had to trust that they would be here, too.

That night, after dinner, Isa was able to go off with the kids, promising Captain Bane she'd meet him at the cabin, and not late. The kids had decided he was Captain Bane, and he didn't seem to mind. Some of the kid's evening was devoted to music. Isa loved the beautiful tones of the acoustic guitar and the lovely, sweet sound of the children singing some of the songs they'd been taught. The Argons, who had settled Yenna, had some rich folk traditions, music was important to them as it helped to record and tell their story. TJ, that cute little blond, asked if she'd like to learn to play.

"Really? Yes, I would!"

Someone handed her a guitar and helped her fingers form what he called a "D" chord on the strings. The first attempt to strum the strings didn't sound very good, but she was hooked. Assuring her that she could borrow the instrument, another girl, Grace, gave her a chord chart and explained how to read it. Then they showed her where an empty cubby was, so she could store the guitar when she wasn't using it. By the time everyone had to start getting ready for bed, Isa's fingers were sore and red from pushing the strings against the neck of the guitar. Grace told her that if she practiced every day, she'd soon have calluses, making it easier to play.

TJ came up with a small, quiet girl, "Isa, this is Lucy. She thinks you sing well and she wants to learn about horses."

"Well, hello, Lucy. Thank you, and I'm glad you want to learn about horses."

Lucy's black hair fell over her face as she looked down at her shoes. She was a thin wisp of a waif next to TJ's solid confidence. It was obvious who had befriended who and knowing that was part of how TJ operated made Isa like her all the more. She squatted down and pulled both girls in close.

"You know, I really need some help checking the horses tonight. See, we turned them out and I have a hard time finding them all by myself. Do you suppose the two of you could sneak out with me if I promise to have you back for story?"

Lucy's big brown eyes gazed up at her and she very slowly nodded her head up, then down. TJ could barely contain her enthusiasm for this against-the-rules bonus. Isa put a finger to her lips and winked.

"We wouldn't want to hurt anyone else's feelings, so let's keep this just between us."

She held a hand out to each of them, catching the girls' counselor's eye and mouthing to her that she'd bring them back. If someone got upset with her for breaking the rules, well, she'd deal with it. This was one little girl who needed a horse to talk to and Isa hoped they'd find the animals by the pasture fence leading up to her cabin where they'd been last night when she'd explained to them how important their work was here.

It was a shorter route to go through the barn and she told them that in a day or two they'd come here for a barn orientation and learn all about what horses need to stay healthy and happy. Lucy's hand tightened her grip; Isa took that as the counterpart to TJ's "Yes!" On the other side of the barn, the trail led to Isa's cabin.

She could see the dark shapes of horses, and began, "Now, let's see if we can find those ponies."

"Is that them?" TJ was pointing and a horse nickered a greeting.

"I believe it is, TJ, and one just said hello to us. Come on."

She led them over to the fence where the roan was standing. Isa leaned in and blew into his nostril, stroking his head with her left hand. Lucy was still holding tight to her right.

"Lucy, do you want to pet him?"

Isa brought her hand up, still holding Lucy's from the back, pressed her palm to Roan's cheek and slowly followed the line of his face down to his soft muzzle.

"Listen, sweet pea, can you stay here and pet him while TJ and I check the others? He gets a little afraid and likes to hear your voice."

Lucy's eyes were on her.

"Can you do that for me?"

She nodded.

"Thanks, love. TJ, how are the others, did you count them?"

They only walked off a short distance while Isa helped TJ count. TJ had attracted several noses and indulged each one with a scratch on the cheek and a kiss. Isa could hear a high, very soft voice whispering behind her; she and TJ smiled at each other.

"I think we found them all. Thanks so much you two, you've been a great help."

Isa stroked the roan's face and as Lucy tucked her hand back into Isa's she beamed.

"All right then, we'd better get back—and remember, this is our little secret."

She took them back, giving each one a goodnight hug and said she'd see them at breakfast. Meeting Bane in the barn on her way back, he'd been on his way to escort her back as it was late, she ran right into him, a squeak escaping and she ducked, gathering to run.

"Isa, it's me, Bane. It's all right."

She'd been so involved with her thoughts that she'd not even noticed him. Reflex took over, but she recovered quickly.

"Sorry. I'm sorry—I was thinking and—I'm really late, huh?"

"I was on my way to get you. I called out to you, but you just ran right into me. You okay?"

"Yeah, just scared myself silly. That hasn't happened in a while."

"Come on, talk to me while we walk." He listened as she explained about Lucy and how she'd handled that.

"I'm sure no one will mind but, Isa, remember that you have to leave after the warm season, and the children will have to follow the rules, so be very mindful of that as you go. It wouldn't be fair to them or their counselors if all they hear is 'But Isa let us...' right?"

"You're right. I'll be careful and explain to the kids too in special circumstances."

43.

Bane rode out again with them the next day, and they took different horses and the Ambassador, too. It was a beautiful morning; the trail followed a creek up a gentle incline. The water rushed down over rocks with abandon from the thaw of the snow in the high country. Isa was enjoying the loud crashing the water made when it careened off the larger boulders, she could talk to her horse without anyone asking, "What?" because the creek was so loud. She had a tall brown gelding called Brownie today. If she did nothing, he just went right along as if he'd taken this trail a million times, but when she'd warmed him up before they left, Brownie had responded to the slightest cue she'd given. A subtle shift of weight or a light leg on his side and he was yielding and bending. He'd been well trained and had an outstanding attitude, enjoying a good scrub on his head without being pushy. Isa had him in mind for some of the boys who needed help with self-control.

Soon, the path led them away from the water and through a series of switchbacks going up the steep hill. The woods were quiet and she could hear Bane talking with Frankie and Skeeter about growing up here and asking how they felt about the Savarins helping with this program. She turned to look behind her, and there was Ambassador Kine smiling at her.

Smiling back, she asked, "Are you enjoying the ride, Ambassador?"

"Yes, very much, and please, it's Lee."

"Well, maybe when the Captain isn't listening," she returned, happily.

"How about 'Lee' unless the gathering is formal?"

"Deal, and likewise with the 'Lt Torunn,' just Isa."

"Okay Isa. My staff tells me you took a couple of girls out after curfew last night." He saw her stiffen and added, "It's okay, really, and I'm not so rigid with the rules that I don't know they need to be bent or broken once in a while. I appreciate you letting someone know. Our little Lucy has so much to overcome."

"She is a darling and needs this program in her life. I do have a tendency to jump on my ideas and go with them, which gets me into trouble now and again. If I really get out of line, please tell me. I certainly don't want to irritate anyone."

"I will, of course."

Captain Lucas had touched briefly on this in their discussions, letting him know that speaking to his lieutenant privately was the best way to solve problems that might arise, but that other than caring so much about what these children needed that she'd do anything to make it happen, she was not in trouble. Lee had assured him that Isa's passion was why he'd spent the last year and a half throwing himself into this work—he believed in making a difference. He was also glad he'd made time to come with them today.

Lee could see the strength in Isa and she seemed to glow with it when around a horse. He'd thought of her as confident when he'd met her in the Astro engineering lab, and quite spirited when they'd met privately so he could receive more information about a possible horse program. But seeing her today, working, she was simply a different person—he thought of her as beautiful.

Putting up the horses in the barn, Lee regretted not being able to join them for lunch. He had a meeting scheduled in his office that included a meal. Thanking his "horse staff," he said he'd see them at dinner.

After lunch, the horse staff had finished riding and made notes on all the horses. Skeeter went off in search of their first group of kids for barn orientation and horse chores. Twelve hardly-able-to-contain-themselves children came into the barn aisle behind Skeeter.

"Well done, gang; one of the first things to learn is that you can't run around and scream. I know it's hard to believe, but these big animals can startle and get scared when something happens that they aren't expecting."

"That's right, Frankie, and it's also why we spend so much time talking to and touching our horses, so they know we're there, well, that and they like the sound of your voice and for you to find that one scratchy spot they can never reach."

The orientation went on with the three of them tag-teaming, offering information, lots of hands-on work and plenty of laughter. Isa partnered each younger child with an older one and she, Frankie and Skeeter supervised two pairs each. Skeeter had been deliberate about scheduling half older kids with half younger ones so they could help each other. They'd allowed a full two hours before dinner so there'd be time for questions and petting horses.

Not one complaint was voiced, even when Skeeter showed them which end of the manure fork to use, how to scoop up the poop, and where to dump the wheelbarrow when it was full. Everything they did reinforced the idea that the humans were responsible for the well-being of the horses. These kids completely understood this and took it seriously.

Turning the horses out for the night had twelve bodies hanging over the fence to watch, some horses immediately dropped to roll and cheering erupted when one rolled all the way over, legs kicking up in the air, as others stopped at the nearest patch of green to munch. The three wranglers stood back, smiles filling their faces, nodding to say that yes, this is how it should be.

Frankie's hand touched Isa's arm and she turned. Frankie pointed toward the far end of the line of kids. It was Lucy, TJ next to her, Lucy had a hand through the middle rail at her eye-level and she was calling softly, "Here, boy." Isa watched as her roan put his nose into Lucy's hand and was still. She stroked him and then blew gently into his nose.

"I think he loves you, and you gave him your breath, like Isa," TJ encouraged her.

"I watched her do it last night, and I love him, too."

Lucy spoke as she continued to hold her hand to the roan's face. The grace in the moment was unmistakable. Isa's heart filled with gratitude to be a witness to it. She sent out a prayer of thanks for whatever caused the horse to walk over and offer himself to that little girl, remembering how her dad would call opportunities like that "God moments." She and Frankie hugged each other while Skeeter, who'd been at the other end of the line, began peeling kids off the fence and sending them to dinner.

Pizza night was buzzing with barn talk. The kids who went couldn't stop talking and the kids who hadn't, couldn't wait. There was joy in this room, every adult was glad for these young hearts; hope had been in short supply, but was making a comeback in the growing sense of community here.

Isa told the kids she'd be back for more guitar practice and a snack. Captain Bane, charged with setting the schedule for communications, wanted to sit with her and Lee.

"It isn't like Academy, Lieutenant. You're on your own much of the time, and at night. Given the situation, and even though the peace treaty has been established, I want you to check in with Bounty every night the first week."

"Okay, sir. Uh, what if I get in late?"

"Then you contact me late."

She nodded. Bane knew she was just wondering how this would work, and he had a feeling she was relieved to be under orders to make contact. The Ambassador would not be monitoring this, but Bane wanted him aware of this requirement.

"If you have any trouble with the comm-link, just let me know."

"Okay."

"We'll test it tonight, Lee."

Bounty would be leaving in three days, but they'd be close enough to return if the need arose, although no one anticipated that it would. Everything was going well and Bane was happy to provide this opportunity for Isa, for Lee, and for those kids who would really benefit from it.

"Captain?" Bane looked up, hearing formality in her tone. The look on her face was anxious. Lee was also focused on her intently.

"Yes, Lieutenant, what is it?"

"May I speak freely?" This rushed out.

"Of course."

"I'm sorry if I seem rude, Captain, Ambassador. I promised I would be back for another guitar lesson and snack, and I don't wish to disappoint Grace, or be late."

Her attempt to smile appeared more like a painful grimace. Lee covered his laugh with a cough, while Bane's perplexed face had been expecting something entirely different.

"We wouldn't dream of making you late. Get going and we'll test the comm-link when you return."

The thanks came over her shoulder as she high-tailed it out the door. Lee began laughing as soon as she was out of sight, while Bane stood shaking his head.

"Captain, I'd imagine there are very few dull moments with that fine lady on your ship!"

"Mmm. Very few indeed."

While Isa practiced what she'd learned, plus two new chords, Lucy and TJ sat like groupies listening. Her fingers were very sore, but she tried her best and Grace told her the more she practiced, the sooner the calluses would form.

"Well, I hope I wake up with them!" The girls giggled.

"Who's ready for a snack?"

Their counselor, Hannah, was the best. She always knew just when to start something new or let an activity run late to meet the girls' needs. She was young and enthusiastic, confident in her leadership ability and style. Hannah had been there the previous evening when Isa had slipped out with TJ and Lucy. TJ had told her that Lucy had talked to Isa's horse; Lucy hadn't spoken at all since coming to Yenna. Hannah had mentioned then that Isa could take them to the barn anytime, day or night, if those were the results.

The snack that night was popcorn. Isa took the bowl held out to her, growing quiet as the girls sat around the soft sofas chatting about their day. TJ, busy popping the kernels into her mouth stopped and paused as she saw Isa sitting still, not eating the treat, "Don't you like popcorn Isa?"

"I used to love popcorn. Guess I'm just not hungry, you can have it."

She passed her bowl to a very excited TJ. She hadn't eaten popcorn since that night, as a little girl, when she'd tried to make her mom happy. She was sitting there trying to hang on, felt like she was clawing at the top of a cliff overhand, desperate not to fall. Shaking with the effort she was making in front of all these children not to come apart, Isa felt a small hand twine with hers.

Lucy was staring up at her. Isa considered her upturned face, tried to speak, to smile, but all she could do was stare back into Lucy's brown eyes, her own wide and sad with remembering. Lucy's right hand tightened on Isa's left hand, and she reached up, stroking Isa's cheek with her left hand, her fingers warm and gentle.

She tipped her chin up and blew slowly into Isa's nose, whispering, "It's okay, you're safe."

Tears slid down Isa's cheeks along the crease her nose made, as two little girls put their foreheads together in the comfort of friendship. The world stilled even as chatter and crunching popcorn went on around them.

When TJ finished both bowls, she stood up and laid a hand on each head, "Friends forever, that's what we are."

She'd brought them together as surely as if she knew they were kindred spirits who just hadn't met yet. That was a blessing for all of them.

When it was time for Isa to leave, she shared an extra long hug with Lucy and then TJ, kissed them on the cheek, and whispered thanks. Lucy held onto her hand, making Isa turn back. Isa nodded at the question in Lucy's eyes and said, "I'll be okay now, I'll tell the roan on my way by." Satisfied with that answer, Lucy let go and turned to go with the other girls.

Tonight, the horses were far out in the pasture. Isa stopped at the fence, knelt in the grass, putting her folded hands on the wooden rail, and prayed. She prayed for courage for that little girl who'd come out tonight missing her mom and dad so much it hurt, courage so that she wouldn't run and hide, alone and so frightened, courage to share her pain and fear with these kids who needed someone to trust and who could understand, courage for them to enjoy the things she couldn't herself because the memories were too blistering. When she'd emptied her heart to God, she opened her eyes, looking up from where she knelt into the brilliant night sky.

Filling her lungs, out loud she said, "Thank you for the love I've known in my life, the special people you always seem to send my way when I need them most, even when I didn't know I needed them. Thank you for those little girls, who have already touched my heart so deeply, and help me to bring healing to their lives. Thank you for this beautiful world and most especially for horses. Your Heaven must be full of them. God, tell my mom and dad that I miss them and love them. Amen." The last came out in a subdued hush.

Rising, she followed the path the rest of the way to the cabin. Stopping, she saw Bane sitting on the bench on the little porch. She couldn't move, suddenly exhausted, spent. He came to her and held out his hand. She clasped it, her tremor apparent. "Come. Sit with me a while." Sinking into his shoulder, she fell asleep, her quiet tears soaking into his shirt. He held her close, then picked her up, took her inside and, removing her boots, tucked her into bed.

Sometime in the middle of the night, she woke from a dream. She had fallen off the back of the pick-up tailgate when she tried to help her dad unload hay. The bale landed on top of her. It hurt and she was afraid, the bale was heavy, crushing her. It was only seconds, and then her dad's strong arms lifted the bale away and, picking her up, hugged her close.

"Are you hurt, little love?"

"I'm scared, and I think my jeans ripped."

"Don't you worry, we'll fix them. You were very brave and you stay right here in my arms until the scared goes away." She didn't want to wake up; it felt so safe, but something pulled at her and she opened her eyes to the dark sky filled with stars.

"Are you okay?" Bane apparently had heard her stirring.

"Popcorn. The snack tonight was popcorn. I came apart inside. One of the kids, Lucy, took my hand and told me it was okay. I," she heaved a heavy sigh, "Bane, what will I do here if I find myself trapped remembering and I want to hide?"

"You'll go the barn and your horse. You'll come here and get on the comm-link and we'll talk it through. You'll let those kids help you, knowing it will also help them. You'll try not to be alone with it. You'll find someone to share a cup of cocoa and sit with them until you're okay again. And you *will* be okay again."

She was nodding at him in the dark. "Goodnight, then."

"Sleep well."

44.

The next few days flew by and Bounty with her crew was ready to depart. Bane had run with Isa that morning, asking her to meet him at her cabin after breakfast. Reminding her one last time about checking in, they said goodbye.

"Make the most of your time here, Lieutenant, and try not to break too many rules."

"I won't, sir. I hope your mission goes well and that someone makes you cookies while I'm gone."

"You'll owe me when you're back onboard. Now, off to the barn with you, you have a job to do." She began to leave then about-faced. Isa hugged him and his arms wrapped around her. He held her a moment, then put his hands on her shoulders, turned her toward the door, letting her loose with a, "Go and do what you love." This time she went out the door and down to her waiting students at the barn without looking back.

Isa, Frankie and Skeeter each had a particular group of kids assigned to them. Of course, they did various activities with all the kids, but focused on riding skills in the arena with one group. Their kids knew who the "go-to" person was for them on the horse staff. It was working well as they built relationships and solved situations that came up. Sharing in this way eased the emotional burden and they could share ideas, depending on who had tried what. Certain kids, they'd noticed, had an abundance of resilience and cared deeply for other kids who were having a much more difficult time understanding what had happened to them, and facilitated talking about it in order to begin healing. TJ was one of these and she'd made Lucy her mission. They were both in Isa's group.

Isa had assigned Lucy to a sweet sorrel gelding called Buster; TJ had a black and white paint, Smoke; Grace was with a brown and white paint mare, Trix; Tess was on a roan mare, Lessa; Reid on a small sorrel mare, Scooter; and Alex was on a buckskin named Barley. Alex and Grace had been teaching Isa guitar and Isa was telling the kids stories about her horses. TJ was interested to hear about Isa's Smokey and whether or not he was like her Smoke. Captain Bane's status had been elevated when TJ found out that he'd ridden Smokey. Isa wanted to be sure to tell him about that one of these nights on the comm-link.

Ever since the popcorn incident, Lucy had been slowly rediscovering her voice. Her soft voice carried to the others when she talked to Buster, and she made a special point of greeting the roan each day, but Isa had also heard her giggling with TJ and she spoke freely with Isa and now Hannah, too. It had happened over time, but after a month into the horse program, many positive changes had occurred. The horse staff would meet on a regular basis with the dorm and teaching staff to talk about kids and any concerns—at this point, there were mostly celebrations and brainstorming for ways to ensure everyone was growing.

Most evenings, the riding staff joined the kids in whatever they were doing. Sometimes they went out after dark, lay in the big meadow and gazed at the stars. If they wanted star facts, Isa could be counted on. Mostly though, they picked out shapes and outlines and named them. One such evening, Justin, the boy's counselor, asked Isa if they could talk. Moving away from the group, he began, "Isa, I know Reid is in your group and he seems particularly troubled tonight. Will you come and sit with us for a while?" Isa thought the world of Justin; he was kind and caring, knew how to rough-house and wrestle without hurting anyone, could tease and get a laugh out of anyone, and had found the ticklish spot on every kid, Isa and Frankie included.

Justin had come upon her one night when she was feeling low and she'd discovered that he was someone she could share a cup of hot chocolate with, even though he preferred a beer, still she could find reassurance in his company. He always added plenty of marshmallows and never pushed her. "Of course I will. What's going on?"

"Remember that night I found you?" She nodded. "I think it's something like that, just feeling overwhelmed and unable to put the words to it." Isa saw Reid sitting with his back against a tree, knees pulled into his chest and his arms wrapped around his legs. Her heart ached for him. Sitting down next to him, she gathered his smaller frame into her arms and, leaning back against the tree, just held him close as Bane had done so many times for her. No words, just warmth, love and acceptance. Justin left them. Soon enough, Reid was crying softly into Isa's chest.

"I miss them so much. Why? We never did anything wrong, why couldn't they leave us alone? I want them back. I want to go home. I want to kill them!"

Isa held him as his pain poured out, recognizing the desperation and utter loss at the unfairness and injustice, feeling like you should have been able to stop it somehow, but you just weren't strong enough or smart enough.

When he was depleted, she pulled him in even closer, saying, "I don't have any answers, Reid, all we can do is hold on to each other and learn to love again. I'm here for you, so is Justin, and the others. Captain Bane tells me not to be by myself when I feel bad, so I come find one of you guys."

"You do?"

"She does," Justin reappeared with mugs of hot cocoa heaped with marshmallows. He raised an eyebrow at Isa, who nodded. "Isa was real sad, like you, a while back and she came and sat with me 'til she felt better."

"Did you give her this many marshmallows?"

"Nah, she's a girl, she can't eat as many as us guys." He winked at Reid, who laughed. "Good to see your smile back."

"Thanks, Justin, and you, too."

"You just remember, we're always here, you don't have to be alone." Justin's focus was on Isa when he said that, his hand on Reid's shoulder.

45.

Ambassador Kine had requested a meeting with Isa before breakfast, Frankie suggested that she better just go and they would handle the morning chores. Isa woke early, doing the five-mile route she'd worked out. Listening to music while she ran gave her mind rest. It didn't stop her thinking, but distanced her from it, and she always came back with more energy, ready to tackle whatever came her way. As she ran this day, she wondered what Lee could possibly want.

After her shower she was unsure whether she should be in uniform but decided since nothing was mentioned her barn "uniform" should suffice. She walked the path filled with wood chips to the administration center, a warm red-brown adobe building with lots of glass, including the doors. She found her way down the hall to the Ambassador's office, his door was open; she didn't think she had ever seen it closed. Isa hadn't made any noise, but Lee said, "Come on in, Lieutenant" before he looked up. All she heard was the Lieutenant part, and she regretted not having worn her Alliance uniform as she entered and stood at attention.

"Oh, I'm sorry, Isa, at ease. This isn't formal, please have a seat."

"Ambassador...?"

"Lee. Really. Sit. I just want to talk."

"I've been in regular contact with Bounty. I did see the medic about my arm. I haven't had any of the kids out late, well, not too late. I did take an extra bag of marshmallows, but this was only the second place I've ever had them and well, I wanted more. I did leave a signed I.O.U. And I did take my horse to the dorm, but I never took him into the lobby, I kept him outside the kids' windows. They just needed cheering up and it was a full moon...." She went on like she was at confession and Lee, the priest.

"Stop, Isa. I'm sure the marshmallows were forgiven, s'more experience and all, you haven't done anything wrong, although Captain Lucas has mentioned that your check-ins have been late recently. None of that is what this is about. I couldn't have asked for a better person to run that barn. You are doing an amazing job."

"Then, what is it?"

"It's your work, or rather, your time off. I've been told that you've yet to take any, and before you say anything, know that I am requiring you to take time for yourself, now, today." Her mouth opened and closed several times.

"But, I don't need it. I love what I'm doing."

"I insist." His tone was quiet, similar to Bane's "this is not up for debate, my final word" tone. She really didn't understand and dropped her eyes down at her lap. "Isa, everyone needs time just for themselves. Surely there is something you'd like to do, just for one day. I can make suggestions if you want." Now she knew why Frankie and Skeeter were so willing to cover barn chores and send her off. They wanted the best for her and maybe she could use a day off to explore the place. It hadn't occurred to her because she had no family here to visit and working with horses was her life.

"Am I outlawed from taking my horse?"

"Of course not, is that what you'd like to do?"

"There is a trail I've wanted to ride—I'll need to fix a lunch—can you make that happen?"

"Done, what would you like?"

"Peanut butter and honey would be fine."

"I know it seems restrictive, but to avoid your being detained, I suggest you eat breakfast here with me, I'll have a lunch brought to you, and you can head off before the kids go to the barn. They'll be told you're taking a day off and you'll see them tomorrow at breakfast."

He'd thought of everything. She guessed her horse would be saddled and ready at the barn, and she wasn't wrong. They ate in his office; she left him a rough map of where she intended to go, telling him she'd contact him when she returned, and off she went. Saddlebags with snacks, lunch and water she'd secured behind her saddle with her rain duster tied on top of that. Isa tacked up a thank-you note to the barn board, mounted the roan after checking her tack, and set off, happy to have the day in front of her and the roan for company.

She let herself out the pasture gate, practicing opening and closing it from Roan's back; he'd proven a quick and willing learner. Finding the trail that Skeeter had told her went up through fairly rugged country and then opened, coming into a meadow with a river, had been in the back of her mind for a while. She realized that she hadn't really ridden by herself since she'd left the farm. This day was a gift and she planned to savor it.

The morning was crisp, but the bright sky told her she'd be shedding the flannel shirt by noon. The trail was rugged, and hadn't been cleared from what looked to be the last couple of winter's deadfall. She and the roan wound their way around several large trees across the path, and she dismounted a few times to pull smaller ones away, others they gingerly stepped over. Coming to a little run-off stream, Roan put his head down to drink and Isa took the opportunity to get her water out, too. They were looking down a steep drop, but she knew her Roan had no notion to go tumbling down it, and she trusted his footing.

Coming down this side of the ridge, the trees were wider and taller, like big old grandpa trees, Isa thought, taking care of some very young saplings and all the critters that must live here. Making their way down and out of the trees, she discovered the large meadow. The river had cut through it, and the bank was craggy with uneven footing. Isa rode the roan carefully down into the water, as it was above his knees and hocks and she thought the cold would be good for his well-worked legs. They stood, the roan drinking and playing with the water. His pawing had soaked Isa's legs as she laughed at his antics.

When she decided his legs had had a good soak, she rode up out of the creek bed and over to an old fallen trunk. Bringing out her lunch and water, untying her duster, Isa loosened the roan's cinch, took off his bridle and, leaving his halter and lead rope on, turned him loose to graze. She didn't think he'd go far, so wasn't worried about facing a very long walk back to the barn. She climbed up on the log, found a comfortable spot and began to eat her lunch.

Lee had been good to his word. The peanut butter and honey was the best she'd ever eaten, the thought made her chuckle, thinking of Josh rolling his eyes. There were also some cheesy crackers, and the salt was just what she wanted, followed by chocolate chip cookies. Isa took a bite, setting the rest of the cookie down, held both arms skyward and yelled, "Thank you, God, for the food! It's yummy!" She had an apple, too, but she was saving it to share with the roan. He was busy filling his belly, and had barely acknowledged her shout-out prayer. Isa leaned back, closing her eyes and soaking in the sun's heat. She dozed, but soon found that she was too hot.

Leaving boots and socks on the bank, she decided to cool off in the river. As she stood on a rock, a tentative toe dipped in the water and came out like it had been bitten. This was fed by melting mountain snow, so her feet took turns going in and out and splashing, although she shouldn't spend too much time here, as the clouds moving in signaled the strong possibility of an afternoon storm.

She turned to jump back to the bank, but the rock was slick and she slipped, narrowly missing a meeting of the rock with her head, but plunging into the icy water. She came up spluttering and soaked, climbing back up the bank. It was going to be a cold ride back. Pulling on her socks and boots, she brought Roan over to the rock and prepared to leave. Before she mounted, she took a bite of the apple and gave her grateful horse the rest. Dripping, she found her seat in the saddle and headed home. When the clouds closed in and opened up, Isa had the duster on and snapped closed around her, but wet on the inside, she was already shivering.

Soon, her hands had gone past painful and cramped to numb and she couldn't feel her feet in the stirrups. Her legs, wet and molded to leather, were wooden, but she was still shivering uncontrollably, and she knew that was a good sign. Forcing herself to sing, with Jack's words of warning about the dangers of high mountain lakes swimming through her head, kept her brain active. She wondered about stripping off Roan's saddle to take advantage of his body heat, but she wasn't at all sure she could keep her balance bareback on this trail in this condition.

46.

The barn chores were finished, the kids had gone off to dinner. Skeeter and Frankie had seen no sign of Isa; they figured she'd show up while they were at dinner, feed and turn the roan out and then eat in her cabin, since Lee had made it clear she was to have 24 hours to herself. The weather was miserable, but it had been warm until mid-afternoon, so they didn't think Isa would have been caught in the rain until the last few miles.

"Well?"

"She isn't back yet."

"Should we be worried?"

"Not yet, Lee, she's probably at the barn now and she said she'd let you know when she's back, right?"

"She did."

Frankie, hands on her hips, said, "I guess you could go down to the barn and wait for her. I'll come down and wait with you if you want."

He looked out toward the barn, back at the tables full of kids eating, his stance divided. Frankie watched as his head turned back and forth and then, finally, at her. "Yes. I think I will. If you want to eat and then come down...."

"K, I'll be down in a bit."

Quiet greeted him in the barn. He took a deep breath, letting the smell of horses and hay settle within him. He hadn't had a lot of exposure to this kind of life, but he decided he liked it; he had also found pleasure in the riding he'd done, seeing this planet from a new perspective.

Looking around, he wasn't sure how to decide whether or not Isa might have arrived back already and gone to her cabin. There was no sign of wet, dripping tack, saddle bags or dusters, nor was there any sign of disturbance in Roan's stall. Rain was coming down in sheets by turns with light sprinkles in between squalls. Lee settled for pacing between Roan's stall and the opening to the corral.

"I don't think that will get her back any sooner." Frankie, with half a piece of chicken in her hand, came in.

"I need to do something, so this seemed as good as anything."

"How long do you want to give her before we start looking?"

"I don't even know how to consider an answer, you tell me?"

Frankie talked about how Isa might have found somewhere to hold up until the storm eased, or she may have spent more time at the meadow and got a late start back so the going would be slow. If either of these were the case, it could be dark before she got back, but the riding staff agreed that when they took the kids out on trail rides and weren't back by dinner, then whoever was at the barn would wait an hour depending on circumstances and weather before coming out to look. Isa had insisted, with no resistance, that they leave a plan for trails they would use, and if something changed that they make an obvious sign so the search would not be futile.

By the time she had talked this through with Lee, it was more than past the allotted time frame for a late return that included unforeseen delay. They found dusters and went out to the corral to get the horses Skeeter had left in, just in case. Doc nickered toward the gate, where Roan stood, a lump bent over his neck with one arm making a feeble effort to open it, reaching out, but misfiring like a dart without enough energy behind the throw to reach the target.

Frankie and Lee moved together to open the gate, Roan making straight for the barn with his cargo. The horse did not head for his stall, but stood quiet in the wide aisle while they peeled Isa off his back, stiff and shaking. "He, he, c, col."

"I got him, Isa-pal. Lee, there's dry saddle blankets back there in the tack room." Frankie pointed, began unsaddling the roan, rubbed him down and stalled him. She'd wait to feed his grain, but gave him a flake of hay and a bucket of water. He watched Isa over the stall door. "She'll be okay, boy. You got her home and we'll take care of her." That seemed to be what he needed as he turned to his hay.

Isa had crumpled against the wall in the aisle. Lee got the duster off, but found her soaked underneath. He wrapped her in the blankets. Frankie offered, "I'll start a fire and get the hot water going in the tub, can you get her to the cabin?"

"I'm right behind you." Lee had scooped the shivering mass up, blankets and all.

Frankie had the bathtub filling and had Lee set Isa on the closed toilet, telling him to start the fire when she had a firm hold on Isa. She closed the door and began helping Isa out of her cold, wet clothes, while talking to her and assuring her that she'd soon be warm and feel human again. Isa's blue eyes watched her with little comprehension; she was cold beyond tolerability and could do nothing to help herself. Lifting her into the warm water, Frankie had to hold her up.

"Lee, can you find something warm she can wear, and some thick socks?" They were shoved through a partially opened door.

"I can't do this without your help—I'll cover her as best I can, but I need to lift her." Isa was still shaking, and her eyes had closed. Frankie drained the tub, awkwardly covering her in a towel and then as Lee lifted and held her, dressed her under and around the towel, pulling the thick wool socks on last. It would have to do. Lee carried her out where he'd already turned the bed down and tucked her in. He and Frankie were soon down to short sleeves in the small space.

"I'll stay with her; we shouldn't leave her alone."

"Agreed, go get what you need and I'll stay here."

Frankie found Skeeter and explained. He went to care for the roan, and she took her things and went back to Isa's. Lee had pulled the rocker next to the bed. Isa was asleep, her body exhausted from the effort to stay warm. They figured she'd sleep for a while, so Frankie went in search of some soup to heat up so they could get something warm and nourishing into her when she came to. It was still fairly early in the evening, so Lee went back to his office, telling Frankie to call him when she woke. He wanted to let Bane know what had happened.

47.

Isa opened one eye, seeing Frankie next to her reading a book. She was so warm; she'd thought she would never be warm again. Residual shivers still shook her muscles, but had subsided for the most part. Trying to stretch, she realized how stiff she was, her legs would not obey her brain. "Hey." It didn't sound like her, but she had Frankie's attention.

"Hey, yourself." Isa was struggling to get out from under the mound of blankets; Frankie stood and pulled her up and out, supporting her until her legs remembered they were supposed to hold her up. "Where are you goin'? Want to sit?"

"Bathroom." Isa tried to grin, but it was more of a grimace.

"C'mon." Closing the door after getting her to the sink, "Holler if you need me. I'll call Lee, promised I would when you were more human."

When Lee came in, Isa was sitting by the fire in the rocker, drinking soup from a mug. She glanced quickly at him and then refocused on the soup like her life depended on it. Frankie had pulled the chairs from the table over and they sat down.

"So, what the heck happened?" Frankie did not mince words; and Isa was completely mortified that Lee had seen her like this, especially in the tub. She asked what happened and Frankie was honest.

Isa recounted her day, emphatic that she hadn't meant to be immersed in the icy mountain water, it had been an accident and she was so grateful that when she could no longer ride, the roan had carried her slowly and carefully back to the gate.

"Thank you both for finding me and, um, helping me."

"We were following the plan you formed, so we were just getting horses to come look for you. Doc tipped us off, or we might not have seen you at the gate right away."

"Bless Doc, then, and I hope you gave Roan extra oats, he had quite a burden getting me down. It was all I could do to stay on his back."

"I'm sure Skeeter did."

Lee had been quiet as Isa told her story. "You're still cold. You're shivering." He moved to grab a blanket and gently covered her.

"Not really, but it feels nice. I just can't seem to stop."

"More soup?"

"No, thanks, Frankie. I'm tired, though, feel like I could sleep for a year or two."

"Go ahead. I figured I'd stay here tonight so we can have a little slumber party."

"You don't have to, I'm okay now."

"I know. I want to."

"Well, I'll leave you ladies to it then. Isa, take tomorrow if you need it to sleep. At some point, we'll talk to Captain Lucas. I did contact him to tell him what happened and that you were back safe." At her look, he added, "I felt that he'd want to know, and should. I'm glad you're safe." His words came out awkward, rushed. "Call me if you need anything, anything at all. Goodnight, then." Closing the door behind him, he left.

In the days that followed, Isa was tired and cut her evenings shorter to get to bed earlier, gradually regaining her energy. Her conversation with Captain Lucas had not been entirely pleasant. At first he'd said she was never to go out alone again, but after they'd spoken a while and he'd seen that she was okay and she explained the system they'd come up with for possible search and rescue scenarios, he relented.

"I was frightened, too, sir. I remembered what Jack had said about how dangerous getting wet in the mountains could be. I knew I was getting fuzzy and the cold wasn't bothering me so much. I just tried to concentrate on Roan's neck, as I knew he'd bring me home. I also knew that Frankie and Skeeter would follow our plan if I didn't get back when they thought I should. I didn't expect the Ambassador to be there, but Frankie said he was the one who went to the barn to wait."

"I see, and it does sound like your emergency procedures are sound, and now tested. That was good work, Lieutenant."

Softly, she told him, "You know, Captain, I never had anyone to worry about me on the farm. I was on my own with a horse constantly and just dealt with whatever happened. It felt good to know that someone would notice if I didn't come back."

"That's how it should be, Isa. Always."

"Yes, sir."

48.

Isa was torn. She was planning an end-of-season pack trip for the older kids who wanted to go. She had a few kids who were really excited, but were too young for such a trip. They'd need another season to hone skills, and grow taller; Isa had to tell them and was trying to dream up something special they could do instead to celebrate all they had accomplished. So far, she had nothing.

She was at her secret, now favorite, thinking spot. Making a habit of taking a walk in the evening before she went to bed, she'd followed what looked to be an old game trail behind her cabin. Oddly, it ended at a tall pine tree with needles she didn't want to tangle with. Razor-thin, and long, she couldn't resist the impulse to set the end of her finger up against those points. Bracing for the poke, her hand moved of its own accord, and as it brushed the ends of these, a slow smile spread across Isa's face and her other arm came up toward the branches. Finding them feather soft, she was soon inside the branches, letting them tickle her exposed skin. Whatever animal had made that trail knew a trick or two about not being followed.

When Isa emerged from the tree, a little valley stood before her with a lake at the bottom of fairly steep sides. She was struck by the picture before her. Wandering the perimeter of the lake, she adopted the large trunk of a tree to lean against and made herself comfortable. She felt supported by the planet's core and a great sense of peace settled around her. Hearing the lap of water against the shore, and feeling the breeze lift strands of her curly brown hair from her face; Isa just sat, relaxed.

She made a habit of returning to her spot every night before she went to bed, sometimes praying, sometimes writing or thinking, or just being. Tonight, her mind kept coming back to her riding group. They were fairly young and could use another year, but she wanted to give them a challenge to end this season and something to look forward to for the next. Isa remembered the meadow, the one she'd ridden to on that first day off. It would be a taxing ride, and long, but they would love it, and having lunch up there would be special. She'd see what Frankie and Skeeter thought first and then talk with her group. Ducking back under the needle tree, she returned to her cabin and went straight to bed.

After everyone had groomed and saddled, Isa called her group together for a pow-wow.

"Guys, I want you to know that I've given a lot of thought to this decision, and that I have loved working with you and watching you grow this summer. I know it's hard to hear, but you aren't yet ready for the pack trip." Six faces were riveted on hers. "Another season, maybe two for some of you, and I don't want you thinking that I don't believe you're good riders. You've done so well with your horses and I'm certain you will continue to do so. A pack trip requires too much of you, and even though I know you'd all try so hard, I don't want to put you in a position where you could get hurt."

"What? Isa, what are we good at?" It was TJ; she'd become a leader for this group, and was the one rider Isa had considered for the trip.

"Okay, TJ, let's start with you. Your balance has so improved; remember when that dog scared Smoke and he startled sideways? You got up close and personal with that bush."

TJ giggled.

"I don't think that would happen now, because you've learned how to keep your body even and relaxed in the saddle." Isa went on, telling each of them what she'd noticed about them as riders that they had learned and reminding them what their skills had been at the beginning. "It's just like me and the guitar. Don't you remember how I struggled with that D chord and how I wanted the calluses to form overnight so my fingers would stop hurting? And now, thanks to Alex and Grace, I can play so much better. I'll keep practicing when I go back to Bounty, and I'll get even better."

"But we don't want you to go." A chorus of "Yeah, please stay" followed.

"I thought we weren't going to have that discussion again, gang. I have to go. Bounty is my home and my work. Of course, I'll miss you every day and in my heart, we'll always be together, even if I can't sit by the fire and roast marshmallows with you. So, let's make the most of these last days, and don't forget that you're supposed to be making memories so you'll have them when you need them." They surrounded her in a hug and, laughing, she told them to get their horses, do their tack checks, and mount up.

Isa's group sat together at lunch and she told them her plan for their end-of-season challenge. Having heard her story of that first ride to the meadow, they were eager to go there with her. Lunch was spent making plans and deciding what to take for snacks on the ride and a meal to share when they arrived.

The day finally came for the group's all-day adventure. Isa, Frankie, and Skeeter had returned from the five-day pack trip with the older kids. Jack had taught Isa well, and everyone agreed that the experience was one they'd never forget. One morning, Isa had climbed out of her tent and, checking on the horses, discovered five deer wandering through the trees where the horses were tied. Each was curious about the other; it was magical to Isa.

Verifying that everyone had rain gear and a warm jacket tied on, plus water and snacks accessible, they left the corral shortly after breakfast. Isa and Frankie carried the lunches and Skeeter stayed behind to manage the barn and the rest of the kids.

At the top of the first ridge, they stopped to drink and to take in the view. Bright blue sky met the green of the pasture below them and framed the massive rock face they'd be riding around. "You want a butterscotch?"

"Thanks, TJ, you're always looking out for me." Isa winked at her, popping the sweet hard candy into her mouth. "Okay, remember, as Frankie leads us down, we need to sit up straight, even with the trees, keep our heels down, and watch out for branches." Once they crossed the small stream with the drop-off and entered what Isa called the "grandpa forest," she told the kids to watch for the meadow.

Riding down into the river, Isa explained how the cold water was good for the horses' legs. When all the horses had soaked and had as much water as they wanted, they rode out, dismounted, loosened cinches and hung bridles over saddle horns, tying them with the saddle strings, then turned the horses loose to graze. Each of them was responsible for keeping an eye on his or her horse. Peanut butter was the sandwich of choice, along with crispy chips, a granola bar, and an apple – most of which were fed to a horse. After they had a chocolate chip cookie, the kids explored the meadow, climbing all over the log. Frankie and Isa sat watching, careful that no one strayed too far.

"So, you ready to go back? To Bounty?"

"It's weird, I feel so torn. I'm gonna miss everyone so much, and my Roan. If I could think of any plausible way to take him on board...."

"At least I'll be on the same planet. Believe me, I plan to spend some time with Doc in the cold and I told you, I'll check up on the kids and your Roan and keep you posted on how everyone's doing. S'pose they'll let you come back for another season?"

"I have no idea."

They rounded up the kids and helped them all mount. Cautioning everyone to be extra careful and diligent about paying attention on the way home, they set off. Isa loved to ride the back of the line. She could watch the kids interacting with their horses and each other and correct anything she saw going wrong. Frankie was busy up front torturing the kids, singing the ping pong song over and over, and laughing at Doc's antics as he looked cross-eyed at a stump and side-stepped around it.

When they came to the top of the ridge with the craggy rock again, the line had fallen silent. Stopping to marvel at the view, Isa and Frankie encouraged their charges to drink and eat something, and to get a piece of hard candy into a pocket easy to access. "You want my last butterscotch?"

"No, sweet pea, you save it for yourself on the way down. Thank you, though." Isa smiled at TJ. "You doin' okay?"

"Yes. I'm just tired. I think you were right about us needing more time before the pack trip."

"You're doing great, and just think, we have pizza night when we arrive, along with campfire and s'mores. What's not perfect about that?"

"Isa, will you play tonight?" Lucy had been listening.

"Course I will, Lucy-love, as best I can."

Frankie and Isa sang all the way back to the corral, where Skeeter and his crew were waiting. Isa's group welcomed their help, and they soon had everything unpacked and squared away. The work of feeding the horses and turning them out for the night provided great entertainment as they dropped one-by-one to roll in the soft dirt. All the kids cheered when any horse managed to roll all the way over without having to stand up.

Pizza restored their energy as Lee was inundated with stories of the day when he sat down to join Isa's group for dinner. After hearing from most of the kids who were now devouring pizza, he turned to Lucy, who was sitting quietly next to him, to ask, "And how was your day, Lucy?"

"Magnificent, couldn't have dreamed of any better. Buster took care of me, just like Isa said he would, even though I was pretty scared sometimes."

"I'm glad Buster watched over you and that you had such a great day. I'm sure it was beautiful."

"Maybe Isa will take you up there when you have a little more experience riding. Are you coming to our last-night campfire? We're having s'mores and Isa is gonna play and sing," she said, as her voice got so quiet, Lee had to lean in to hear, "she has to go, y'know, back to Captain Bane." Lee put his arm around Lucy.

"We'll all miss her, and we have to hold on to all the fun we had with her and be happy when we think of her, she'd want us to. Of course I'll come tonight; someone has to make sure Isa doesn't eat all the marshmallows!" He tousled her hair, making her giggle. Isa hadn't realized how much impact she'd had on these young lives, but Lee was going to make certain that the Alliance did, and Lucy would be his prime example.

Later, around the campfire and after many s'mores, everyone settled in for some guitar music and singing. The kids sang along, proud of what they had taught Isa, and that what she had practiced all season was now evident. Lee was quite taken with her clear, sweet voice. The kids would miss her terribly, and he would also miss her easy-going, pleasant way. Bounty was due back any time, and it was time to prepare for Yenna's cold season.

After she sang, Isa said goodnight to every child, saying something special to each one and encouraging them to continue to grow, to hold on to each other, and to never lose hope. Her riding group gathered around her and they stood quietly by the dying fire. Lee watched as Isa guided them back to the dormitory. Alex volunteered to put her guitar away and as the kids went in slowly, Isa knelt down and hugged TJ and then Lucy, who clung to her. After a long moment, they came apart, Lucy and TJ holding hands as they went in.

Lee felt he was intruding on a private moment, so he didn't ask if he could walk Isa back to her cabin. He stood in the shadows until she moved off, then he returned to his office. He had some thinking to do.

49.

Bounty arrived two days later and while Bane wrapped things up with Lee, Isa, Frankie and Skeeter planned for the horses in the cold season. Frankie was off to school soon; Skeeter would go back to work the ranch, but would be in charge of seeing to the horses. They closed the barn down; they cleaned the tack, oiled and put it away, and ensured everything was in order and ready for the next season. Frankie and Skeeter would both continue to work the horse program and Isa was so glad it would go on in such capable hands. They were to stay in contact and with the kids, too, so they gave each other great big bear hugs, now lifelong friends.

Isa had made, thanks to some help from Frankie's mom, beaded bracelets for her charges. Each one was a different color, and she'd showed them how she'd made one for herself incorporating all the colors so she'd have a piece of theirs with her. Whenever she looked at it, she'd remember each one of them and their horse. In a top-secret mission, Alex called it, they'd wrangled permission from Lee to give her a guitar. It was a beautiful honey-colored acoustic guitar with twelve strings. Each had signed it. Isa sat with her hand over her mouth while Alex demonstrated. Sweet sounds emerged, flowing around them, raining joy. Isa had no words for what this meant to her. She simply held her hand to her heart, looking from one child to the next, with tears glistening.

Frankie's mom had helped her pack up the cabin, readying it to be winterized. The water would be shut off and the pipes drained. Now, she stood in the middle of the main room, saying, "You've been a good home to me, sheltering me from weather and keeping me safe. I'll always have a picture of those stars I gazed at through your window before I drifted off to sleep each night. I hope whoever comes next will have that same sense of peace that I had here." She'd done this at each place that had touched her over the season, a thank-you for the blessing, and good wishes for those who would come next.

Finished, Isa took the path to Ambassador Kine's office, practicing, once again, the military stride she learned from her stay at the Academy. She stood straight, waiting for permission to enter.

"Isa, come in."

"Ambassador, sir." She addressed them both, but didn't look at either. She was trying to hold herself together.

Bane kept it formal. "Is everything in order, Lieutenant?"

"Yes, sir, I'm ready any time."

Lee came around his desk to stand in front of Isa. "Lieutenant, it has been my great pleasure and fortune to have you here. I can't begin to tell you my appreciation for what you've done for these kids and the horses. You gave more than anyone had the right to expect, and we will all miss you and are grateful."

"Thank you, and know that I've loved every minute."

She was quiet during transport and back on Bounty. Bane told her to go unpack, take what was left of the day, and to come see him for dinner. She went, but was too pent up to do much but stare at her belongings. Having already run that morning, she didn't know what to do to get rid of, or at least keep at bay, these emotions. Going over to the viewport, she spotted her ballet slippers at the bottom of the closet. Changing into a leotard and tights, she then headed toward the room Mary used as a dance studio. She found the music for bar exercises and, turning it up extra loud, began the routines.

She wasn't punishing herself, but working hard not to think. Ballet looked graceful and elegant, but was deep muscle work—difficult and equal to any intense workout. Isa was soon sweating, and although she knew she'd pay the price tomorrow, she did the routine like she hadn't missed three months of class. Switching the music for floor exercises, she loved to put arms and legs together, feeling the music through her movements like Mary had taught her. A dancer needs to embody the music to make it come alive for the audience. Isa used the entire floor as she danced and her feelings about leaving Yenna, the kids, her friends and the roan, became a deluge she couldn't stave off.

She hadn't heard him come in, but was soon aware that the Captain had been watching her, which meant, she realized, that she was late. Isa went over and shut off the music, grabbed a towel and then sat leaning against the wall, her sweaty face in the towel.

"Did it help?"

A muffled "yeah" came out of the towel.

"Come on." His hand grabbed hers and hauled her to her feet. "Let's get something to eat."

"I'm all sweaty."

"I can see that, you have something you can change into?" She shook her head. "We'll swing by your quarters and you can get whatever you need." She nodded.

Reaching Bane's quarters, he told her to shower and he'd fix dinner. The cold water felt good, reviving Isa, but a knock on the door told her it was time to get out. Refreshed and dressed, all the sweat washed away, Isa emerged less of an emotional wreck. Bane had set the table and was holding a chair out for her. Once seated with a plate of food she wasn't really hungry for, she began to tell him about Yenna. He listened, like he always did, and let her get it all out.

"The goodbyes were tough and I knew they would be. I just got so close to my kids, and I'll worry about how they're doing and what it will be like for them without their horses. I told little Lucy that Buster would be close by in the winter pasture and Skeeter or Hannah or Justin could take her there to see him. She and TJ promised to keep an eye on my Roan and let me know how he's doing."

She went on for a while and then got quiet. Bane glanced at her untouched plate. "Still not hungry?" She shook her head. "How about some hot cocoa on the sofa?"

Tentatively, she asked, "With marshmallows?"

"Absolutely."

50.

Bounty's way of life, her very breath, drew Isa in and she gave herself back to her work there. It had been simple to maintain communication with those on Yenna and she didn't overdo it. She received a copy of Ambassador Kine's report on the horse program's first season and her part in making it successful. This would become part of her official record and she was pleased by Lee's kind words and, more, for his high recommendation of the program and the possibility of replicating it in other places.

Isa had several long chats with Jack over the months after her time on Yenna. It was good to be able to share those stories with him. He chuckled when she told him about her first day-off ride and hearing his voice in her head as she was plunged into the icy water.

As Yenna prepared for three more months of cold before the warm season came again, Isa was summoned to the conference room. A rebellious streak had surfaced. She hadn't directly disobeyed orders, but had put herself on the cutting edge several times. Isa was wondering how the Captain had already found out about the late night party in the common room and her raid of the soda stores; she'd been very careful to clean up and planned to confess to Lieutenant Hamilton and pay restitution in whatever way he saw fit. The after-hours party without permission was another matter.

"Captain, sir. Lieutenant Torunn reporting."

"At ease. Have a seat." He motioned her to a chair opposite his and close to the vid-screens, which were on and projecting both Academy President Wilson and Professor Kolter.

"So, this isn't about the party, is it?"

"Party? No, Lieutenant, but we can discuss the party later." From the way he emphasized the word party, Isa knew she'd just blown her cover.

"Isa, it's good to see you." President Wilson always addressed her familiarly.

"Thank you, sir, and you as well."

"Lieutenant Torunn, aside from any mention of parties, we were very pleased with your work on Yenna, and I'm glad you heeded my advice to be open to possibilities and opportunities."

"Yes, we were discussing with Captain Lucas another such opportunity that has come up with your name attached."

She looked at her Captain, eyebrows raised and her breathing quickened. She couldn't believe he was considering sending her off again. She'd just come back, and yet here she sat and realized this was a serious request that Captain Lucas had already considered or she wouldn't be hearing it. He reached across, his hand gripping her arm, and said with a serious, but kind, demeanor, "Just listen."

51.

Isa couldn't believe it. She was going back to Yenna for another warm season. Prof K. and President Wilson had asked if she would consider the assignment again. Asked. She took one look at Bane, saw that they meant it, and jumped out of her chair, whooping. When the meeting was over, Bane let her contact Frankie, who said she'd tell Skeeter. They discussed the new development for a while and Isa's excitement. "All right, Lieutenant, back to work, we'll discuss details," he paused until he had her attention, "and that unauthorized party, later." He ushered her out the door.

***

She felt fortunate enough to be assigned to this place again. Although she enjoyed her "real" job, especially the crew she worked with, there was something special about being here. Surrounded by rugged peaks still harboring snow from the winter, and the incredible indigo of the mountain lake, it was a protected haven where her skills were put to good use.

Isa's skills at riding put her in charge of the warm season program for orphans and she couldn't wait to start again. She recognized the value of putting horses and children together, and had seen so many kids benefit from a big, warm friend they could trust and tell all of their troubles. Isa missed having horses on her ship, and looked forward to sharing her secrets with her beautifully built roan gelding.

She had spent most of the last warm season building trust with the orphans, listening and simply spending time with them. She was not threatening, on the short side of average in height, with unruly curls in her shoulder-length dark brown hair, cobalt blue eyes, and mischievous grin. She had a slight build, jogging daily to maintain good physical condition, and had a passion for the discipline of ballet. Since some of the kids had taught her to play guitar, and she enjoyed singing, especially the local folk music, as when Isa sang, people stopped to listen, forgetting the difficult grind of daily routine. It was her voice and her empathy for the children that had Ambassador Kine requesting her return this season.

Lee Kine had been assigned to Yenna for three years now, having spent the first year supervising the building and organizing the programs. It was a planet of beauty and grace, and the refugees from a close-by civil war needed the healing it provided. Lee was here to guide the people, and help them rebuild their lives and the lives of the kids whose parents died in the war. War was almost unheard of now; most cultures understood that people are unique and different and those differences provide a richness for all. The Argons who had settled Yenna, were a generous people. They were glad to be able to house the center to help the children from other cultures who had been orphaned by war. These children had witnessed horrible atrocities, and needed time, understanding, and love to heal. Lee thought Isa was the right one for this job, having learned about her own painful past and the demons she lived with, and watching her at work last season.

"Ambassador Kine, it is good to see you again."

"Lieutenant Torunn, it is my pleasure to welcome you back to Yenna." Lee stood a foot taller than Isa, with his brown hair short, light blue eyes, and a friendly grin on his boyish face. He had strength in his formal handshake. Lee turned to Isa's Captain who had accompanied her down to settle some details. "Captain, thank you for granting my request. Isa has her work cut out for her, and the kids have missed her."

Captain Bane Lucas responded, "Ambassador Kine, I am sure you will make good use of my Lieutenant. The Bounty will remain in this sector for several weeks, if you require further assistance."

"Thank you, Captain. Isa, I believe you know your way around. If you'll excuse us, the Captain and I have some timelines to work out."

"Of course Sir. Captain, Ambassador."

Isa left them to their details to go in search of the barn and her horse. Outside the main administrative building, she was startled when she ran into a tall man pushing his way into the building. As she started to excuse herself, a shock raced up her spine, prickling her scalp, leaving her unable to speak. Her shoulders hunched, quad muscles bunching up for a fast take-off. His dark eyes threatened as he looked down and she backed away. He continued past, staring back at her as he muscled through the tall glass doors. Isa froze against the reddish-brown adobe wall. As the dark man disappeared from view, her breath rushed out and her hand held to the wall for a moment. The hatred and anger had crept into her bones, his eyes a conduit of his emotions.

Finding the wood-chip path to the barn, she wondered who that man was, and why he was so filled with fury. Isa felt sorry for whomever he was going to see. Shaking off the dark emotions, she began to lose the measured military stride, and stepped back into the loose, easy walk of a horsewoman. She spotted Lucy, such a quiet little girl.

"Lucy, hey sweet pea, I missed you." Lucy turned, the breeze pulling her black hair from her brown eyes, and stared at Isa as though she was a ghost. "It's me, Lucy." Isa knelt down and waited. Lucy hesitated and slowly approached, considering Isa for a long while and then quietly put her arms around Isa's neck. Isa gathered her in, understanding that she wasn't yet real to Lucy. "It's okay, I'm here."

They held on to each other until Lucy relaxed. "I wasn't sure you would come back. Your roan wasn't either. I've brushed him every day since they brought the horses back." Clasping hands, Isa and Lucy headed to the roan's stall. Leaning over the half-open stall door, Isa breathed in the scent of the horses, fresh hay, and sighed.

"Hey boy." Clucking to him, she had imagined this moment a million times. "Lucy, he looks great, you've done a beautiful job taking care of him." Lucy's eyes lit up with the compliment, and she squeezed Isa's hand. The big roan had perked up his ears hearing Isa's voice, and wuffling, came over to the door. Four hands reached up to scratch and love on him. He was the horse no one wanted to ride. Big and fast, he has always been known as "the roan." Isa loved riding him, his powerful muscles moving with her, losing herself in his thick russet mane, and his soft muzzle blowing warmth to her like a campfire.

52.

The roan soon went back to his hay, leaving Isa and Lucy to wander down the barn aisle, swept clean from the morning chores. Lucy filled Isa in on each horse and what all the kids were up to. Leaving the barn, they walked over to the dormitory that housed the kids and the adults who looked after them. Isa was soon surrounded in a happy reunion of hugs and smudged faces. After a lunch of grilled cheese, tomato soup with crackers, and Isa's favorite chocolate brownies, it was time to settle in.

The little cabin was constructed with a synthetic material that could withstand the harsh winter climate, and keep the occupant cool in the warm season. It reminded Isa of the old log cabins of the early Earth pioneers. The cabin was up the hill from the barn, close enough that Isa could hear the horses stomping and neighing, yet secluded by pine trees towering over the roof. Behind the cabin was a shortcut trail to the lake Isa had found the season before, and she relished having the place to herself. It was one room, a double bed on one side, with a small kitchen for convenience, an old rocking chair by the large window, and a door into a compact bathroom. She kept her clothes in her trunk under the bed. Frankie's mom had ensured that she was supplied with sheets, pillows, blankets, and a warm comforter, as even in the warm season it was cold at night. The kitchen had a small fridge, a warming plate, and a few dishes; most of her meals she ate in the dining hall with the kids. The bathroom had a small supply of thick, cushy towels. Isa's small cache of possessions arrived before her and waited to be put up. She noticed that the com-unit had been set up for her communication with the Bounty. She turned and stuck her tongue out at it.

Arranging everything to her satisfaction, Isa changed her formal uniform for the blue jeans, boots, and short-sleeved shirts that were more common around the barn. She tied a blue and green flannel shirt around her waist, prepared for possible weather changes, and headed down the rocky path to the barn to give her first lessons. She could see the kids were saddled and ready, waiting in the arena, each one's head leaning against their horse's neck, no doubt whispering or softly singing to their horse partner.

Isa greeted each child and horse by name, taking the time to hug each one and scrub their equine partner's ears. Teaching this group, she felt like they had all been put under a spell, so rapt was their attention. "Keep the heels down, Grace, and your back straight but relaxed. Good, let the horse move you and your rear will stay in the saddle where it belongs!" Grace smiled back at her, and settled into the paint mare. "You look beautiful up there, Tess, I can tell you've been practicing that gentle hand, and your Lessa mare appreciates it." Tess had worked hard, last season she rode with the hands of a dead person, stiff in formaldehyde. The horse had suffered but Tess spent so much time grooming and finding Lessa's favorite scratchy spots that she had been forgiven. Isa paced slowly from the middle of the arena over to one side and fell into step with the little red mare, Scooter, and Reid.

"Reid, your balance is incredible. You and Scooter are like one animal. I understand you have spent a great deal of time with her."

"It's true, Isa. She asked me to, I mean, I, well, I just know she did. I can't explain it, but she talks to me, and she listens to me when no one else will. I want to ride her in the mountains on the pack trip."

"I know she talks to you, Reid. Pack trip, huh? Do you think you are ready? It is a rough trail, and this is only your second year. I'm not saying no, I just want to be absolutely certain you are ready, and Scooter too." Isa had seen the smile leap off his face when she hesitated. She had to think quickly to fix it.

"Okay." Isa was constantly amazed by how soon these kids could recover. She thought about that as she went back to the center to finish the lesson. As usual, she learned more from them about living than they learned from her about riding. Just that morning, she had again overreacted to a male presence that she sensed was upset. She wished she had more control over her instinct to duck and cover whenever she felt a threat. She spent a pleasant afternoon with kids and horses, had supper at the dining hall, and retired to the cabin.

The sun was setting into dusk when Captain Lucas showed up. "Lieutenant, all settled in? I envy you this quiet place, all those horses. I'd love to stay and ride with you, but the Bounty calls." Bane folded his long frame into the rocker by the window. Isa admired the muscled shape of his thighs, and the contrast of his trim waist and broad shoulders.

"Captain, I hope you can find the time to spend a few days down here. I'd enjoy riding out with you again in these rugged mountains."

"Hmm, buttering up the Captain, are you? Well, I would enjoy a ride, too, so I'll see what I can do. You will check in as we discussed. The Ambassador has provided you with a communications link, and I expect you to use it."

"But Sir, do you really need to hear from me so regularly? My duties here at the barn and with the children are time consuming. There are days when I don't return to the cabin until late. Many days. Sometimes I even end up sleeping in the barn with a sick horse or a sad kid."

"Enough. I understand, more than most, what you do here. I still expect regular check-ins. This planet is housing those who have had to flee from war and violence. Although everyone knows this is a neutral planet, there are still possibilities for violence, and I won't have a member of my crew jeopardized. You will check in."

"Yes, Sir." Isa was aware that her closeness to the Captain was unique. She also understood that he took his duty seriously, and expected no less from his crew, close or not.

"Very good, Isa, I leave you in the capable hands of Ambassador Kine. I will have regular contact with him as well." His shrewd gray eyes held her gaze for a moment. The message was clear, and they both understood the "threat" behind those last words.

"Where is Bounty off to?"

"Bounty is going to study the Raimos System. It holds life-supporting planets and we will begin the process of mapping the system and determining life forms in existence, and possible contact. We won't be out of range should you need anything."

"I have everything I could possibly need from my quarters. I even remembered the guitar I received from the kids, and I hope to impress them with my growing talent. They were so excited by the video message I sent of myself singing the songs they taught me."

"You are good for these kids—they have faced so much loss in their lives, seen atrocities that no young person should have to see. I know you give everything you have to them and to this project. I also know that it comes from deep within you, and I appreciate your willingness to share that, as hard as it is for you." His sturdy arms wrapped around her for a brief moment.

"Thank you, Captain, and yes, my nightmares can still haunt me. If you hadn't given me a chance, I would not be here now. You helped me escape from a very dark place, and gave me hope for a different future. If I hadn't come to Bounty, I wonder what hole I would have locked myself into. I want that same chance for these kids."

"I recognize that, as does Ambassador Kine. Did I tell you that he requested you to come back? He pleaded with the Alliance, and a plea from Lee Kine does not go unheeded."

"I didn't know that. I am glad though. He does an incredible job here with these refugees, and they obviously respect him. He is also good with the children. He never talks down to them, and he even comes along riding once in a while."

"Well, you'll have to get him out into the mountains if I can't manage the time away. I'm sure he would enjoy it. I'd like you to help him with the report he will be making to the Alliance. The work here is important, and having your perspective will be convincing to certain members of the board. You do have a way of telling a child's story."

"I'd be happy to, Sir. Does he know that you want me to help him? Could you tell him so it doesn't seem like I am getting in his way?" Isa looked forward to working with Lee. He believed in the beauty and grace of this planet and the role it played in healing for the people of this region. He was aiding them in rebuilding their lives after an ugly decade of war. Besides, his light blue eyes always seemed to be inviting her to share something with him.

Captain Lucas responded with, "All right then, I'll be sure to let him know. As for you, remember that just because you are working a little more closely with the Ambassador, does not excuse you from checking in with Bounty on the agreed-upon schedule."

"No Sir, I got that message loud and clear!"

"I'll say goodbye and, Isa, be careful and keep yourself safe until the warm season is over and you can be back onboard Bounty."

"I will, goodbye, Captain." Standing, his shrewd gray eyes held her gaze for a moment, followed by a brief hug, his comforting arms wrapping around her. He cupped her shoulder in his hand, nodded, and strode out the open door of the cabin. Isa watched his graying black hair disappear, savoring that hug, the strength and fondness in it. Her day had been full, but before she could sleep, she had to walk to the lake. Sighing, she pulled on the flannel shirt and buttoned it.

She stepped out to meet the darkening night, closing the door behind her. It had been her routine to walk through the woods, finding stillness and solitude on the shore of the lake, and she intended to reinstitute this pleasant task. The low-hanging branches of a tree, thick with deep sea green needles, obscured the path. The previous season, she remembered exploring behind her cabin, discovering that the needles of this tree looked razor sharp, but were actually soft, like a feather. Crawling under to get a closer look, she had discovered a path and followed it to the lake. She ducked under that tree now, and made her way to the lake.

53.

The crescent moon was just rising, giving minimal light from reflection in the water. Isa sat, her back against a tree, and gazed out at the cold, blue lake. Breathing seemed easier. The pulse of this planet rested far beneath her and she could sense the beating of it in time with her own heart. The connection she had with the natural world was a source of deep joy.

Sitting up suddenly, Isa looked around. It was dark. She felt that someone was watching her. Quietly, Isa moved toward the path, listening for signs of movement. She reached the big tree, the feathery needles caressing her as she slid through. The evening breeze stilled as she reached the cabin door, and pausing, Isa wondered if she had imagined that presence.

"It was real, whatever it was," she mumbled to herself. The Argons were a peaceful people, and she was sure no harm would come to her here. Passing it off as some other night wanderer enjoying the lake, she brushed her teeth and changed into the soft cotton long johns she preferred for sleep. Sinking into the smooth sheets, pulling the blanket and comforter up to her shoulders, Isa whispered a prayer of gratitude and slept deeply.

***

"Lucy, you are more than ready for an overnight ride in the mountains. You have worked so hard this season, and you have a beautiful seat. So, what's the matter? Talk to me, love." Lucy stood by the paddock fence, her whole body sagging, with Isa's arm around her.

"Oh Isa, it is almost over, and I wish you could stay forever." Lucy turned and let herself be enveloped by Isa's arms.

"I'm going to miss you, too, but I'll send messages like I did before. I'll talk to the Ambassador about letting you use my com-link once in a while so we can talk directly."

"Really? I'd like that. And Isa...I would like to go on that ride."

"Now you're talkin'. Come on up to the cabin. I'll fix us lunch, and we can do some planning. I think there will be six or seven of us."

Isa remembered as they arrived at the cabin that she was supposed to check in with the Bounty. She set Lucy to work making sandwiches while she sat in the rocker by the window to report to Captain Lucas. Prepared for a reprimand, Isa wondered at the best way to counteract it. "Lieutenant Torunn reporting, Captain. I have the perfect horse for you, Sir. He's spirited and an excellent jumper."

"Lieutenant, you are late again. You had best remember that it is a short time until you are back onboard, and your horse tactics will not work."

"Yes, Sir, I apologize. Are you coming planet-side?"

"I'm afraid not. Bounty will arrive on time to pick you up, but we have not finished our study of the Raimos System. You'll have to ride that spirited jumper for me."

"Okay, I'll do that. Captain, have you been able to send the items I requested?"

"Lieutenant, I have never known you to misplace so many things. Is there a problem?"

"No problem, some of my belongings have simply vanished. I think some of the kids may have them."

Lucy and Isa spent the afternoon outlining the overnight ride. Lucy had been thrilled to speak with the Captain again, thinking him quite handsome; despite his lack of experience with children, Bane was friendly enough. It was good to have company in the cabin, as Isa didn't feel that unknown presence so much. The season had been a strange one for her. She hadn't looked over her shoulder so much in a long time. As a child, Isa suffered under Frank's steel hand. He had helped her to hone her sixth sense, making it easier to avoid his violent blows. She rarely walked to the lake at night, feeling a menace there she didn't understand. There had been nights when she slept in the stall with the roan, feeling secure wrapped in his warmth.

"Well, Lucy, we'd better head back. I'm to sing for the masses tonight."

"All us kids get to come, and you will sing my favorite song, right?"

"I could never disappoint my biggest fan, so you bet, I'll sing 'Moon on the Meadow'." Giving Lucy a hug, they went back to the dorm. Isa hurried on to the administrative center. She was to have dinner with the Ambassador and his guests, and then provide the entertainment for the settlement's harvest celebration.

"Isa, we are all looking forward to hearing you sing, and the Argon have prepared a gift for you. It is a traditional costume, and they would be thrilled to have you wear it tonight."

"Ambassador, it is beautiful. I am honored." The costume was a brilliant azure, skillfully woven with love and pride. Holding the flowing pants with a matching waist-length jacket, Isa was surprised by how light and soft it was. Now having donned it, she rejoined the Ambassador, her sparkling blue eyes highlighted by the striking cloth. "Isa, you are lovely. May I escort you to the hall?" Isa took his arm and they strolled together.

Truth be told, Lee Kine had a crush on Isa, finding her light touch on his arm exhilarating. Looking forward to hearing her lovely voice, and the inspiration it would bring to the Argon, he guided her onto the makeshift stage. Lee introduced Isa, noticing the children right up front smiling and clapping as loud as they could. He leaned down to kiss her cheek for good luck, and went to sit with the people. The first clear, true notes enchanted them all, "Moon on the meadow...." After the concert, he would ask her to join him, wanting to be more intimate with Isa, and kicking himself for waiting so long.

Lee hadn't counted on the adoring children. They embraced her on the stage, laughing, hugging, and admiring the beautiful costume. Isa bowed gracefully to the Argon elders who thanked her for wearing their gift, unknowingly scoring high marks for the Space Alliance, the Bounty, and Captain Lucas; Lee would be sure to mention it in her evaluation. He soon lost her in the crowd, and decided he would go out to her cabin later. Isa was making her way to the door, accepting the compliments and giving credit to the exquisite Argon folk music. Once outside, she breathed in the crisp night air, walked the crowd of children back to the dorm, and tucked Lucy in with a special cuddle.

"Thanks for singing my song. I love you, Isa."

"I love you, too, sweet pea, sleep well."

54.

Alone in her cabin, Isa savored the touch of the Argon fabric as she packed it away in her trunk. Tugging on her long johns and warm wool socks, she felt a prickle at the back of her neck. Too late she turned, catching a glimpse of that immense dark man, his hatred filling her pores, and she was knocked into blackness.

He was over six feet tall, lithe and light for his height. His skin was dark chocolate, taut across his toned muscles, his hair and eyes were dark and he was dressed in black. He lifted Isa's inert form across his shoulder, thinking she was lighter than he'd estimated, they would make better time. Leaving the cabin, he hauled her down the hidden path he'd watched her take several times. Disappearing would not be a problem; he'd been here through the warm season exploring and detailing his plan ever since that accidental meeting outside the Ambassador's building. Lieutenant Torunn would be the first step in paying for all the damage done to his culture by the Space Alliance, Captain Bane Lucas, and Ambassador Lee Kine.

Leif's people were a race of warriors. It was how they lived, and they had kept their planet rich and powerful for generations. Now they were reduced to begging from the Alliance, a kept people, devoid of pride since the wars stopped. Retribution was required, and Torunn would be the source. He soon reached the shore of the lake and began climbing the east side. Midway to the ridge, a rocky outcrop hid a large cave. Leif squeezed through the opening, dumping his burden against the far wall. The effects of the drug would soon wear off, and he sat down to wait.

She struggled to open her eyes, and when she did, everything was blurry. It was cold, the dampness clinging to her clothes. Isa lay very still, confused and trying to stop the shaking inside. He was here with her, hating her. He jerked her up and struck her hard across the face. Isa's hands reached up to protect herself.

"What do you want? Please, what have I done?"

"You will make up for the wrongs your Alliance has done to my people. I will crush you as you have crushed us."

She fought him as long as she could, finally overcome by his weight and the single-minded assault. Isa's lungs could not bring enough oxygen, and she sank into unconsciousness on the cold, hard rock. Leif stood over Isa, staring at her bruised and bleeding flesh. He was still seized by his rage. This was the weak point in his plan; from here Leif wasn't confidant of the outcome, having let anger lead him. They would be searching for her by morning, and he intended to be long gone. Leif would have Lt. Torunn deliver his message, and his culture would thrive with war again.

55.

Lee finally emptied the hall, eager to be on his way. Arriving at Isa's cabin, he was pleased to see the windows glowing with the soft light of the lamp. Lee had enjoyed riding with her several times, discovering Isa's love of the outdoors and her gentle hand with the horses. Smiling, he reached out and knocked on her door. When she didn't answer, Lee opened the door, calling as he stepped in, "Isa, it's Lee, come for a walk with me." Checking the bathroom, and calling around outside, he wondered if she were still at the dorm. Using the com-link, he asked to speak with her. There was some confusion about when, but it was obvious she had left to come back to her cabin. Lee checked back with the duty officer in administration, but Isa had not returned there.

Two hours later, a full-scale search was on. Lee was at the cabin, his stilted voice speaking with Captain Lucas, "Bane, we don't know where she is. She was here after she left the kids at the dorm. I found her costume folded away in her trunk."

"Have you checked the barn? She may have gone to see her horse and fallen asleep."

"I thought of that, but the roan is alone in his stall. How far out are you?"

"Lee, at this speed, we'll be there within the hour. I'll come directly to the cabin with a search team."

Lee left his own team at the cabin to coordinate the search while he went out to look for her himself. He could not simply sit and wait for reports. Switching on the headlamp, he made his way to the back of the cabin, focusing on the ground for tracks. There were footprints, too large to be Isa's, but Lee followed them until they disappeared. Kneeling down, he noticed bunches of feathery needles on the ground under the tree. Pulling the branches aside, he found a path and kept on it to the lake.

***

Isa came to and was overcome with terrible pain. She lay quite still, afraid he would continue his attack. Isa had trained herself to listen, falling back on skills she hadn't been forced to use in a long time. The bitterly cold rock walls of the cave echoed silence. Slowly cracking open her eyelids, Isa peeked around. He was gone, but she lay motionless and freezing for a long while. Awkwardly rising to a sitting position, she leaned against the stone wall, her breathing fast and burning. He must have broken some ribs. Tenderly testing out arms and legs, Isa tried to cover herself with the torn remains of her long johns. Her wool socks were whole, and her feet the only part of her that didn't hurt.

Isa wanted to curl up in a ball, escape this hell somehow. She crawled to the cave's entrance, tentatively poking her head out, sure he would be there. Isa peered out, seeing the lake below, wondering how far she could get. Bleeding and raw, she pulled herself out of the cave expecting him to pounce. At the edge of the outcropping, Isa felt her way into the cover of the trees. The hill was steep, but tree-by-tree, clinging to the trunks and low bushes, she crawled her way down. She lay there, under the cover of a scraggly bush, and prayed that he wouldn't find her.

Lee had begun searching the edge of the lake. He'd switched off his headlamp when he found the old, hidden path, feeling in his heart that Isa was in trouble. Coming around to the east, he stopped, thinking he heard something, like an animal scratching around in the underbrush. Silence. Lee kept on, searching every rock by the shore. Reaching his starting point, he was ready to widen the perimeter to the rise of the hillside. Lee switched on his com-link for any update. "Ambassador Kine, the Bounty has arrived, and Captain Bane is here and ready to see you."

"Put him on."

"Lee, have you found any sign of Isa? Your teams here are coming up empty thus far, and my teams are heading out."

"Captain, bring a headlamp, and I'll meet you at the back of the cabin. I'm going there now."

***

"I found some large footprints leading me to this tree, where I discovered an old path to the lake. I've focused my search there and was just ready to widen it."

"Lead the way. Do you have any inkling of what could have happened, Lee?"

"My gut feeling tells me she's been taken, but I can't explain why."

Lee and Bane began to search the widened shore zone together. Dawn was not far off now and the sun's light and warmth would facilitate the search. Both men were concerned about Isa's exposure to the cold. Back on the east side now, above them the sky was just showing pink. Lee discovered her first. He said her name softly as his heart seized with fear, thinking she was dead, she lay so still. She was half-covered by the bush. Gently, Lee touched her shoulder, breathing her name again. Isa opened her eyes, wide with terror, and opened her mouth to scream, but no sound emerged. She tried to slide back into the cover of the bush. Bewildered, Lee backed up as Captain Lucas ran to her.

Bane subdued her easily, saying her name over and over.

"It's all right, Isa; you're safe now. It's Bane and Lee. Shhhh, it will be okay."

Bane carefully picked her up, cradling her in his arms. Lee led the way, eyes bright with tears as he began to understand what had been done to her. There was a lot of blood under that bush. He heard Captain Lucas crooning softly to her like a mother to a frightened baby.

Back at the cabin, Bane held her while the ship's medic sedated her. Isa seemed to retreat inside herself as the medication took effect. Lee had cleared everyone out, wanting to protect Isa's vulnerability. Her injuries were extensive, her right wrist and four ribs broken. She was covered with blood and dirt. Tenderly, Bane and the medic cleaned her wounds, disinfected them, and gently dressed her in the loose clothing Lee had found in her trunk. Tucking the comforter around her, Bane finally addressed Lee.

"What the hell happened here? Who could have done this?"

"I don't know, Captain. It doesn't make any sense. The Argons love her and they wouldn't hurt anyone, especially like this."

The two men would have to wait until Isa could help them.

56.

Isa slept through the day, sometimes sweating and shaking, sometimes as still as death. Bane and Lee kept watch with the medic, soothing her with whispered reassurances. At dusk, she woke wide-eyed with terror; recognizing Bane, she gripped his hand. Isa pulled at every ounce of courage she possessed to get her breathing under control so she could speak. Reliving it as she conveyed what happened, Isa trembled uncontrollably. Bane held her, his rage at her story palpable. Lee stayed just behind him, not wanting to panic her further. He'd heard of this warrior, Leif, and speaking softly to the com-unit, issued orders to find him.

Isa asked if it were true; had the Alliance abused Leif's people? Captain Lucas told her no, but some were struggling to let go of war, and it didn't excuse the horrible things Leif had done to her. Bane was amazed by Isa's concern for these people after what Leif had perpetrated against her. The healing process would be a long, difficult road, but Bane was certain Isa had the character and spirit not only to survive, but to learn to love life again.

"Captain, please stay with me, I don't want to be left alone." She looked lost under the thick comforter.

"Isa, we won't leave you alone. You are safe, sleep assured," Bane lightly touched her hand reassuringly. She drifted in and out of sleep through the night, the Captain and Lee Kine taking turns at the watch. Around midnight, they heard a soft scratching at the door and a small voice whispering, "Isa, are you okay? Please let me in."

Lucy had been sure Isa was dead. No one would tell her anything, except that Isa was sick and getting better in her cabin. When the dorm fell silent, she crept out and made her way up the path to the cabin. Startled when Ambassador Kine opened the door, she stepped back, her eyes on the ground. "Is she dead?"

Lee knelt down, tipping her chin up with his thumb, "No, Lucy, Isa is very much alive. She was hurt badly, and it will take time for her to get better."

"Can I see her? I can take care of her."

"I know you can, Lucy. Captain Bane and I are caring for her, and you should be in bed. Let me take you back to the dorm, find TJ, and you can see Isa tomorrow."

"No, please, I won't be any trouble, I promise. I'll sleep right here on the porch."

Unable to dissuade her, Lee brought her inside. Lucy tiptoed over to Isa, reached over and lightly laid her hand on Isa's forehead. Leaning toward Isa, Lucy whispered against her cheek, "I love you." Straightening up, Lucy addressed Bane and Lee.

"My horse, Buster, was real sick one time. He couldn't get up and had a bad bellyache. I stayed with him and patted him. He got better and pretty soon he got up."

Lee reached out to wipe the tear sliding down her cheek, and then gathered her up. Bane arranged blankets on the floor next to Isa's bed; content that she'd be allowed to stay, Lucy drifted off to sleep. Isa calmed and rested easier the remainder of the night.

Lucy's presence gave Isa courage to fight her way back, and something to focus on. After three days, Isa wanted to get up and be outside. She felt too helpless lying there all that time. She had her chance later when Captain Lucas and Lee left to meet with Alliance mediators. Isa struggled to move her legs over the side of the bed. Lucy slipped an arm around her waist, straining to help her up.

Step by step, Isa and Lucy aimed for the rocker by the window. One shaky leg slowly shuffled after the other, her breathing moving her chest in and out, her heart pounding against ribs to get out. Reaching the rocker, Isa crumpled into it, her breath shallow and fast. Grinning, Lucy flung open the door for Isa to look out. "It's so sunny today, Isa, can you feel it?"

"Thanks, Lucy. It is good just to sit up and have the world upright."

"I'll be right back, Isa, I won't go far." Lucy took off running down the path.

Alone suddenly, Isa stopped breathing, eyes wide, as if the planet had stopped spinning, and she felt she couldn't move. Through the haze in her head, Lucy's sweet, high voice filtered in. She was singing, "Moon on the meadow, bugs in our ears..." at the top of her lungs, and continued all the way down to the barn.

Isa found her smile; leave it to Lucy to figure out how to comfort her. Isa knew his name, and she would never forget his face or his crushing weight. Frank had merged with this dark giant in her mind. She had survived a brutal childhood; she vowed now to survive this, too. She refused to live a life that was fear-filled again, and was grateful to Lucy for bringing her back from it.

"How the hell?" Lee stood in the doorway, eyes wide, and his mouth open.

"I couldn't stay in that bed any longer. Lucy helped me get this far, and I'm counting on you to get me out to that chair on the porch. Please, Lee."

"You aren't even supposed to be up. You could tear something and start bleeding." As Lee spoke, he put an arm around Isa easing her up, ignoring her flinch reflex. Fifteen small onerous shuffling steps had her seated on the hard wooden chair. Studying her face, pale and strained, Lee concluded the unyielding chair was hurting her. "I'll bring the rocker out."

Lee set the burled maple rocker on the porch, cushioned with pillows, lifted Isa and lowered her gingerly into it. Lucy appeared on the path leading the roan. The big gelding snorted, walking right up to the uncovered porch and touched his velvety muzzle to the top of Isa's head, his breath stirring her hair.

"Hey, bud, I'm glad to see you, too." Isa, eyes bright, lifted her left hand to his tear-shaped nostrils, enjoying the warmth.

Lucy tucked her hand into Lee's, startling him for a moment. He looked down at her face, focused in awe at the horse and the woman before them. Following her gaze, he almost wanted to turn away from the incredible intimacy of what was enacted here. The roan seemed to be holding her. Isa sighed.

***

Isa's goodbyes had been emotional, but she had to return to Bounty, called away for urgent duty. Lee had gladly agreed to allow Lucy use of the com-link, and they'd spoken several times. Lucy was a sprite, full of wisdom, and Isa was thankful for the gift that had brought her so far from the grip of terror.

Ambassador Kine, Lee, had gently kissed her, and with a light embrace, let her go. He said as she left, "I'll be here next season, Isa." The phrase played over in her mind, each time bringing joy in the memory of him. Isa was aware of Captain Lucas' respect for Lee, and that said more for him than anything else.

Back on board, she was not on active duty; the healing was progressing slowly. Isa was sleeping on the couch, set up for her in the Captain's quarters. Night terrors snatched at her like long, thorny branches. Isa, drenched in sweat, would find herself rocked like an infant in Bane's embrace. He never complained, and only repeated to her that it would get better. When the night had passed, and all seemed safe, she would ask the Captain about returning next season.

Thank You

Thank you for purchasing Windows In The Loft. I hope you enjoyed Isa's story. To get updates on future releases, receive excerpts, and win prizes join my mailing list. Write to sallygerardmmza@gmail.com with "subscribe" in the subject heading. I promise I won't spam you or share your address.

About the Author

Sally Gerard is a writer and teacher who lives in rural eastern Colorado. She has a Master's degree in English, and spent twenty-five years running a horse camp program for kids and adults in the mountains of Colorado. Windows in the Loft is her first novel.

You can find Sally on the web here:

Facebook: www.facebook.com/pages/Sally-Gerard
    Twitter: www.twitter.com/mssallygerard
    Blog: www.sygoerner.wordpress.com
    Email: sallygerardmmza@gmail.com

Reading Group Guide

1. What are the various ways Isa uses to cope with the different situations she finds herself in?
2. Pick one challenge that Isa faces, explain how she approaches it and then discuss how you might have handled it.
3. There is rich sensory detail throughout much of Isa's story. Pick one of your favorite descriptions and explain how the details add to the story, situation, and characters.
4. Isa continues to have strength and resolve, even in the midst of untenable circumstances. What is it that gives a person this kind of spirit? What details can you provide from the text to support Isa's personal strength?
5. Who do you know that has faced difficult situations in life? How have they handled those situations? What could they learn from Isa?
6. What can you tell about Isa's faith? How is it similar or different from yours?
7. How would Isa's life be different if she hadn't found horses in her Alliance life? What would it be like to give up something that feels like it has been a part of you since you were born?
8. Isa had a loving family when she was very young, and then had to give up her childhood as she became the

parent for her mother. When she is free of Frank, where do you see her reclaiming the joys of growing up?

9. Isa wants people to be good, and when they aren't, she seems to need to see the why of it—almost a justification beyond normal expectations. Why do you think she needs this? How does it develop her character?

10. Isa says she can sense when to trust someone or when to duck and cover. How reliable is "gut" feeling?

11. After Isa's mother dies, she spends a lot of time with her horses, and planning various escapes that she never follows through on. How do you think the title of the book plays into this?

12. Many people in Isa's life support and love her. Discuss some of these people and how they have helped to shape her, heal her, and allow her to grow.

CPSIA information can be obtained at www.ICGtesting.com
Printed in the USA
LVOW06s1930170314

377759LV00025B/1103/P